BLACK MAMBA BOY

It's 1935 in Aden. Jama is ten years old, living in the slums of the ancient city, learning to survive amongst the cosmopolitan ragamuffins and vagabonds of the port. But when he loses everything in Aden, his only chance of survival lies in finding his father who disappeared years before. His search will be dangerous and lonely, and he faces a world preparing for war. Jama's epic journey, by foot, camel, lorry and train, will take him through war-torn Eritrea and Sudan, to Egypt, Palestine and finally, to the icy realms of Britain he heard about in Aden.

NADIFA MOHAMED

BLACK MAMBA BOY

Complete and Unabridged

ULVERSCROFT
Leicester

First published in Great Britain in 2010 by
HarperCollins*Publishers*, London

First Large Print Edition
published 2011
by arrangement with
HarperCollins*Publishers*, London

British Library CIP Data

Mohamed, Nadifa, *1981 –*
Black mamba boy.
1. Orphans- -Somalia- -Fiction. 2. Fathers and sons- -Fiction. 3. Somalia- -History- -Fiction.
4. Large type books.
I. Title
823.9′2–dc22

ISBN 978–1–44480–523–9

C46012057.

Published by
F. A. Thorpe (Publishing)
Anstey, Leicestershire

Set by Words & Graphics Ltd.
Anstey, Leicestershire
Printed and bound in Great Britain by
T. J. International Ltd., Padstow, Cornwall

This book is printed on acid-free paper

For Nadiifo, Daxabo, Axmed, Xasan, Shidane and all the others we lost.

Now you depart, and though your way may lead
Through airless forests thick with hagar trees,
Places steeped in heat, stifling and dry,
Where breath comes hard, and no fresh breeze
   can reach —
Yet may God place a shield of coolest air
Between your body and the assailant sun.

   Gabay by MAXAMED CABDULA XASAN

O troupe of little vagrants of the world,
Leave your footprints in my words.

        From *Stray Birds* by
        RABINDRANATH TAGORE

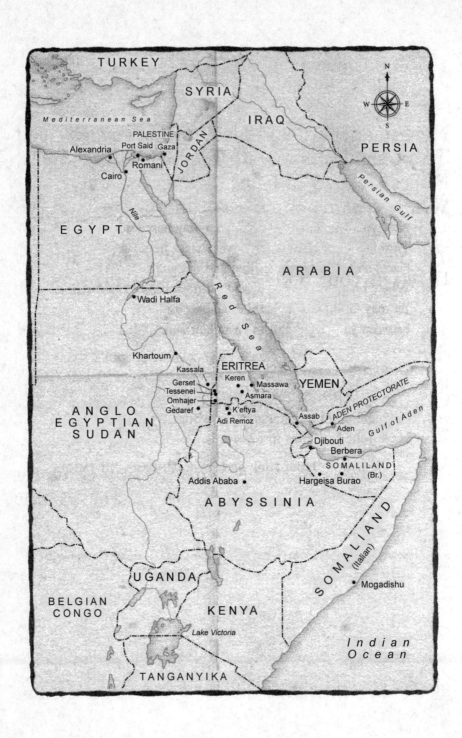

London, England, August 2008

Dark clouds are gathering in the twilight sky, the moon and sun admire each other but my eyes are on him. His oversized glasses perched on his bulbous nose, the flashing blue and white lights of the television dancing on the lenses, his ma'awis hitched up around his knees. To see his knees buckling under the weight of his thin body hurts me, but I respect those knees for walking across continents, for wading through the Red Sea. I will sing the song of those knees.

I am my father's griot, this is a hymn to him. I am telling you this story so that I can turn my father's blood and bones, and whatever magic his mother sewed under his skin, into history. To make him a hero, not the fighting or romantic kind but the real deal, the starved child that survives every sling and arrow that shameless fortune throws at them, and who can now sit back and tell the stories of all the ones that didn't make it. I tell you this story because no-one else will. Let us call down the spirits of the nine thousand boys who foolishly battled on the mountains of Eritrea for Mussolini, who looked like my

1

father, lived like him but had their lives cut off with blunt axes, the ones who starved to death, the ones who lost their minds, and the ones who simply vanished. Boys like Shidane Boqor. Our fiery boy! Our pilferer of canned goods! Our dead child! Light the torches for his flight to heaven. Let his shadow always haunt his tormentors. Let them bathe for all eternity in the Shebelle and Juba before their sins are washed away.

★ ★ ★

My father's life has been an exercise in a strange kind of liberty; if he outwitted death then his life was to be completely, perfectly his own, owing no debts to anyone or anything. Like his mother before him, he sharpened his spirit on the knife edge of solitude; stylites on their pillars, they saw loneliness, aloneness, oneness as divine states. The mother of all sailors is meant to be the sea, but Ambaro was more powerful, more tempestuous, more life-giving than any puddle of water. She gave life to my father over and over again, guarding him as Venus did Aeneas. She took his paltry little life and moulded it into something epic. Her love was violent, thick lava that she poured into her son's mouth, she cut her veins and transfused

2

her hot wild blood into his soul. She was all that he needed in life and he remains here testament to what a mother's love can do, it turns wax into gold.

*   *   *

My father is an old sea-dog who sailed to freedom on a prison ship. Jama with his Somali Argonauts, who remembers each one of his ships like other people remember lost loves. Life as a sailor was ideal for him; wherever he was in the world, his steel leviathan would blast its horn and call him back to his cabin. Even now, see-sawing engravings of galleons surf along his walls as we watch the exploits of Sinbad the Sailor. As a child I would plunge my hands into a King Edward Cigars box of coins, some ancient, some strange, some from countries, like ours, that don't exist anymore. In another box were cufflinks with glass stones that I mistook for rubies, emeralds, sapphires and coveted with all my heart; his golden pirate's treasure chest buried under old maps and certificates. He spun me briny old sea yarns, 'You see, I was being chased by deadly Zulu gangsters, tsotsis they called themselves. I ran along the wharf in Durban in the dead of night with them snapping at my heels, desperate to rob me and cut my throat, my heart was going BOOM BOOM, when a policeman came and fired at them. When the ship got to Venice I bought an ivory-handled pistol for our next journey to South Africa.'

★ ★ ★

Long ago, with a mouth full of clumsy braces, I would allow my father to take my hand and lead me on long purposeless walks. We usually ended up in Richmond Park, sitting amongst the broken trunks of oaks, elms and hawthorns pulled up by the great storm of eighty-seven. In our matching anoraks, we watched bats fly awkwardly from nook to cranny, and listened to the feral Somali parakeets that hid in the park, saying 'Maalin wanaagsan, Maalin wanaagsan, good day.' With fugitive African birds chattering above our heads, and the red and fallow deer hiding in the long grass, we could almost have been in the Serengeti or back in the Miyi. My father would reminisce about Eritrea, Aden, and the camel bells he played with as a child in the Somali desert. I would sullenly wait for him to finish; what could I imagine of life as a child soldier or as a street boy in Aden, I was not allowed out to the corner shop alone. With a distant sigh, my old father Time would become quiet again and I would tell him what was on my mind, perhaps a new pair of trainers or a puffa jacket. I wanted to be a ragamuffin, never knowing that my father was the biggest ragamuffin, vagabond, buffalo soldier of them all.

And all around us the other vagabonds still pour in. Underneath lorries, stowed away in boats, falling out of the sky from jumbo jets. Even old grandmothers pack up their bags and start the tahrib. Those fortune men like my father who set their footprints in the sand, fifty, sixty, a hundred years ago, are the prophets who led the Israelites out of the wilderness. Whatever Pharaoh says, they will not be tied down, they will not be made slaves, they will make the whole world their promised land.

Aden, Yemen, October 1935

The muezzin's call startled Jama out of his dream, he pulled himself up to look at the sun rising over the cake-domed mosques and the gingerbread Adeni apartments glowing at their tips with white frosting. The black silhouettes of birds looped high in the inky sky, dancing around the few remaining stars and the full pregnant moon. The black planets of Jama's eyes roamed over Aden, the busy, industrial Steamer Point, Crater the sandstone old town, its curvaceous dun-coloured buildings merging into the Shum Shum volcanoes, the Ma'alla and Sheikh Usman districts, white and modern, between the hills and sea. Wood smoke and infants' cries drifted up as women took a break from preparing breakfast to perform their dawn prayers, not needing the exhortations of the old muezzin. A vulture's nest encircled the ancient minaret, the broken branches festooned with rubbish, the nest corrupting the neighbourhood with the stench of carrion. The attentive mother fed rotting morsels to her fragile chicks, her muscular wings unhunched and at rest beside her.

Jama's own mother, Ambaro, stood by the roof edge softly singing in her deep and melodious voice. She sang before and after work, not because she was happy but because the songs escaped from her mouth, her young soul roaming outside her body to take the air before it was pulled back into drudgery.

Ambaro shook the ghosts out from her hair and began her morning soliloquy, 'Some people don't know how much work goes into feeding their ungrateful guts, think they are some kind of suldaan who can idle about without a care in the world, head full of trash, only good for running around with trash. Well, over my dead body. I don't grind my backbone to dust to sit and watch filthy-bottomed boys roll around on their backs.'

These poems of contempt, these gabays of dissatisfaction, greeted Jama every morning. Incredible meandering streams of abuse flowed from his mother's mouth, sweeping away the mukhadim at the factory, her son, long-lost relatives, enemies, men, women, Somalis, Arabs, Indians into a pit of damnation.

'Get up, stupid boy, you think this is your father's house? Get up you fool! I need to get to work.'

Jama continued to loll around on his back, playing with his belly button. 'Stop it, you dirty boy, you'll make a hole in it.' Ambaro slipped off one of her broken leather sandals, and marched over to him.

Jama tried to flee but his mother dived and attacked him with stinging blows. 'Get up! I have to walk two miles to work and you make a fuss over waking up, is that it?' she raged. 'Go then, get lost, you good for nothing.'

Jama blamed Aden for making his mother so angry. He wanted to return to Hargeisa, where his father could calm her down with love songs. It was always at day break that Jama craved his father, all his memories were sharper in the clean morning light, his father's laughter and songs around the campfire, the soft, long-fingered hands enveloping his own. Jama couldn't be sure if these were real memories or just dreams seeping into his waking life but he cherished these fragile images, hoping that they would not disappear with time. Jama remembered traversing the desert on strong shoulders, peering down on the world like a prince but already his father's face was lost to him, hidden behind stubborn clouds.

Along the dark spiral steps came the smell of anjeero; the Islaweynes were having breakfast. ZamZam, a plain, teenaged girl, used to bring Jama the mealtime scraps. He had accepted them for a while until he heard the boys in the family call him 'haashishki', the rubbish bin. The Islaweynes were distant relatives, members of his mother's clan, who had been asked by Ambaro's half brother to take her in when she arrived in Aden. They had done as promised but it soon became clear that they expected their country cousin to be their servant; cooking, cleaning and giving their family the appearance of gentility. Within a week Ambaro had found work in a coffee factory, depriving the Islaweynes of their new status symbol and unleashing the resentment of the family. Ambaro was made to sleep on the roof, she was not allowed to eat with them unless Mr Islaweyne and his wife had guests around, then they were all smiles and familial generosity, 'Oh Ambaro, what do you mean 'can I'? What's ours is yours, sister!'

When Ambaro had saved enough to bring her six-year-old son to Aden, Mrs Islaweyne had fumed at the inconvenience and made a show of checking him for diseases that could infect her precious children. Her gold bangles had clanked around as she checked for nits, fleas, skin diseases; she shamelessly pulled up his ma'awis to check for worms. Even after Jama had passed her medical exam, she glared at him when he played with her children and whispered to them not to get too familiar with this boy from nowhere. Five years later, Ambaro and Jama still lived like phantoms on the roof, leaving as few traces of their existence as possible. Apart from the neatly stacked piles of laundry that Ambaro washed and Jama pegged out to dry, they were rarely seen or heard by the family.

Ambaro left for the coffee factory at dawn and didn't return until dark, leaving Jama to either float around the Islaweyne home feeling unwelcome, or to stay out in the streets with the market boys. Outside the sky had brightened to a watery turquoise blue. Somali men asleep by the roadside began to rouse, their afros full of sand, while Arabs walked hand in hand towards the suq. Jama fell in behind a group of Yemenis wearing large gold-threaded turbans and beautiful, ivory-handled daggers in their belts. Jama ran his hands along the warm flanks of passing camels being led to market, their extravagant eyelashes batted in appreciation at his gentle stroke, and when they overtook him their swishing tails waved goodbye. Men and boys shuffled past ferrying vegetables, fruits, breads, meats, in bags, in their hands, on their heads, to and from the market, crusty flatbread tucked under their arms like newspapers hot off the press. Butterflies danced, enjoying their morning flutter before the day turned unbearably hot and they slept it off inside sticky blossoms. The smell of leather harnesses damp with human sweat, of incense lingering on skin from the night before filled Jama's nostrils. Leaning against the warm wall, Jama closed his eyes and imagined curling up in his mother's lap and feeling the reverberations of her songs as they bubbled up from deep within her body. He sensed someone standing over him. A small hand rubbed the top of his head and he opened his eyes to see Abdi and Shidane grinning down at him. Abdi was the nine-year-old, gappy-toothed uncle of eleven-year-old gangster Shidane. Abdi held out a chunk of bread and Jama swallowed it down.

The black lava of the Shum Shum volcanoes loomed over them when they reached the beach. Market boys of all different hues, creeds and languages gathered at the beach to play, bathe and fight. They were a roll-call of infectious diseases, mangled limbs, and deformities. Jama called 'Shalom!' to Abraham, a shrunken Jewish boy who used to sell flowers door to door with him, Abraham waved and took a running leap into the water. Shidane's malnutrition-blond hair looked transparent in the sunlight and Abdi's head jiggled from side to side, too big for his paltry body, as he ran into the surf.

Abdi and Shidane were two perfect sea urchins who spent their days diving for coins. Jama wanted them to take him out to sea so collected wooden planks washed up on the shore, and called the gali gali boys to attention.

'Go and find twine so we can go out to sea,' he ordered.

Jama sat on the seaweed-strewn sand while Abdi and Shidane tied the planks into a makeshift raft. Together they pushed the rickety contraption out to sea. 'Bismillah,' he whispered before they took off, holding on desperately while Abdi and Shidane propelled him forward. When Abdi and Shidane tired, they clambered on, panting beside him, their faces upturned to the rising sun. Jama turned on his back and smiled a contented smile, they floated gently on the young waves and linked arms, water droplets scattered over their skin like diamonds.

'Why don't you learn to swim, Jama?' Abdi asked. 'Then you can come pearl fishing with us. It's beautiful down there, all kinds of fish and animals, coral, shipwrecks, you could find a pearl worth a fortune.'

Shidane shifted position and the raft spun around with him. 'There aren't any pearls down there, Abdi, we've looked everywhere, they're all gone, taken by the Arabs. Look at those stupid Yemenis, they don't deserve a boat like that,' sneered Shidane. 'If we had a gun we could take everything those fools had.'

Jama lifted his head up, he saw a sambuk hurrying back to port with crates piled up on its deck. 'Get a gun then,' he dared.

'Ya salam! You think I can't? I can make one, boy.'

Jama pulled himself up onto his elbows, 'What?'

'You heard me, I can make one. I've been watching the soldiers, some people are always active, always thinking. It's simple for someone like me to make these Ferengi things; you get a piece of hardwood, make a hole all the way through, get gunpowder, stuff it into the hole, then fill one end with pebbles and in the other put a lit string, then blow fools like those into the sea.'

'More likely you would blow your burnt futo into the sea,' chuckled Jama.

'Laugh all you like, you big-toothed Eidegalle donkey. I will be the mukhadim, if you are lucky you can be my coolie.'

'Yes! We could be shiftas of the sea, covered in gold, wallaahi everyone will shake when they see our ship,' enthused Abdi, firing imaginary bullets at the sun.

Jama felt water against his skin. 'Yallah,

yallah, back to the beach! The twine is loosening,' he cried, as the planks fell apart.

Abdi and Shidane sprang into action, grabbing his arms and bearing him aloft like two well-trained dolphins.

★ ★ ★

Walking out into the dust and scorching heat, Jama instinctively headed for the warehouse district. He kicked a tin can down the streets of Crater, a town in the heart of a volcano, its hellish heat spilling people and cultures over its sides like a lava flow. Sunlight reflected against the tin roofs of the warehouses, blinding him momentarily. The smell of tea, coffee, frankincense, myrrh swept up the hill and swathed him in a nauseating, heady mix. Reaching the first warehouse, bare-chested coolies chanted as they pushed heavy wooden crates onto the backs of lorries, slightly smaller crates onto the backs of camels and sacks onto donkeys. Standing outside Al-Madina coffee stores, Jama walked through the stone entrance and peered into the darkness, sunlight splintered through the tin roof, illuminating the dust rising from the coffee beans as they were thrown up and down to loosen the husks. A field of underpaid women in bright, flowery Somali robes were bent over baskets full of

14

coffee beans, cleaning them ready for sale. Jama weaved around them looking for a woman with smallpox scars, copper eyes, canines dipped in gold and inky black hair. He found her in a corner, working on her own with a sky-blue scarf holding her hair back. She brought his head down to kiss his cheek, her soft freckly skin brushing against his.

Ambaro whispered in his ear, 'What are you doing here, Goode? This isn't a playground, what do you want?'

Jama stood in front of her, legs entangled like a flamingo's. 'I dunno, I was bored . . . do you have any change?' He hadn't been thinking of money but now he was too embarrassed to say he just wanted to see her.

'Keleb! You come to my place of work to hassle me for money? You think of no-one but yourself and may Allah curse you for it, get out now before the mukhadim sees you!'

Jama turned on his heels and ran out the door. He hid behind the warehouse but Ambaro found him, her rough dry hands pulled him against her. Her dress smelt of incense and coffee, he let his tears soak through to her skin.

'Goode, Goode, please, you're a big boy. What have I done to you? Tell me? Tell me? Look at the life I'm living, can't you take pity on me?' Ambaro asked softly. She pulled his

15

arms up and dragged him to a small wall facing the sea. 'Do you know why I call you Goode?'

'No,' lied Jama, hungry to hear of the time when he had a real family.

'When I was pregnant with you I grew incredibly large, my stomach stuck out like you wouldn't believe. People warned me that a young girl of seventeen would die giving birth to such a child, that you would tear my insides out, but I was happy, at peace, I knew I was expecting someone special. Following camels around is terrible work and I got slower and slower. I was often separated from my father's large caravan and would hobble with my swollen ankles until I caught up with the family. But maybe in the eighth month, I was so exhausted I had to stop even though I had lost sight of the last camel. There was an ancient acacia in a savannah called Gumburaha Banka, and I sat under the old tree to rest in the little shade it provided. I sat and listened to my heavy breath fall and rise, rise and fall, I was wearing a nomad's guntiino and the side of my stomach was exposed to the sun and breeze. Then suddenly I felt a smooth hand caress my back and move towards my bellybutton, I looked down in shock, and hoogayeh! There was not a hand but a huge mamba curling around my belly. I

16

was scared its heavy body would crush you so I didn't move even one inch, but it stopped and laid its devilishly wise face against you and listened to your thumping heartbeat. All three of us were joined like that for what seemed like a lifetime until, having decided something, the snake flexed its sinews and slipped down my body, massaging my womb with its soft under-belly till with a flick of its tail it disappeared into the sand. I wanted to name you Goode, meaning Black Mamba. Your father just laughed at me, but when you slithered out with your beautiful dark skin and your smell of earth I knew what your name was meant to be, I kept it as my special name for you.'

Jama melted in the warmth of his mother's words and he felt the liquid gold of love in his veins, he was silent not wanting to break the spell between them, and she carried on.

'I know I'm tough on you, sometimes too tough but do you know why I ask things of you? Things that you don't understand are good for you? It's because I have such high hopes, you are my good luck baby, you were born to be somebody, Goode. Do you know the year you were born became known as the year of the worm? Fat worms poked their noses out of the earth during the rainy season and came out to consume the grass, the trees, even our straw houses, until finished, they suddenly disappeared. Everyone thought it was a sign of the end but the elders said they had seen it before and it was barako as the rains were plentiful afterwards and our camels would breed fantastically. One old woman, Kissimee, told me that as my child would be born in the thick of that plague he would have the most beautiful luck, as if he had been born with the protection of all the saints and he would see the four corners of the world. I believed her because no one knew that woman to ever make a false prophecy.'

Despite the beauty of her words, Jama felt his mother was threading pearl after pearl of expectation into a noose that would sit loosely around his neck, ready for her to hang him one day. He pulled in close to her for an embrace and she wrapped her golden brown arms around his mahogany back, rubbing her fingers along his sharp spine.

'Let's go back home to Hargeisa, hooyo.'

'One day, when we have enough to go back with,' she said with a kiss on his head. Untying a knot at the bottom of her dress, she pulled out a paisa coin and gave it to Jama, 'See you back on the roof.'

'Yes, hooyo,' Jama replied and stood up ready to go. Grabbing his hand, his mother looked up at him. 'God protect you, Goode.'

* * *

Mrs Islaweyne had a problem with Ambaro, and she didn't inconvenience herself by concealing it. In the mother's long absences she went for the cub. When she realised in her sickly-sweet interrogations that Jama would never speak badly of his mother or let slip embarrassing secrets, she volunteered her own criticisms. 'What kind of woman leaves her child alone to roam the streets every day?' and 'I'm not surprised Somalis have a bad reputation, the way some of these newcomers dress, all naked arms, with their udders hanging out the sides.' The resentment was mutual and Ambaro and Jama mocked her behind her back. When Ambaro saw Mrs Islaweyne wrapping her nikaab around her face she would raise an eyebrow and sing in a bittersweet voice, 'Dhegdheer, Dhegdheero, yaa ku daawaan? Witch, oh witch, who will admire you?'

Dhegdheer was a strange, vain woman with short, plump limbs, always oiled from head to toe, her eyebrows drawn on thickly with kohl, a fat, hairy mole on her cheek blending into a luxurious moustache, small, swollen feet squeezed into shoes that Ambaro could never afford. Sometimes Dhegdheer would appear on their roof glaring at them for no particular

19

reason, marking her territory. When she returned downstairs, Jama would copy her signature waddle and squint to perfection. 'Go eat yourself, witch!' he shouted when she was safely out of earshot.

'The one thing that woman is good at is breeding, she must have a highway between her legs, she gives birth to litters of two and three as if she was a stray bitch,' Ambaro would say, and she was right, Jama had counted eight children but behind every door there seemed to be more sleeping or crying. The older Islaweyne boys went to school and chattered away in Arabic, even at home. Jama had learnt a rough, street Arabic which they mocked, mimicking his bad grammar and slang in slow, imbecilic voices. Although ZamZam was not the most alluring of girls, Dhegdheer had her eye on one of the wealthy Somali men who imported livestock from Berbera and wanted her daughter to appear a delicate flower cultivated in the most refined of settings.

Jama heard Dhegdheer complaining to her husband that Ambaro and her guttersnipe son lowered the honour of their family. 'How can we be first class when we have people like that in our own home?'

Mr Islaweyne grunted and waved her away, but it was clear to Jama that his place in the home was precarious. As Jama spent more time on the streets to avoid Dhegdheer and her sons, the more their complaints about him increased.

'Kinsi said she saw him stealing from the suq.'

'Khadar, next door, said that he hangs around the camel mukhbazar joking with hashish smokers.'

Jama did joke with the hashish smokers but it was because he did not have brothers, cousins or a father to protect him like the other children. He knew his powerlessness so did not argue or make enemies. He had recently befriended Shidane and Abdi who were kind and generous, but friendships between boys of different clans tended to form and collapse like constellations of new stars forged in the heat of Aden, never lasting.

In the apartment the cold war between the women was thawing and simmering in the summer heat. Ambaro, tired and frustrated after work, became more combative. She used the kitchen at the same time as Dhegdheer, helped herself to more flour and ghee, picked out whichever glass was clean instead of the ones set aside for them, and left the laundry waiting for days at a time. Even with Jama she was like a kettle whistling to the boil; one day she wanted him to work, another day to attend school, another day to stay on the roof and keep away from those market boys, and yet another day she didn't want to see him ever again. Jama at first tried to soothe her, massaging away all the knots in her body with his keen, sprightly fingers but soon even his touch irritated her and he left her to spend the nights with Shidane and Abdi. He returned every few days to wash, eat a little and check on his mother, until one evening he came in to find Ambaro and Dhegdheer in the kitchen, bosoms nearly touching, nails and teeth bared, ready to pounce on one another. From what he could tell through the shouts of 'Slut born of sluts!' and 'Hussy!', Dhegdheer was ordering his mother out of the kitchen and she was cursing back and standing her ground, looking as if she was ready to spit in Dhegdheer's face. Jama grabbed his mother's arm and tried to pull her away. Dhegdheer's sons, older and stronger than Jama entered the kitchen, unable to ignore the shouting women any longer. Ambaro and Dhegdheer were now grappling with each other, pushing and shoving amongst the hot steaming pots. Jama hustled the pans off the fire and put them out of harm's way. Ambaro was younger, stronger and a better fighter than the housebound Dhegdheer and she pushed the older woman into a corner, daring Mrs Islaweyne to lay a finger on her.

'Soobax, soobax, come on,' jeered Ambaro.

Dhegdheer's oldest son grabbed hold of Ambaro and jostled her onto the floor.

'Stop that shameful behaviour,' he squeaked in his breaking voice.

Seeing his mother lying on the floor, Jama without any thought, picked up a pan of boiling soup and slung the steaming liquid in the boys' direction. The soup fell short of their bodies but cascaded over their bare feet. Dhegdheer was beside herself. 'Hoogayey waan balanbalay, my precious boys, beerkay! My own livers,' she keened. 'May Allah cut you up into pieces Jama and throw you to the wild dogs.' Dhegdheer picked up a long butcher's knife and began sharpening it, while Ambaro tried to wrench it out of her hands, Jama darted beneath their legs and escaped from the apartment.

Shidane and Abdi applauded Jama when he told them he was never going back to the Islaweyne house. Aden was a huge, dangerous playground for market boys and Shidane knew all of the secret nooks, crevices, holes and storerooms that made up the map of the unseen Aden. Together they could avoid older boys who would rob or beat them.

It was only when they became a gang that

Jama realised Abdi was nearly deaf, he would put his ear right up to your mouth to compensate and hold your hands while he listened. As they sat on their rooftop, watching the setting sun turn the pools of water in the ancient tanks into infant suns, Jama and Abdi snuggled up under an old sheet. Shidane laughed at their canoodling and they laughed at his big ears.

'No wonder your poor uncle is so deaf! You have taken enough ears for both of you,' said Jama grabbing hold of Shidane's flapping ears.

'You can talk!' exclaimed Shidane in response, pointing at Jama's big white teeth. 'Look at those tusks in your mouth! You could pull down a tree with them.'

'You wish you had teeth like mine, rabbit ears, with a lucky gap like this in my teeth, you wait and see how rich I become, you would die for my teeth, admit it.' Jama displayed his teeth for them to envy.

★ ★ ★

Ambaro had spent days holding her breath when Jama had disappeared. Mr Islaweyne had allowed her to move into a tiny room in the apartment while Dhegdheer took quiet satisfaction from Jama's disappearance. Ambaro searched for Jama in dark, filthy alleys late at night, long after her twelve-hour shift had finished she was still looking, she went to his old haunts, asked around the other market boys but could not find him. She had no friends amongst the coffee women and unlike other Somali women whose troubles gushed forth at every opportunity, her anguish stayed locked up within her without release. Jama regularly disappeared but Ambaro had a panicky feeling that this time he would not come back. Her daughter Kahawaris began appearing in her dreams and she hated dreaming of the dead.

Unlike many Somali women, who abandoned four- and five-year-old boys on the street when their fathers absconded, she had guarded Jama as best as she could, and thought day and night 'How can I keep my baby safe? How can I keep my baby safe?'

Jama was the only family she had or wanted, she had not seen the rest since leaving for Aden. Ambaro had grown up in the care of her aunt after her mother, Ubah, had died of smallpox. Izra'il, the angel of death, had barged down Ubah's door fourteen times to decimate her legion of children, spiriting them away with diarrhoea, petty accidents, hunger, coughs that had wracked tiny rib cages until they had cracked. Ubah had left one live child, a heartbroken sickly little girl, who haunted her grave waiting for the day of judgement to arrive and restore her mother to her. Smallpox had laid its pockmarked hand on Ambaro's body but she had survived, wearing her scars as proof of her mother's ghostly protection. As she grew older Ambaro became a lean, silent young woman. Grief for her mother and lost brothers and sisters kept her detached from the other members of the family, who feared her and worried that misfortune might lead her to perform some evil witchcraft on them. Ambaro's eyes were too deep, too full of misery to be trustworthy. It was only Jinnow, the level-headed matriarch of the polygamous family, who showed her any affection. Jinnow had delivered Ambaro into the world as a baby, had named her, and had demanded a veil be drawn over her growing intimacy with her cousin Guure. Guure the orphan lived with his elderly aunt and Ambaro imagined him a kindred spirit as well as a kinsman. She thought only he would understand how it felt to be an outsider in their family, to be called 'cursed' and 'miserable'. She watched him for a long time before he noticed her, but then he began sneaking up behind her as she trekked to the well or collected firewood.

When Ambaro heard that her father and uncles had rejected Guure in favour of another man, she asked Jinnow to send word to Guure to meet her. She wrapped herself in her newest shawl and escaped into the night. Guure stood waiting under the great acacia as she planned, lithe and smiling, his skin shining in the moonlight. His brown afro formed a halo around his head and with his luminous white robes she felt she was running away with the archangel Jibreel. He had brought with him a cloth bundle. He kneeled down to open it and brought out a pomegranate, and a gold bangle stolen from his aunt; he passed these to Ambaro, kissing her hands as she took them. Then he removed a lute and pulled her down to sit next to him, placing the cloth underneath her. He plucked the strings sparsely, delicately, watching the shy smile on her face grow mischievously; he then played more confidently, easing out a soft bucolic melody. It sounded like spring, a lover's lullaby. They sat entwined until the moon and stars tactfully dimmed and took their leave of the secret lovers. They were married the next day, in a wedding witnessed by strangers and conducted by a rebellious sheikh who laughingly placed two goats in the role of the bride's male guardians. They returned to the family camp and the admiration of their cousins but the elders were furious and gave nothing to the young couple, who were forced to build a ramshackle aqal of their own. Ambaro quickly learned that her husband was a hardened dreamer, always stuck in his head; he was the boy everyone loved but would not trust with their camels. Guure could not accept that his carefree youth was over; he still wanted to wander off with his friends while all Ambaro wanted was a family of her own. Guure played the lute with all of his passion and attention but was listless and incompetent with the practical details of life, they had no livestock and depended on Jinnow's charity. In the blink of an eye, Ambaro became Guure's judge, his overseer, his jailer. When Jama arrived a year later in Ambaro's eighteenth year, she hoped it would force Guure to start providing but instead he carried on endlessly combing his hair and playing his lute, singing his favourite song to her, 'Ha I gabin oo I gooyn'. He occasionally dangled the baby from his thin fingers before Ambaro snatched Jama away. Ambaro carried both a knife and a stick from the magic wagar tree to protect her son from dangers seen and unseen, she was a fierce, militant mother, her sweet mellow core completely melted away. Ambaro tied the baby to her back and taught herself how to weave straw baskets, make perfume, sew blankets, intending to barter these items in neighbouring settlements for food. Whatever Ambaro did, they remained destitute, and she was reduced to foraging in the countryside for edible plants and roots. When Guure began to spend his days chewing qat with young men from whom he caught the Motor Madness, Ambaro was ready to tear her hair out. He bored Ambaro with obsessive talk about cars and the clansmen who had gone to Sudan and earned big money driving Ferengis around. It all seemed hopeless to Ambaro who had never seen a car in her life and could not believe that cars were anything more than the childish sorcery of foreigners. Ambaro tried desperately to extinguish this fire that was burning in Guure but the more she criticised and ridiculed him, the more Guure clung to his dream and convinced himself that he must leave for Sudan. His talk stole the hope out of her heart and made her wonder how he could desert his family so easily; she would cry and he would hold her but she knew only heartache lay ahead. Guure quietened down when a daughter arrived a year after Jama, a smiling golden child with big happy eyes that Ambaro named Kahawaris, after the glow of light before sunrise that heralded her birth. Kahawaris became the light of their lives, a baby whose beauty the other mothers envied and whose giggles rang through the camp.

Jama had grown into a talkative little boy, always petting his little sister, accosting the adults with questions while he carried Kahawaris on his back. With his two children pawing at him, complaining and crying with hunger each night, Guure promised that he would take any work he was given, even if it meant carrying carcasses from the slaughter-house. He began to help Ambaro with the chores, scorning the jeers of his friends to collect water from the well and milk the goats alongside the women. Life carried on bearably like this until after a long exhausting day, Ambaro unstrapped her daughter from her back and found her limp and lifeless. Ambaro screamed for Guure and he took the child from her arms and ran to Jinnow. Ambaro's soul emptied after her baby's death, she wept in sunshine and moonlight, she refused to get up, to feed herself or Jama. She blamed Guure for making her carry a young baby from village to village in the heat and dust. Ambaro had feared for Jama, she had constantly put her ear against his heart to check it was still beating but he had thrived with her. Now she felt that she had failed Kahawaris, had been a bad mother to the beautiful child. Guure hopelessly struggled to look after them, he fed and bathed Jama but he could not trade and barter like Ambaro so

30

they often went hungry or begged. Guure's father had died before he was born so he had no idea what a father did or didn't do, he just floundered along guiltily, frightened that Jama would also die. Finally, when a drought decimated the clan's camels, sheep and goats, everything disintegrated and families dissolved as people sought survival down every dirt track.

Guure cupped Ambaro's face in his hands and said, 'Look, either I go and make a living for us or you do. What will it be?' Ambaro took his hands away and kept silent.

The very same day Guure set off on a mapless, penniless journey to Sudan. That was the last they saw of him, though they heard tales of his wanderings. Ambaro waited and waited for him, not knowing if he had died, gone mad, met someone else. Her family demanded that she divorce him, the clerics told her that she had been abandoned and was free but still she waited. She went to Aden and its factories hoping to earn enough to track him down. She cursed her admirers and sent them away in the hope that one day Guure would appear over the horizon with his lute strapped to his back.

★ ★ ★

Returning to the Islaweynes' house was too bitter a fruit for Jama to stomach; the bloated, pompous pig of a woman treated Jama and his mother like flies hovering around her heaped dinner plate. He had grown tired of making his small body even smaller so that false queen could feel like the air in the room was her sole reserve. Jama had also grown weary of his mother, she did nothing but give him a headache. Living in the open had furnished him with a wolfish instinct for self-preservation; he could sense danger through the small hairs on his lower spine and taste it in the thick, dusty air. He thought from the primitive, knotted tangle of nerves at the base of his spine, like Adam — his needs were primal, to find food, find shelter and avoid predators. Sleeping on roofs and streets had changed his sleep from the contented slumber of an infant, safe within his mother-sentried realm, to a jerky, half-awake unconsciousness, aware of mysterious voices and startling footsteps. His favourite place to sleep was an earth-smelling crook on the roof of a teetering apartment block. The crook was made up of a mud wall that curled over to make a three-walled tomb, inside it Jama felt as safe as the dead, in this world but not of it, floating high in the sky. At dawn he would wake up and watch the little insects as they carried on with their busy lives, scurrying across the wall with so much self-importance, crawling over his fingers and face as if he was just a boulder in their way. He felt as small in the world as them but more vulnerable, more alone than the ants with their armies or the cockroaches with their tough shells and hidden wings. But this night he would return to the new apartment block he had been sleeping in with Shidane and Abdi. Days and weeks and months came and went but Jama rarely knew where he would be eating or sleeping on any given night, there was no order to his life. Jama could easily imagine growing old and weak on these mean streets, eventually being found one day, like other market boys he had seen, cold and stiff on the kerb, a donkey cart carrying him away to an unmarked pauper's grave outside town before stray dogs made a meal of him. Letting himself into the building, Jama wished the sleepy-eyed caretaker goodnight and went up to the roof, feeling a hollowness in his chest from wanting to be with a mother whose company he found too difficult to bear. On reaching the roof, he saw his inner emptiness matched by complete silence. Abdi and Shidane were not there. The loneliness Jama felt carved even deeper into his soul, he needed Abdi's small warm body to huddle up with tonight, his wet nose buried in Jama's neck. Jama stepped onto the ledge and looked up at the unblinking stars and the still pregnant, indifferent moon.

He hung there, enjoying the vast drop inches away from his feet, and at the top of his lungs called out, 'Guure Naaleyeh Mohamed, where are you? Come find your son!'

His voice echoed against the buildings and drifted out to sea.

★   ★   ★

Shidane led his gang through the streets of the Arab part of Aden, Ma'alla, filling-in his little uncle and Jama on the local goings on, passing on the information he had gleaned from his errand work. Men and women moved behind curtains like jerky Indian puppets, their lives framed by windows and back-lit by lamps as the boys watched them from the twilight street.

'The woman in that house is really a eunuch, I have seen him take off his sharshuf and underneath he has a gigantic club sticking out, hair all over his arms and feet, oof! He looked like a wrestler, wallaahi, I swear.'

Jama looked incredulously at Shidane and pushed him away. Extravagantly-red roses the size of Jama's face flopped over the exterior walls of the houses, filling the air with their molasses-sweet scent. Jama picked one off its stem, stroking the petals that felt like the down on a butterfly's wing, he waved it in a circle in the dusk breeze, trailing a ballet of insects that urgently followed the arcing fragrance.

'And that man, see him up there? In the turban? He is always in and out of jail, all of his teeth are gold, he's a diamond smuggler, he can take out his teeth and hide diamonds inside, I've seen him do it at night through the window.'

Abdi with a rapt expression exclaimed, 'Inshallah I will be a diamond smuggler when I'm older, that's even better than being a pearl smuggler. I would buy sparkling black pointy shoes like rich men wear and buy hooyo a house and more gold than she could ever wear.' Silently the three boys looked at their naked feet shod only in sand and dirt.

'Do you know what I would buy?' asked Jama.

'A car?' replied Shidane.

'No, I would buy an aeroplane, so I could fly through the clouds and come down to earth whenever I wanted to see a new place, Mecca, China, I would go even further to Damascus and Ardiwaliya and just come and go as I wanted.'

'Allah! They are the work of the Shayddaan! You wouldn't get me in one of those things,' Shidane harrumphed. 'My mum says they're haram, it's only angels, insects and birds that God intended to fly, it's no surprise that they burst into flames. Then when you die your body is turned into ash so you can't even have a proper burial and you go straight to hell. Serves the Ferengis right though.'

The rose torn from its bush wilted in the stifling heat and Jama tore it apart petal by petal. 'Hey, do you remember that flower merchant that we worked for last Ramadaan?'

'That shithead, how could we forget him? We are still waiting for our pay. We can't all flutter our eyelashes at the women like you, Jama. The old hags would open the door, see me, and slam the door back in my face. He still owes me for the few flowers I did sell,' said Shidane.

Jama held his finger to his mouth. 'Be quiet and listen Shidane, I heard that he is now a seaman and earned enough on one voyage to take two wives and buy a large house in Sana'a.'

'Two wives!' said Shidane with a whistle. 'That ugly sinner! I would be surprised if he managed to trick one blind old baboon into marrying him.'

Abdi creased up at his nephew's cruel tongue. Abdi's face was usually set in a grave, contemplative expression but then with a flicker of light in his eyes, a smile would crack it open, revealing teeth that tumbled over one another. A crooked smile made up of a hundred broken pearly whites.

Jama had enjoyed carrying the big baskets laden with jasmine, frangipani and hibiscus door to door in the cool quiet twilight, smiling at the pretty wives and daughters of wealthy men in the rich neighbourhoods. By nightfall his skin and sarong would be infused with an intoxicating smell of life and beauty. He would return home and decorate his mother's black hair with pink, red and purple flowers.

As the three boys padded down the street, a racket broke the silence of the neighbourhood. A woman's screams rose above the general shouts and Jama nervously looked at the boys. A small, middle-aged woman came around a corner, running barefoot past them with the front of her gown ripped open revealing an old grey brassiere, her face contorted in unseeing terror.

Behind her chased a group of older men, one of them bearing a knife, another a thick cane. They hollered after her, 'Ya sharmuta! Whore! Adulteress! You have brought shame on our street, by God we will catch you.'

Behind them a rag tag of children came,

some crying, some cheering and laughing. This human storm engulfed Jama and then flew away just as quickly. Jama stood stock still, bewildered by what he had seen, his head still turned in the direction of the lynch mob.

'Let's chase them!' shouted Shidane, and they pelted after the crowd. 'Which way did they go?' Jama asked, trying to pinpoint where all the commotion had gone.

The screams were piercing when they reached the dirty alley where the woman had been cornered. Her children clung to her, a howling, shaking little girl holding her mother around the waist, and a teenage boy desperately trying to put his slight body between his mother and the man holding the knife. Shidane pushed through the crowd to the woman, the knife frozen in the air above their heads.

'Let go of her!' he screamed. 'Let go of her you son of a bitch.' Jama saw the man with the cane slap Shidane around the back with it, the other thug held him back as the old man cursed and lunged at Shidane. 'Get away from here! Ya abid, slave,' he raged.

The crowd of excited children shifted around Jama, their eyes wide with terror and joy at what they were seeing, one boy kept climbing Jama's back for a better look but he threw him to the ground. Abdi was hanging from the arm of the man with the cane. Jama, worried that Abdi would be beaten, crept up to the knifeman, grabbed hold of his arm and sunk his teeth in. Jama bit harder and harder until the knife dropped to the ground. Shidane picked up the knife and dragged Jama and Abdi away. They fled into the night, the dagger tucked into Shidane's ma'awis.

★ ★ ★

The next day, the boys stalked the outdoor restaurant of Cowasjee Dinshaw and Sons like a pack of hungry hyenas. They placed themselves to the left, right and front of the seated, cosmopolitan diners, who ordered heaped plates of rice with chicken, spaghetti with lamb mince, stew with huge hunks of bread. The clinking of full glasses and chatter drifted up into the air along with faint arabesques of cigarette smoke. Jama wiped his salivating mouth, and made eye contact with Shidane, who was standing behind the table of a suited Banyali merchant and his elegantly sari'd companion, her juicy flesh peeking out from underneath her fuchsia choli. The boys had barely eaten or drunk anything for days and they had to restrain their desire to knock the waiters down and snatch the steaming plates from their hands. The waiter took the white towel hanging over his forearm and flicked Abdi roughly around the back of his legs with it, 'Yallah! Yallah abid! Leave our customers in peace,' he shouted. The boys pulled back from the restaurant and regrouped at the palm trees lining the road. Hunger was the motivating principle in their lives, whether they were searching together or alone. Abdi gestured towards the Indian couple who were settling their bill. Jama and Shidane sprinted to the table and in one desperate movement tipped two plates of leftover spaghetti into their sarongs, which they had pulled out into makeshift bowls. Abdi collected all the bread and then ran after Jama and Shidane as they scrambled up the road. They stopped the instant they realised they were not being pursued and dropped down by the side of the road with their backs against a wall. They pulled the food to their mouths as if they would never eat again, silently and with a fixed attention to the meagre meal in their laps. Abdi tried to pick spaghetti from Jama's and Shidane's laps but had to dodge their frenetically moving fingers. They in turn grabbed at the bread in his hands and it was only after he shouted in despair that they slowed down and allowed him his share of the booty. Jama and Shidane wiped their greasy fingers on the sand beneath them and watched as Abdi lethargically finished off the scattered breadcrumbs. Jama's eyes scanned over the little boy's protruding ribs and matchstick-thin ankles and wrists. 'Abdi, why do you eat like a chicken? You're always getting left with the crumbs, you have to be fast!'

'Well I would eat more if you two pigs didn't swallow everything before I can even sit down,' Abdi replied sullenly.

Abashed, Jama and Shidane giggled but did not meet each other's eyes.

'I want to go see my hooyo again,' said Abdi sadly. 'I think she's ill.'

'Don't worry, we'll go tomorrow. We'll all be going back to Berbera soon anyway, the dhows are already leaving for Somaliland. I can't wait for this year's fair, coffee from Harar, saffron, tusks, feathers from our great Isse Muuse, Garhajis with feathers, myrrh, gum, sheep, cattle, ghee, and the Warsangeli with their bloody frankincense. And all those Arabs and Indians to pickpocket before our morning swim. Are you not going, Jama?' asked Shidane.

'No, I'm staying here, in the big city. I've got nothing to go back for,' lied Jama.

Shidane stared at him, a smile pulling at his mouth.

'Where is your father anyway? Why did he run off? Was it you or your mother that got on his nerves?'

'Shut up, Shidane,' Jama replied sternly. Shidane picked on people the way he picked at scabs, desperately trying to get to the red, pulpy stuff underneath. Jama hated Shidane when he was like this. Shidane's mother was a prostitute in a port brothel but he still never dared insult Shidane back. The boys never took Jama with them when they visited Shidane's mother but Jama had followed them once, he watched from behind a post as Shidane and Abdi embraced a small woman in a Ferengi shirt, her red hair flying in the breeze. She was surrounded by the hard-living women of the port who drank, chewed tobacco and qat and attracted sailors by shaking tambourines and dancing. Shidane's mother looked like a lost bride with her red lips, kohled eyes and copper jewellery, but behind the make-up was a face that had lost all innocence, bloated and yellow with alcohol.

Shidane's father had been killed by a British bomb left behind from the campaign years earlier against the Mad Mullah, and the rage that this had spawned in Shidane sometimes made his temper flare up as brightly as magnesium. He would seek out fights and get pulverised, Jama and Abdi would then huddle silently around him, tentative, as he wheezed and swore at them for being cowardly, stupid, pathetic, his eyes bloodshot with held-back tears. Jama and Abdi loved Shidane, so they tolerated his foul-mouth, his unreasonable demands, his cruelty; he was too charming to hold a grudge against. His gigantic eyes could be so sincere and full of compassion that they could never stay angry with him for long. Without Shidane and Abdi, Jama's days would be long, lonely and almost silent, they had insinuated themselves deep down into his heart and Jama fantasised that they were his brothers. The only time they were separated now was when Shidane and Abdi went to Steamer Point to dive for pennies. Cruise ships on the way to India or the Far East stopped off in Aden and idle passengers would throw coins into the water to watch the gali gali boys risk their lives to collect them. Jama occasionally watched them, Shidane dangerously sleek and elegant in the water, Abdi struggling always with a mouthful of saltwater. After hours in the sea they would come ashore with their cheeks full of coins and spit them out at Jama's feet; it was begging, but they made it look beautiful.

★ ★ ★

At Shidane's instigation the gang would sometimes go looking for trouble. Indian kids, Jewish kids, and Yemeni kids, all lived with their parents however poor they might be. It was only the Somali children who ran around feral, sleeping everywhere and anywhere. Many of the Somali boys were the children of single mothers working in the coffee factories, too tired after twelve hours of work to chase around after boisterous, hungry boys. Their fathers came and went regularly, making money and losing it, with the monsoon trade. With no parental beatings to fear, the Somali boys saw the other children as well-fed and soft enough to harass safely. Jama, Shidane and Abdi liked to prowl around Suq al-Yahud and the Banyali area as well as old Aden. Today, they penetrated the Jewish quarter, walking under the flapping laundry crisscrossing the alleys, looking for boys their age to fight. The Jewish boys looked so prim and proper in comparison to them, over-dressed with little skullcaps balanced on their heads, books tucked under their arms as they returned from yeshiva.

Shidane picked up a stone and lobbed it at one. 'Hey Yahudi, do they teach you this at your school?' he said with the secret envy of

44

the illiterate. Abdi and Jama although hesitant picked up smaller stones and threw them as well.

The Jewish schoolboys piled up their books in a heap. 'Somali punkahwallahs, your fathers are dirty Somali punkahwallahs!' they shouted and started bombarding the Somali boys back.

Adrenaline flowed on both sides, and soon vile insults in Arabic against each other's mothers were exchanged along with the stones, Jama chipped in with a few Hebrew insults he had learned from Abraham, a boy he used to sell flowers with, 'Ben Zona! Ben Kelev.'

The Jewish boys had sweat dripping down their temples into their ringlets, and down their backs onto their tunics. Jama and Shidane cackled as they avoided the sharp stones, pushing Abdi out of the way whenever one was targeted at him. Hearing the commotion and obscenities, Jewish matrons came out onto their balconies to hector the little brats. They went un-heeded until one no-nonsense woman went indoors and returned with a large basin, tipping half of the dirty water on the Somali intruders and splattering the rest on the Sabbath-disrespecting Sons of Israel. All of the boys ran away, Jama, Shidane and Abdi fled together, passing fabric shops as they closed for the Sabbath.

Abdi pinched a black waistcoat that was hanging from a nail and they ran even faster, their booty held aloft while a burly, bearded man chased them. 'It's the Sabbath, you shouldn't be running!' shouted Jama over his shoulder, and Shidane and Abdi roared at his wit.

The man huffed and puffed behind them but eventually gave up, cursing them in Hebrew. 'You shouldn't swear on the Sabbath either!' shouted Jama in a parting shot, as they bolted out of the neighbourhood.

★   ★   ★

The camel mukhbazar was a small, white-washed greasy spoon serving pasta and rice dishes to Somali migrants. A few round tables were placed inside the mukhbazar and Somali baskets hung from the wall in an attempt at decoration. Most of its customers preferred to stand or sit outside in loud groups, metal plates balanced in their hands. The camel mukhbazar had become a meeting place for all the Somalis who washed up on the Yemeni coast looking for work. Merchants, criminals, coolies, boatmen, shoemakers, policemen all went there for their evening meal. Jama often hovered around its entrance hoping to see his father or at least someone who had word of him. Jama did not know what his father looked like, his mother rarely talked about him. Jama always felt, however, that if he ever had the chance to catch his father's eye, or watch him move or talk, he would instantly recognise him from amongst the untidy men with shaved heads and claim him as his own.

One windy day as Jama's legs and feet were being buffeted by flying refuse, he joined a group of men gathered around Ismail, the owner of the mukhbazar. The Somalis were flowing out into the road to the consternation of Arab donkey drivers and coolies, who struggled past with their heavy loads. Jama heard them cursing the Somalis under their breath, 'Sons of bitches should go back to the land-of-give-me-something,' one hammal said, Jama fought the temptation to tell the men what the Arab had dared say. He eased his way into the crowd until he was at Ismail's shoulder. Ismail was reading from an Arabic newspaper, 'Italy declares war on Abyssinia, Haile Selassie appeals to the League of Nations,' he translated.

'To hell with that devilish imp!' shouted out a bystander.

'Coloured Americans raise money in churches but the rest of the world turns its gaze,' Ismail carried on.

'Good! They turned their gaze too when the Abyssinians stole our Ogaden, if they can take our ancestral land then let the Ferengis take theirs,' shouted another.

'Runta! Ain't that the truth! Look at this small boy.' Ismail suddenly lifted his head from the paper, and pointed an angry finger at Jama. 'Selassie is no bigger than him yet he has the nerve to call himself a king, an emperor no less! I knew him in Harar, when he was always running to the money lenders to pay for some work of the devil he had seen the Ferengis with, I bet he needs his servants to pick him up before he can relieve himself in his new French pisspot.'

Jama inched back, the finger still pointed at him as Ismail returned to reading. 'The Italians have amassed an army of more than one million soldiers, and are stockpiling weapons of lethal capability.'

Ismail stopped and screwed up his face. 'One million? Who needs a million of any-thing to get a job done? This war sounds like the beginning of something very stupid.' Ismail impatiently scrunched up the newspaper, wiping the ink from his fingers with a handkerchief and padded back inside his mukhbazar.

Jama was eavesdropping on the men's war talk; the names of strategic towns, disloyal nobles, Somali clans that had decided to fight with Selassie were thrown about over his head. Ismail leaned out of the kitchen window and whistled at Jama, 'Come in and make yourself useful, boy!'

Two cooks were working in the kitchen, a bald-headed, yellow-toned Somali man cooked the rice and pasta and another taller man made vats of the all-purpose sauce.

Ismail fluttered around moving dirty dishes to the basin on the floor. 'Get here, boy, and wash these dishes, do them well and you've got yourself a job.'

Jama's eyes widened with happiness at the prospect of regular money and he rushed towards the pyramid of dishes as if it was a newly found goldmine. The hot water scalded his arms but he scoured and rinsed the heavy pots and pans without complaint. Ismail stood behind him scrutinising his work but soon left to talk with new customers. Within a few minutes the dirty pyramid had been transformed into a sparkling display of almost new-looking dishes. Jama turned around with a jubilant look but the two cooks were uninterested in his achievement. Ismail came back into the kitchen and after casting an eye over his rejuvenated dishes said, 'Come back tomorrow, Jama, you can start at seven in the morning, there's a plate of rice waiting for you inside.'

Jama skipped past as Ismail slapped the back of his neck. A large plate of steaming rice and stew was placed on a table and he stopped to smell the delicious aroma and wonder at all this food that was entirely his own. Eating slowly was a luxury he rarely allowed himself but he chewed the lamb meditatively, removing all the meat from the bone and sucking out the marrow. He licked the plate clean then sat back as his stomach strained against his knotted sarong. Jama couldn't sit still he was so excited about this unexpected good luck. As soon as he felt able, he waddled out and stumbled towards the beach, where he expected Shidane and Abdi to be. Jama laughed at the memory of stealing from the camel mukhbazar, Shidane's idea was to tie a fresh date to a stick, and use the contraption to pick up paisas left on tables for the waiters. Jama was the best at casually, innocently walking past and picking up the coin with the stick. When they had finally been caught, they had moved onto the Banyali quarter. Shidane would throw a bone into the shops of the vegetarian Hindus and Jama would offer to remove it for a price.

Shidane and Abdi were kicking at the surf. The waistcoat Abdi had stolen looked ridiculous hanging from his bony shoulders and Jama burst into laughter at the sight of

Abdi in a fat Jewish man's clothing. Jama skipped up and jumped onto Shidane's shoulders, Shidane shook him off in irritation and said, 'Leave me alone you donkey.' Abdi looked gloomily at them both, rubbing his red, teary eyes, silently gathering the waistcoat around his ribs to stop the sea breeze blowing it away. Shidane was in one of his moods, he kept staring at Jama and his nostrils were round and flared, his face set in a stony grimace. 'Something has happened to Shidane's mother,' Abdi tried to explain, but Shidane hushed Abdi with a stern finger against his lips.

'What's the problem, walaalo? You need money? I've just had some good luck.'

'What?' asked Shidane defensively.

'I've got a job starting tomorrow at the camel mukhbazar, Ismail wants me to do the dishwashing from now on.'

'Ya salam! You Eidegalle really know how to look out for each other, don't you?' interrupted Shidane.

'What do you mean by that?' asked Jama in shock.

'Well, it just seems strange that you're always getting work and you never think to ask for us as well, all you care about is yourself.'

'Have you gone mad?' exclaimed Jama.

'Don't raise your voice to me, saqajaan, do

you hear me? What do you want from us anyway?'

'Stop it, stop it,' pleaded Abdi. 'Just leave Jama alone.'

'What's going on with you, Shidane? Why are you acting like this? You know I'll look after you, you can come and eat there anytime now.'

'Do you think we need your charity, huh? Is that it? Do you think we need the charity of a saqajaan bastard like you?' spat Shidane.

Jama froze, Abdi froze, the children playing nearby froze, even Shidane froze once these spiteful words had left his mouth. Jama felt his pulse beating hard in his temple, in his throat, in his chest, and he felt a trickle of shame running down his back.

'Take that back now, Shidane,' threatened Jama.

'Make me.'

There was only one way to save face after Shidane's insult and Jama threw up his fists and charged. A crowd of boys surged forward emitting a savage cry for blood. Jama pounded his fists clumsily against Shidane's soft face and slapped away Abdi's attempts to tear them apart; unable to watch his friends hurt each other Abdi preferred to take the blows himself. Jama pinned Shidane down on the sand, between his knees was the face he had looked for in crowds, the body he had slept next to for months, it was as if the world had been turned upside down. Jama couldn't bring himself to look into Shidane's eyes as they fought, a shadow Jama stood to the side and frowned at the pain he was inflicting on his friend. Abdi unable to stop this cataclysm threw in his towel at playing peacemaker and waded in to defend his nephew, he pulled at Jama's hair and feebly tried to pull him off Shidane. Jama turned around and punched Abdi hard in the mouth. Seeing this Shidane pulled the trophy dagger from his sarong and plunged it deep into Jama's arm. Jama jerked away as Shidane lunged forward for another stab but was caught in the hand. Red blood poured onto the sand and was lapped up by the surf. Jama rose woozily from Shidane and squeezed his bleeding arm. Tears gathered burning hot behind his eyes but he kept them hard and unblinkingly focused on Shidane.

'Jealous of me, you're just jealous of me, because you're a sea-beggar, diving for the pennies that Ferengis throw you and your hooyo opens her legs for them,' Jama yelled.

Shidane clutched howling Abdi in one hand and the bloody dagger in the other. 'Don't ever let me see you again or I will cut your throat.'

The crowd of children, who all knew the

combatants, kept a respectful distance and noted this shift in alliances. From now on Jama was on his own, a true loner, a boy without a father, brothers, cousins or even friends, a wolf amongst hyenas. Jama slunk away, intending to walk and walk until he found himself at the end of the world. He wanted to escape like the fake prophet Dhu Nawas, who had ridden his white horse into the waves and crests of the Red Sea, who let the sea bear him away from pain and misery.

★ ★ ★

Approaching the camel mukhbazar the next morning, Jama's eyes were sunken and dark, his back aching, but worst of all his hand bled every time he tried to use it. He had a strip of his sarong tied around his arm which stopped that bleeding but he was unable to staunch the flow from his hand. He had walked around the eating house from dawn watching the white walls become more and more luminous against the dark cloth of the sky. He now saw Ismail walking with that camel-like gait that people had named his mukhbazar after.

'Nabad Jama,' hollered Ismail.

'Nabad,' mumbled Jama, his hands behind his back.

'You have a long day ahead of you, start by

54

sweeping the floor and wiping the tables and when the first customers have eaten, start on the dishes.'

Jama nodded and followed Ismail into the yellow painted room. He picked up an old broom propped up in the corner and started attacking the piles of sand that had rushed in during the night through the cracked door. Pretty soon springs of blood popped up from Jama's hand, rivering down the earth of his hand and the broom handle to splash red pools on the white cement floor. Ismail returned to find Jama trying to sweep away the blood but just smearing it over a larger area.

'Hey, hey! What are you doing? Why is there blood all over my floor?' shouted Ismail, as he lunged towards Jama. Ismail pulled Jama's hand up into the air and marched him back outside. 'Kid, why is your hand bleeding?'

'Someone cut me yesterday, I was only protecting myself, but now it won't stop.'

'Wahollah, Jama, how do you expect to work today when there is all this najas on your hand, you're dealing with people's food for God's sake! Go home and come back when it's healed,' exclaimed Ismail.

'No, it's fine, please, let me keep my job. It will stop bleeding anytime now,' pleaded Jama, but Ismail was a squeamish man and pulled a disgusted face as the blood dripped down from Jama's hand onto his.

'Jama, I'm sorry, I will keep you in mind if another vacancy arises, go and wash this hand so it doesn't go bad,' Ismail said, dropping the child's hand.

Ismail rummaged in the pockets of his thin, grey trousers and pulled out a handkerchief and a crumpled note. He handed the money to Jama and wiped his hands with the handkerchief. Ismail threw the bloody cloth away and padded back into his café shutting the door firmly behind him. Jama stood motionless, looking vacantly at the dirty money in his hand.

Jama wanted to distance himself from any gloating eyes so he walked away from the market towards the port. The sun was starting to thicken the air into a choking fog, and Jama developed the droopy-eyed, slack-jawed expression of the stray dogs that lived on the city limits. More and more Ferengis appeared in the streets; in the starched white uniforms and peaked caps of the Royal Navy, they ignored the young child and drifted in and out of groups sharing cigarettes and gossip. Jama's eyes fell on a tall, black-haired sailor who was waving goodbye to a group of men; Jama unconsciously followed him and was drawn deeper and deeper into the busy Steamer Point. Massive steel cranes lifted gigantic crates into the air and into waiting trucks. Camels were suspended in terror as they were unloaded from the ships, their legs stuck rigidly out like the points on a compass. Machines belched dirty, hot fumes into the already claustrophobic atmosphere. Jama let his mind and feet wander in this alien land, a comic, strange, technological land so different to his own antique part of Aden. Staring at the workers, their loud cranking, whirring machinery, and the goods both animate and inanimate had made Jama lose the shiny, obsidian head of the sailor. He sat on a decayed section of wall and dangled his legs over the edge, balancing himself on his hands, a frightening drop beneath his feet. In the distance, steamer ships chugged towards the port with all the slow grace of turtles. Jama tried to imagine where the ships were coming from and going to, but could not really believe in the icy realms and green forests that people had described to him. The vessels seemed both monstrous and magnificent to Jama, and he tried to take in every detail as the ships approached. Jama wondered who could create such colossal objects, were they the work of giants, devils, or of Allah? The torrid black smoke emanating from their bellies frightened him and he dreaded the idea that these smouldering ships of fire might at any time erupt into hellish infernos. It was supernatural how they defied the laws of nature, the sea swallowed everything he threw into it so how did these iron and steel cities stay afloat as if they were no more than flower blossoms or dead fish. Jama grew thirstier and thirstier as he looked into the sparkling sea and dreamed that he could drink it all up and float and frolic like a fish in that blue paradise. He climbed off the wall and went to search for a drink from one of the busy port cafés, his money stuck to his sweaty, bloody hand like a stamp to an envelope. He waited behind the broad back of a sailor at the counter, a wiry Arab man scurried about delivering drinks to tables, when it was his turn Jama found the counter was taller than him so he pushed his moneyed hand up, and waved it at the man serving, 'shaah now!' The waiter let out a derisive snort of laughter but took the money and put a glass of watery tea on the counter. Jama carefully brought it down and walked out with his lips placed against the rim of the sticky glass, jingling his change in his other hand.

★ ★ ★

Jama was tired of always turning up a beggar at people's doors, begging for someone's leftover food, leftover attention, leftover love. Everyone is too busy with their own lives to think about me, he muttered to himself as he walked to Al-Madina Coffee. He intended to give the change to Ambaro and buy his way back into her affections. Inside the warehouse, the women had moved positions, new girls were being trained by the Banyalis. A teenage girl was working in his mother's spot and he looked at her disapprovingly. He recognised the large woman next to her, 'Where is my mother?' Jama demanded.

'How the hell would I know? Do I look like her keeper?' the woman said, pushing Jama out of her way.

'Did the Banyalis tell her to go?'

The woman put her tray of coffee husks down and decided to give Jama exactly ten seconds of her precious time. 'She fell sick a few weeks ago, I haven't seen her since then. She never spoke to any of us so I don't know where she's gone but I shouldn't be the one telling you all this, boy, she's your mother after all.'

Jama dragged his feet out of the warehouse, his eyebrows knotted in concentration as he ran through the possibilities. His mother was suddenly the only person that mattered to him. Sneaking up the grey worn steps into the dim hallway of the Islaweyne apartment filled

Jama with unpleasant memories. It still seemed incredible to him that his mother, a woman who had so devotedly tutored him in pride, self-respect and independence, could allow herself to become subject to the petty dictatorship of a fat woman and her overfed family. Jama found the roof empty and snuck back downstairs into the apartment. Ambaro had been moved into a closet-like, air-starved room in which old suitcases lay stacked against a wall, watching her with zipped silent mouths. She was stretched out on a grass mat, her thin headscarf had slid back releasing big black waves of hair. The tobe she was wearing had split all the way down the side, revealing a body shrunk to childlike fragility. A strange odour hit him as he got closer to her; he saw a basin brimming with najas; phlegm, blood clots, vomit all curdling together.

Ambaro's hand was thrown over her mouth, but he could still hear a terrible gurgling sound, every intake of breath made the gurgling louder. Jama crept closer to his mother, his eyes darted from her knees to her ankles, swollen with the same fluid that her lungs were drowning in. 'Where have you been, Goode?' Ambaro gasped.

'I'm sorry, hooyo,' Jama whispered as sorrow, regret, shame seared through him.

'Put me by the window, son.'

Jama threw open the window, picked her up under her arms and dragged her with all of his strength; he gathered her head in his lap and stroked her cheek. Ambaro's heartbeat shook her body, every pulse frantically pounding against her ribs as if there was a butterfly inside of her battling free from a cocoon. A gentle breeze washed over them. Ambaro's lips were a deep, alarming red but her face was pale yellow, Jama could never have imagined seeing her so sickly, so ruined. Ambaro's eyelids were clenched in pain and Jama looked on jealously as her convulsing lungs took all of her attention. He wanted her back, to shout at him, call him a bastard, get up suddenly and throw a sandal at him. Jama placed his mother's head gently on the floor and rushed out of the room.

'Aunty!' Jama cried. 'Aunty, hooyo needs a doctor!'

He ran into each room looking for Dhegdheer, finding her in the kitchen. 'Hooyo must see a doctor, please fetch one, I beg of you.'

'Jama, how did you get in? What kind of people do you think we are? There is absolutely no money for a doctor, there is nothing anyone can do for your mother now, she is in God's hands.'

Jama pulled out the remnants of his pay and held it up to her face. 'I will pay, take this and I will earn the rest after, wallaahi, I will work forever!'

Dhegdheer pushed his hand away. 'You are such a child, Jama.'

She turned her back to him, ladled out soup. 'Here, take this through to her and don't make so much noise, inshallah she just needs rest.'

Jama took the soup, his head drooping down to his chest, his heart a lead weight, and went back to his mother. He gathered Ambaro in his arms and tried to put the soup to her lips. Ambaro jerked her head away. 'I don't want anything from that bitch, put it down, Goode.'

Jama felt a surge of power run through Ambaro. She turned her face to the window and took a smooth, deep breath in.

'Look at those stars, Goode, they have watched over everything.' The sky was as black and luminous as coal, a white-hot crescent moon hung over them like a just-forged scythe, the stars flying like sparks from the welder's furnace.

'It's another world above us, each of those stars has a power and a meaning in our lives. That star tells us when to mate the sheep, if that one does not appear we should expect

trouble, that little one leads us to the sea.'
Ambaro pointed at anonymous specks in the
distance.

Jama saw only a sea of solitude, an expanse
of nothingness impossible to navigate on his
own.

'Those stars are our friends, they have
watched over our ancestors, they have seen all
kinds of suffering but the light in them never
goes out, they will watch over you and will
watch over your grandchildren.'

Ambaro felt Jama's tears falling on her and
grabbed hold of his hand. 'Listen to me,
Goode, I am not leaving you. I will live in
your heart, in your blood, you will make
something of your life, I promise you that.
Forgive me, my baby snake, don't live the life
that I have lived, you deserve better.'

'I wanted to make you happy, hooyo, but
now it's too late,' Jama wept.

'No it is not, Goode, I will see everything
that you do, the good and the bad, nothing
will be hidden from me.'

Jama pushed his face against his mother's
cheek, rubbed his moist face against hers,
hoping to catch whatever she had, go with her
to the next life. Ambaro pulled her face away
from him.

'Stop that, Goode. Shall I tell you what the
Kaahin told your father?' she cajoled. 'A great

Kaahin once told your father when he was a boy that his son, the son of Guure Mohamed Naaleyeh, would see so much money pass through his fingers, I know in my heart that you are a child of fate, you were born with the blessing of the stars.'

Ambaro touched Jama's cheek. 'Guess what your father said to the Kaahin, he asked him, 'What's money?' Neither of us had seen any before, but now I know money is like water, it will give you life. Take the Kitab amulet from around my neck.'

Jama began to unpick the large knots in the string that hung the amulet over Ambaro's chest; in a folded paper heart lay prayer after prayer, it was in this heart that Ambaro kept her hope, she did not trust her body anymore. The Arabic script had smudged and faded on the thin exercise paper the wadaad had used. 'Inside the amulet, I have put one hundred and fifty six rupees, I do not want you using it until you absolutely need to, wait until you have grown up and know what you want to do with your life.'

Jama squeezed the amulet in his palm, he had never seen a rupee, nevermind hundreds of them, his world was of ardis lost in the street, paisas to pay for stale cakes, occasional annas thrown to Abdi from the passenger ships.

'I have been saving that for you, Goode, promise me you will not waste it, don't tell anyone about it either, tie it around your neck and forget about it.'

Ambaro's swamped lungs protested against her chatter and seized up, her face suddenly contorting as she gasped for breath. Jama did not believe a word of the old Kaahin's prophecy, he knew that no boy born for a special fate would have to see his mother choking on strange liquid that poured out of her mouth and nose. Jama wiped his mother's face on his ma'awis and held her in his arms. 'Shush, hooyo, shush,' he soothed, rocking her gently. His mother fell into a foetal curl with her back turned to him and soon fell asleep. Jama watched the rise and fall of her back and grabbed a handful of her tobe to keep himself connected. The fabric dampened in his nervous grip; she was already slipping from him. He would have preferred his umbilical cord never to have been severed but to extend limitlessly like spider's silk between them, he belonged to no-one else, she belonged to no-one else, why couldn't God just leave them together?

Jama's eyes remained open all night, scanning the pitch black room for any figures that might materialise to take his mother away. The gloom was alive with shifting densities, lumps of grey light that hovered slowly along the floor, furry black masses that shivered in corners. Jama's fingers finally loosened their grip on Ambaro's tobe and reached out. Ambaro's arm was relaxed along her side, her fingers resting on her hip. Jama placed his hand on hers, she felt like one of those shells washed up on the beach, cold, hard, smooth, veins making superfluous swirls under her skin. Everything powerful and vibrant about her had gone, only the worn-out machinery of her body remained, and the little life that wondrous machinery had produced was left to grieve over everything she had once been.

Hargeisa, Somaliland, March 1936

The chaperone finally released his hold on Jama's forearm, leaving a sweaty handprint on his skin. Jama's legs shook from the long journey in the back of the old lorry and he clasped both of his thighs in his hands to steady them while his clansman went to replenish his stash of qat. Jama had put up with the mushy green spittle and the acrid stink that had accompanied his chaperone's habit for the day and night it took to cross the Red Sea and get to Hargeisa. Jama's bloated, gaseous stomach bulged out before him and he wondered why it stretched further and further out the hungrier he got. His stomach had been relatively peaceful throughout the journey, but for weeks after the burial it had contracted, cramped, made him vomit, given him diarrhoea as well as constipation, until he had passed blood and little slivers of congealed flesh. A clanswoman of his mother had found him huddled in an alley, covered in dust and flies. It took just three days for a human telephone network of clansmen and women to locate his great-aunt and deliver Jama to her like a faulty parcel. In Aden the

Islaweynes had paid for Ambaro's burial but expected Jama to look after himself, separated from Shidane and Abdi, he had hung out with the dirtiest of Aden's street children. Jama had eaten fitfully and badly, sometimes picking up food from the dirt and giving it a casual clean before swallowing it in a few untasting bites. He became argumentative and loud, often fighting with the other abandoned children. To appease the hungry demon in his stomach, seething and cursing from his cauldron of saliva and acid, Jama had fought with stray cats and dogs over leftover bones. He tried to be brave but sadness and loneliness had crept up on him, twisting his innards and giving him the shakes. Jama dreamt of his mother every night; she followed a caravan in the Somali desert, he would follow, calling out her name, but she never turned around, the distance between them growing until she was just a speck on the horizon.

Jama looked around him; Somaliland was yellow, intensely yellow, a dirty yellow, with streaks of brown and green. A group of men stood next to their herd of camels while the lorry over-heated, its metal grill grimacing under an acacia tree. There was no smell of food, or incense or money as there was in Aden, there were no farms, no gardens, but there was a sharp sweetness to the air he breathed in, something invigorating, intoxicating. This was his country, this was the same air as his father and grandfathers had breathed, the same landscape that they had known. Heat shimmered above the ground, making the sparse vegetation look like a mirage that would fade away if you reached out for it. The emptiness of the desert felt purifying and yet disturbing after the tumultuous humanity of Aden, deserts were the birthplaces of prophets but also the playgrounds of jinns and shape-shifters. He heard from his mother that his own great-grandfather Eddoy had walked out of his family's encampment and into the sands, he had given no-one word of where he was going, and was never seen again. Eddoy became one of the many bewitched by the shifting messages that were left amongst the dunes. Though these stories of people losing their minds and vanishing terrified Jama, his mother used to tease him, telling him that it was no bad thing to have a jinn in the family and that he should call on his great-grandfather if he ever became lost. His ancestors had been crow-worshippers and sorcerers before the time of the prophet, and the people still kept tokens of their paganism. Precious frankincense and myrrh still smouldered in the same ornate white clay urns;

black leather amulets hung from the chubby wrists of infants. His mother's amulet was tied as tightly as a noose around his neck, the sacred pages grubby and hardened together. He lay down under the acacia tree and spread his arms out, the sky covered him like a blue shroud and he felt cooled by the watery blueness washing over him, he guessed the time by looking at the position of the sun and decided to rest. He awoke, disturbed by the sound of two voices above his head, and opened his eyes to see an old woman standing over him as tall as an Amazon. She bent down to wipe the drool from his sleepy face and held him to her bosom, filling his nose with her sour milk smell. Tears beaded up in the corner of his eyes but he drew them back afraid of embarrassing them both. Jinnow took his hand and led him away, Jama floating from her hand like a string cut loose from its kite.

It was only the expanse of emptiness around it that made Hargeisa seem like a town but unlike the straw and skin collapsible desert homes they had passed, the houses in Hargeisa were forbidding white stone dwellings, as utilitarian as beehives. Large barred windows were decorated above with simple, geometric designs, the wealthier houses had courtyards with bougainvillea and purple hibiscus creeping up their walls. Everywhere you looked there were closed doors and empty streets, all the town's dramas were played out by figures hidden behind high walls and drawn curtains.

Finally the door to his grandfather's compound creaked open and a smiling girl said, 'Aunty, is this Jama?' but Jinnow pushed past her, still holding Jama solidly by the arm.

In the courtyard, women stood up to get a closer look at the boy.

'Is this the orphan? Isn't he a spit of his father!', 'Miskiin, may Allah have mercy on you!' they called.

The girl bounced along in front of Jinnow, her big eye constantly peering back at Jama.

Jinnow reached her room, 'Go now, Ayan,' she said, shooing the girl away and pulled Jama in after her. A large nomad's aqal filled the room, an igloo made of branches and hides, she caught Jama's look of surprise and patted his cheek. 'I'm a true bedu, could never get used to sleeping under stones, felt like a tomb, come lie down and rest, son,' she said.

The inside of the aqal was alight with brightly coloured straw mats. Jama lay down obediently but couldn't stop his eyes roving around. 'Do you remember that you once stayed here with your mother? No, look how 'my mind is rotting, how can you remember, you couldn't even sit up,' Jinnow chattered.

Jama could remember something, the snug warmth, the light filtering through woven branches, the earthy smell, it was all imprinted in his mind from a past life. He watched Jinnow as she fussed around, tidying up her old lady paraphernalia. She had the same high cheekbones, slanted eyes and low toned, grainy way of speaking as Ambaro, and Jama's heart sunk as he realised his mother would never be old like Jinnow.

After a restless sleep, Jama ventured into the courtyard; the women carried on with their chores, but he could hear them whispering about him. He ran towards a leafless tree growing next to the compound wall, he climbed its spindly branches, and sat in a fork high up in the tree. Leaning into the cusp Jama floated over the roof and tree tops, looking down like an unseen angel on the men in white walking aimlessly up and down the dusty street. The tree had beautiful brown skin, smooth and dotted with black beauty spots, like his mother's had been, and he laid his head against the cool silky trunk. Jama rested his eyes but within moments felt tiny missiles hitting him, he looked down and saw Ayan and two little boys giggling. 'Piss off! Piss off!' Jama hissed. 'Get out of here!'

The children laughed louder and shook the tree, making Jama sway and lose his grip on his seat. 'Hey bastard, come down, come down from the tree and find your father,' they sang, Ayan in the lead, with a cruel, gappy-toothed leer on her face.

Jama waved his leg at that smile, hoping to smash the rest of her teeth in. 'Who are you calling a bastard? You little turds, I bet you know all about bastards with your slutty mothers!' he shouted, drawing gasps from the women near him.

'Hey Jinnow, come and get this boy of yours, such a vile mouth you would think he was a Midgaan not an Aji. No wonder he was thrown into the streets,' said a long-faced woman.

Jinnow, startled and ashamed, charged over to Jama and dragged him down. 'Don't do that, Jama! Don't drag down your mother's name.' She pointed towards her room and Jama slunk away.

Inside the aqal, Jama cried and cried, for his mother, for himself, for his lost father, for Shidane and Abdi and it released something knotted up and tight within his soul, he felt the storm leave his mind.

★ ★ ★

Jinnow spent her days tending her date palms, selling fruit in the market near the dry riverbed that bisected the town or weaving endless mats, while Jama appeared and disappeared throughout the day. With all the men away with the camels Jama spent time on the streets to avoid the harsh chatter of the compound women who treated him like a fly buzzing around the room, swatting him away when they wanted to talk dirty. Their faces a bright cruel yellow from beauty masks of powdered turmeric, they dragged each other into corners, hands cupped around mouths, and in loud whispers languidly assassinated reputations, they drew shoes in fights as quickly as cowboys drew pistols.

Clutching her brown, spindly fingers against the wall of the compound, Ayan would peer over and watch as Jama tripped down the road. Ayan was the daughter of one of the younger wives in the compound and lived in a smaller room away from Jinnow. Jama would throw stones at her every time she approached him, so now she just satisfied herself with staring at him from a distance, crossing and uncrossing her eyes, flapping her upturned eyelids at him. As a girl she was rarely allowed out, and Jama's bad reputation within the compound and filthy mouth had slowly begun to win her admiration. She hoped to stare him into friendship but he had too long a memory for that and was still planning a revenge for the time she dared call him bastard. Jama slyly observed her daily routine of housework, childminding and standing around, one leg scratching the back of the other, and plotted her downfall. Ayan's mother was a tall shrewish woman with a missing front tooth, a neglected third wife who beat her children down verbally and physically. In front of her mother, Ayan was a well-behaved, hard-working child but in private she was a gang-leader and vicious fighter. Her troupe of scraggly infants would gather behind her after lunchtime, and prowl around the compound, catching lizards by the tail, spying on older children and going through their belongings. If challenged, the younger children would take flight while Ayan fought the angry object of their snooping. Scratches and cuts formed patterns on her skin like the tattoos on a Maori warrior, her young face knocked into a jagged adult shape by the fists of her mother and cousins. Jama had no possessions to filch or secrets to hide but for Ayan he presented an enigma, he was a strange silent boy from a foreign land.

Jama would sometimes see Ayan in the evening as the women gathered around the paraffin lamp to tell stories. Tales about the horrors some women were made to suffer at the hands of men, about the secret lovers some women kept, or about Dhegdheer who killed young women and ate their breasts. Ayan would regularly be mocked as 'dirty' and 'loose' by the women and older children for being uncircumcised and her head would droop down in shame. Her stupid mistakes would be recounted; she had once tried to open a lock with her finger and instead got it stuck. 'I thought that is how people open locks!' Ayan wailed.

'Served you right, that was Allah's reward for your snooping,' rejoiced her mother. Jama's favourite stories were about his grandmother Ubah, who travelled on her own as far as the Ogaden desert to trade skins, incense, and other luxuries despite having a rich husband. 'What a woman, Ubah was a queen and my best friend,' Jinnow would sigh. All the story-tellers claimed to have seen a shapeshifter, nomads who at night turned into animals and looked for human prey in town, disappearing before daybreak and the first call to prayer. Ayan's eyes would form frightened wide circles in the orange light and Jama could see her trying to nestle next to her mother and getting pushed irritably away. Jama hoped that one of these shapeshifters would snatch Ayan away, and take her out into the pitch black night where shadows slipped in and out of alleys. Alleys where hyenas stalked alongside packs of wild dogs, hunting lone men together, ripping out the tendons from their fleeing ankles as they tried to run for their lives, their helpless screams piercing the cloistered night.

★ ★ ★

Jama's life was no different to the goats tied up in the compound, staring blankly as they chewed on peelings. He was just a lump of dull clay that no-one wanted to mould or breathe life into, he was not sent to school, not sent out with the camels, only told 'Fetch this' and 'Get out!' The wives made a show of exchanging glances and locking their rooms if he was nearby, they were all like Mrs Islaweyne in their pettiness. The only comfort he found was at night in Jinnow's aqal, when Jama would allow her to tuck him in under the thin sheets and wait for her to start talking about his parents. With his eyes tightly closed Jama would listen to Jinnow describe how his father leapt out one night in the desert and with a flaming torch scared away hyenas that were stalking the family camels, how his mother had run away as a child and got as far as the sea before she was brought home. Jinnow remembered them at their best, young and brave before hunger, disappointment and illness brought them low.

She recited old gabays to make him laugh: 'Life in this world allows one man to grow prosperous, while another sinks into obscurity and is made ridiculous, a man passing through the evil influence of red Mars is feebler than a new born lamb punched on the nose.'

Jinnow told Jama one night, 'I know you are sick of milk, you think you are a man already but don't hurry to that, Jama, the world of men is cruel and unforgiving, don't listen to those fools in the courtyard, you are not an orphan, you have a father, a perfectly good father who will return.'

'Why hasn't he come to collect me then? What's he waiting for?'

'Don't be like that, Jama, we are all servants of our fate, he will come when he can. Hopefully he has made a good life for you both somewhere.'

'What's wrong with here? This is where we belong.'

'Your father has too much music in his soul for this kind of life, your mother did too but she tried hard to drown it out. Life here is too hard, everyone is peering over the horizon, but one day inshallah you will also see how wide the world is.'

'But where is my father?'

'Far, far away, in a town called Gederaf in Sudan, beyond Ogaden, beyond Djibouti, many months' walk, son, I heard that he was fighting in Abyssinia but now it seems he is in Sudan trying to become a driver again.'

'Can I go to him?'

'Allah, how could I let you do that? I owe it your mother to make sure you don't come to any harm. She is watching me, I feel her here,' Jinnow placed her hand on her stomach. 'She is like a light there, you understand, son? Your mother, Kahawaris, sometimes the dead are more alive than the living, no-one really dies, not while there are people who remember and cherish them.'

★ ★ ★

Jama was ready to explode cooped up in the compound. He needed a job so that he could add to his mother's money and find his father. He scoured the barren town for places to work, but shops and homes operated on the most basic levels of survival and there was no room for luxuries such as paid servants. The market consisted of a handful of women laying out dying fruits and withered vegetables on dusty cloths in the sand, they sat in the sun gossiping, collecting their meagre income in their laps. The eating houses were the busiest places in Hargeisa but they offered only two dishes whatever the wealth of their diners, boiled rice with boiled goat or camel. The cook would serve as waiter and dishwasher as well and would earn a pittance for all three jobs. Children and young men mobbed each other for the leftovers from the eating houses, pushing the smaller ones out of their way. Men chewed qat constantly to stave away the nagging hunger in their stomachs, so they wouldn't succumb mentally to it, wouldn't humiliate themselves. Late in the afternoons, the steps of the Haber Awal warehouses were clogged with men talking over each other, laughing and composing epigrams, but later as the qat left their systems they became morose, reclining like statues as the town darkened around them. Even with qat, the fear of hunger determined every decision every person made, where to go, what to do, who to be. Destitute nomads would come in from the countryside and sit under trees, too exhausted to move any further. Jama thought himself tough but the youth of Hargeisa were desert hardened, belligerent brawlers, uninterested in small talk with strangers, and the boys his age just wanted to sing and dance with the market girls. Jama, not finding any companionship inside the compound or outside, retreated deep into himself and made his mind his playground, fantasising all day about the father he had somehow lost. Conjuring his father was a pleasure, his strong muscles, gold rings and watches, nice shoes, thick hair, expensive clothes could all be refashioned on a whim, he said and did only what Jama wanted without the intrusion of reality. The fact that his father was alive made him everything Jama could want, while seeing his mother in his mind's eye was agonising, he could recall the way she smelt before dying, the sweat running down her temples, the fear she was trying to mask from him.

* * *

Jama had seen young boys working in the slaughterhouse, ferrying the carcasses of freshly killed animals to the eating houses and market. He watched the couriers, their necks awkwardly bent forward by the weight on their shoulders, their feet frantically shuffling forward, propelling whirlwinds of sand up their legs. The work was hard and dirty, but Jama resolved to get money by whatever means necessary.

He woke up early one morning, the sky

grey and the air still cool, and snuck out of the room, Jinnow's snores chasing after him. A hyena rich darkness covered the town and Jama could feel jinns and half men at his back stalking the alleys, making the hairs on his neck stand on end. He sped to the slaughterhouse, the cries of camels and sheep growing in volume as he got closer. He summoned up an image of his father; a dreamboat of a father, tall, strong, elegant in uniform, a smile playing on his dark lips. The slaughterhouse was empty of people; only the penned-up animals, waiting since night-fall for their deaths to come, acknowledged him, fixing their pleading eyes on him, sticking their flaring nostrils into the air. Jama felt the impending bloodshed sizzle in the air and rubbed down the tiny hairs on his lower spine as they nervously stood up, as if they were frightened conscripts standing to attention before a bloodied old general. He paced up and down, avoiding the eyes of the animals, turning his back to them, counting the stars, as they one by one bowed and left the stage. As the sun rose, more tiny figures emerged from the dawn horizon, approaching Jama with hostile eyes. Jama looked around with satisfaction as he realised that he was amongst the tallest of the motley crew of boys which had formed, waiting for the butchers to come and make their selection from them. With the same swift appraisal of strength and value that they usually trained on livestock, the butchers would pick their couriers for the day. The Midgaan and Yibir boys, those too young to believe that they would never be chosen, were insulted out of the line-up, 'Get out of here, you dirty shit, go and clean some latrines!' They moved away, forming a separate line, silent and enraged. The oldest porters were camel herders who had been possessed by jinns in the lonely haunted desert and were now forbidden from approaching the camels. The smallest were barely five years old, bewildered little children who had been dumped in Hargeisa by nomad fathers keen to toughen them up, they had been ripped from their mother's arms and now slept huddled in groups on the street. Hungry and lonely they followed older children wherever they went, their fathers occasionally visiting to ask, 'So, how much have you made?'

The butchers arrived already smelling of blood, with an impatient slap on the shoulder and a grunt they pushed out of the line the boys that they would employ that day. Jama was one of the chosen few. The unlucky ones returned to their mats or patches of dirt and prepared to sleep away the day and its insidious hunger pains. Jama walked towards the killing ground but hung back, hoping to avoid seeing the actual slaughters. A man shouted 'Hey you! Whatever your name is! Come here!'

Jama turned around and saw a broad, bare-chested man kneeling over a dead camel, still holding onto its reins as if it could make an escape. 'Jama, my name is Jama, uncle.'

'Whatever. Come and take this carcass over to the Berlin eating house for me. Wait here while I prepare it.' Jama stood back and waited as the butcher cut off the neck and legs, removed the skin from the camel's torso and emptied it of heart, stomach, intestines and other organs that only the poorest Somalis ate. The carnage shocked Jama, its efficiency and speed making it even more dreadful, he stood before the giant, naked, gleaming ribcage, frightened and awed by its desecration. The butcher got up wiping his red hands on his sarong before picking up the ribcage and balancing it on Jama's head. Its weight made him stagger and the soft, oozing flesh pressed revoltingly onto his skin. Jama pushed himself forward, trying not to career around, but the heavy load drove him left and right. He stopped and pushed the ribcage down his neck onto his shoulders and held it wedged there as if he was Atlas holding up the world in his fragile arms. The broad bones jutted into Jama's back and blood trickled down from his hair onto his shoulders and down his spine, making his brown back glisten with a ruby lustre. His nose was filled with the dense, iron smell of blood and he stopped against a wall to retch emptily. Blood dripped onto the sand, decorating his footprints with delicate red pools, as if he was a wounded man. He finally reached the eating house and hurriedly handed over the ribcage to a cook through a window. The cook grabbed it as if it were weightless and turned back to his talking and chopping without acknowledging the human carriage that had brought the delivery to him. Jama walked back to the slaughterhouse, a grimace set on his face, his sticky arms held away from his rancid body so that they wouldn't rub and release the metallic fumes. He delivered four more carcasses that morning and by the end he resembled a little murderer covered in the juices and viscera of his victims. Jama carefully tied his hard-earned money in the bottom of his sarong and walked home. The blood dried quickly in the noon sun and his hair and skin began to itch, he rolled his palms over his skin and the blood peeled off in claret strips. The insides of his nails were choked with dried blood and his sticky hair attracted fat, persistent flies, their buzzing causing an infuriating pandemonium by his ears. Jama had grown used to his own high, rich smell but the scent of death clinging to him was unbearable. Knowing that the precious water in the compound was only occasionally used for bathing, he hurriedly removed as much of the filth from his body as he could, using sand to clean himself as the Prophet advised. He arrived at the compound door and it was opened by Ayan before he had even knocked, she had fresh cuts on her face and one of her plaits had come apart, her wavy hair fanning out over one side of her head. 'Nabad Jama,' she enunciated slowly, looking into his eyes intensely. 'Where have you been? You look tired, and what is that in your hair?' she reached out to touch his hair but he slapped her hand away.

'Get off, you idiot,' he said gruffly, walking away to Jinnow's room. He could hear Ayan skipping behind him, her rubber sandals clapping the earth. 'I'll get you one day,' he threatened. Tired and hungry, he just wanted to collapse onto his straw mat. Ayan continued to follow him until unable to contain herself any longer, she exploded with her news, 'The ginger cat is pregnant! She's not just fat, there are kittens in there! Come and see, Jama! Come.'

Jama turned around and gave her the most belittling dead eye he could muster, before going into Jinnow's room and slamming the door shut behind him. He heard Ayan squeal in frustration before trundling back to the main courtyard. There was a stillness in the air, the compound was silent, cobwebs floated from the ceiling, cockroaches scuttled into crevices, everyone was dozing. The droning of insects in the air was punctuated by the hammering and ratter-tattering speech of workmen outside, the smell of charcoal, onions, meat, tea boiling with cloves and cardamom drifted from underneath the door. As Jama dozed images of Hargeisa appeared in his mind, the roughness of hot rocks and thorns underfoot, the soft prickliness of camel fur, the taste of dates, ghee, hunger, a parched mouth surprised with the taste of food.

★ ★ ★

A young woman arrived at the compound while he slept, she carried her slim possessions in a bundle on her back and looked ready to collapse. She was one of Jinnow's nieces, who had recently run away to marry a man from another clan.

'Isir? What are you doing back here?' shouted one of the wives.

'That man doesn't want me anymore, he's divorced me.'

'You see! Has he given you your meher at least?'

Through the thin walls Jama was awoken by the compound women scurrying around. 'She has been possessed, I can see a jinn in her eyes, tell Jinnow,' they called. Jinnow brought Isir into the aqal, Jama pretended to be asleep but watched as Jinnow inspected Isir, rubbing her hands all over her body, half doctor, half priestess.

'How do you feel, girl?'

'Fine, I'm fine, just keep those crazy women away from me,' Isir said; she was dressed in rags but her beauty was still intense.

'What happened?'

'That idiot, that enemy of God says I am possessed.'

Isir caught Jama's eyes peeking out from under his arm and he shut them quickly.

'Has he given you any of your dowry?'

'Not one gumbo.'

In the dim light, the women looked as if they were ready to commit some mysterious deed. Jinnow gathered herbs from her leather pouches and told Isir to eat them. She left Isir to rest and called the other women of the compound, as the neighbourhood alaaqad with shamanic powers they could not refuse her.

Isir shook Jama, 'Are you Ambaro's son?'

Jama nodded, Isir's large brown eyes had the same burning copper in them as his mother's had.

'Go and listen to what they're saying for me,' she demanded.

* * *

Jama went as Isir's eyes and ears. 'Our sister needs us, she has been afflicted by a saar, we must exorcise her tonight, as her husband is not here you must bring perfume, new clothes, halwa, incense, amber and silver to my room to satisfy the jinn. I will conduct the ceremony,' proclaimed Jinnow.

'She's always been like this, it's the price for her beauty,' Ayan's mother scoffed. 'Isir has always been leading men on, one of them has finally put a curse on her.'

'Nonsense,' shouted Jinnow, 'she is of our blood, we can not stand aside when she needs us, what if a man threw you out with the rubbish?' The compound women grumbled but agreed to prepare the saar ceremony.

Some cleaned Jinnow's room, some cooked,

some borrowed drums, others collected the gifts. When the children had been fed and sent away, Isir was led by a procession to Jinnow's room. Jama was locked out, but with a pounding heart he climbed the wall and walked over the roof until he could lean over Jinnow's window. The room was brightly lit with paraffin lamps, smoky with expensive incense. Jinnow had brought more old women, mysterious crones with shining dark skin and strong hands. After the incense had been passed around, and the gifts presented to the jinn, Jinnow took the largest drum and pounded it intermittently while shouting out instructions to the jinn. Isir stood in the centre of the room, looking stiff and nervous, with every command the old women chanted 'Ameen' and the young women clapped. Then the old women brought out small drums, got to their feet and started drumming in earnest. Jinnow stood behind Isir, grabbed her around the waist and forced her to dance, the crowd ululated and danced with them. Jinnow tore off Isir's headscarf and pulled at her hair. Jama watched as Isir's movements became more self-willed and definite, Jinnow was an inch away from her face shouting and crying, 'Nin hun, nin hun, a bad man, a bad man, never tie yourself to a bad man, we told you he was useless, useless while you were brave

and strong, Allah loves you, Allah loves you.'
Isir's tears flowed freely down her face, she
looked like a lost little girl to Jama. Jinnow
spun around Isir with more energy than he
could have imagined, steam was rising from
the women and no-one noticed his head hanging upside down in the window. Isir had her
head flung back, her eyes half-closed but staring unseeingly into Jama's, she was saying
things that Jama could not understand. Jinnow
was encouraging her, shouting, 'You are carrying this load on your back and you are staggering
around with it like a tired camel, stop here
and pass your load to me! Send him out of
your soul! You are full of ghosts! Spit them
out! Get your freedom, my girl!'

Isir carried on weeping while the compound women danced around her, clapping
their support and flushing out their own
grief.

* * *

Isir became a small ally against the
compound women; she slept in the same
room as Jinnow and Jama and joined in on
their late night conversations.

'I used to sleep right there next to Ambaro,
where you are now Jama, plaiting our hair,
tickling each other.'

'That's right, that's right,' encouraged Jinnow.

'Jinnow would throw a slipper at us to quieten our laughter.'

'They had no sense of time.'

'Do you remember, aunty, how she would read our palms? Telling us all kinds of things, how many men we would marry, how many children we'd have, she scared the other girls with that talk.'

Jama sat up on his elbows and listened attentively to the women.

'It's because she had the inner eye and she didn't soften or hide what she saw, I saw it in her from an early age, I watched her read the future in shells when she was not yet five, grown men would come and ask her to tell them their fate. Did she tell you all this, Jama?' Jinnow asked.

Jama scanned his memory. 'She only told me that I had been born with the protection of all the saints and that a black mamba had blessed me while I was in her stomach.'

'That is all true, you had a very auspicious birth, every kaahin and astrologer envied your signs, even Venus appeared the night you were born.'

Jama rested his head on his arm and sighed loudy; if only he could meet his father he would believe all of their fanciful words.

Jama went to the abattoir every morning, and his eagerness and industriousness meant he was always picked out, creating enemies for him amongst the other hungry children. Jama saw the sweaty, smelly work as a kind of test, that if passed would entitle him to see his father, a trial of his worth as a son and as a man. He hid all of his abattoir money in a tin can in Jinnow's room. The bundle of coins grew and grew in its hiding place, and he could feel the reunion with his father approaching, whether his father came to him or he went to his father Jama knew it was fated to be. He read it in the clouds, in the entrails of the carcasses he delivered, in the grains of coffee at the bottom of his cup.

After work, he often wandered around town, sometimes as far as the Yibro village that nestled against the thorny desert on the outskirts of Hargeisa. He walked through the pariah neighbourhood looking for signs of the magic Yibros were said to possess, he wanted some of their powerful poison to use against Ayan, to watch her hair and nails drop off. Jama peered into small dark huts, an outcast amongst outcasts, hot dark eyes following his progress. But there was no magic to be seen, the Yibros had yet to find spells that would turn dust into bread, potions to make their dying children live or curses that would keep their persecutors at bay. An Aji boy in their midst could easily bring trouble. If a hair on his head was hurt a pack of howling wolves would descend on the village, ripping and tearing at everyone and everything, so they watched him and hoped that his curiosity would quickly be satisfied. The village had only recently stopped mourning for a young man killed by Ajis, his body had been cut up and the flesh put in a basket outside his family's hut. His mother collapsed when she peered into the basket and realised where the plentiful meat had come from, his head was at the bottom, broken and grey. No blood money could be demanded by them, his father went to work in the town the next day as he did every day, smiling to hide his fury, bowing down to men who had dismembered his child. Jama saw that the village was full of women; Yibro men were usually labouring elsewhere, hammering metal or working leather or in the town cleaning out latrines. The children sat outside picking their noses, their stomachs stretched to bursting point, destitution the way of life. The clan handouts that kept other Somalis afloat were absent here as the Yibros were so few and so poor. Ancient superstitions meant that Aji Somalis ostracised Yibros and Midgaans and other undesirables without any thought; Yibros were just Jews, eaters of forbidden foods, sorcerers. Jama was only dimly aware that these people received a payment from families like his whenever a male child was born and that a curse or spell from a Yibir was more powerful and destructive than from anyone else. Jama could see why they were feared, their clothes were even more raggedy than his, their shacks open to the cruelties of the August heat and the October freeze, their intimacy with misery deeper than that of anyone else.

* * *

On a still stagnant day, Jama returned home from work to find Ayan in Jinnow's room. Standing on tip-toe, her eyes, ringed with stolen kohl, widened as she saw Jama staring at her as she snooped through Jinnow's things; the beautiful, silver kohl bottle rolling on the floor separately from its ornate lid.

'Thief! Thief!' shouted Jama, filled with horror that she might have found the father-finding money. 'What are you doing? You thief!' he said as he lunged at her.

Surprise had frozen a ridiculous expression on Ayan's face, her eyebrows had arched up like the spines of frightened cats and her gap-toothed mouth hung open. Jama pulled her arms around her back, lifting her thin, dusty feet up from the ground.

'Let me go!' she cried.

'What do you want in here? What are you looking for? Has someone sent you?'

'No, no, please, Jama, I was just looking, wallaahi, let me go!' she begged. Jama in confusion held on to her, Ayan was strong and supple for a girl but she was no match for a feral street boy like Jama. He was too embarrassed to check her body for the money so seeing the imposing dark wood wardrobe with the key in the lock, he opened the door and shoved Ayan in. He quickly turned the key and stood back, shaking with sweat beads trickling down his forehead. He stared at the wardrobe door as Ayan kicked and shouted to be let out.

'Jama! Jama! Jama! Let me OUT! I can't breathe! Oh God, oh God,' said her muffled voice.

Jama gathered himself, and with a jabbing finger said, 'You are staying in there, you dirty thief, until Jinnow comes back and checks you.'

Ayan screamed long and loud, her erratic breathing and convulsive tears clearly audible in the room. Jama wiped the sweat off his brow and walked out of the room as Ayan continued to wail and weep, 'It's dark! It's too hot. I'm going to die. Murderer! Murderer! Jama the Bastard Murderer! Please help!'

Jama waited and waited outside Jinnow's room, inside the cupboard Ayan gulped down the warm old air and emitted a low, strange whine. Her jail was lined with nuptial gowns and undergarments given as part of ancient dowries, the relics of dead loves and youthful dreams of glamour and romance. The velvety blackness around her shifted and made room for its young visitor, all the while caressing her damp face into unconsciousness with long, clammy fingers. She felt like she was at the bottom of a deep, deep well, too deep in the earth to ever be found, panic washed over her in rapid waves. The noon prayer came and went as did the afternoon prayer and it was not until it was nearly time for the sunset prayer that Jama could hear Jinnow's voice rising up from a commotion in the courtyard. Jinnow walked down the hallway from the courtyard followed by a loud troupe of compound women, she had a beleaguered look on her wrinkled face.

'Have you seen Ayan? Her mother can't find her,' Jinnow asked.

Jama looked up and it was only then that it occurred to him how long he had spent on that doorstep and how long Ayan had spent in her makeshift prison. Jama got up creakily on weak legs and pushed the door open. With slippery fingers and a roomful of expectant females, Jama turned the key on the wardrobe lock, immediately a stink of urine swelled out of the hot stuffy cell. Seeing only fabrics and bags at head height, everyone's eyes fell down to the floor of the wardrobe and there lay Ayan, barely conscious, her head flung back, her too-red tongue lolling from the side of her mouth. A collective gasp surged from the audience and Jinnow shoved Jama violently out of the way to get to Ayan. She shook Ayan and kissed her face until the girl's eyes snapped open and a long scream coiled out from her. Ayan's mother grabbed her child and hugged her suffocatingly against her bosom, 'May God break your back, you devil,' she said over Ayan's shoulder, her eyes ringed with anti-mony shooting daggers of hate deep into Jama.

Jama stuttered, 'She's a thief, Jinnow, check her, she was trying to steal my money.'

A screech ripped out from Ayan and her mother. 'May God break your balls, you lying bastard, you are cursed by all the saints, what have I done to deserve this Allah? Oh tolla'ay, tolla'ay, my poor child, may God put you under the ground, you eunuch, you devil!' wailed Ayan's mother.

Jinnow's head sunk down and fat tears rolled down Jama's distraught face. Young women bearing water and cloths dragged Ayan from her mother's grip and took her away to revive and clean her. Jinnow watched on aghast, wiping her own tears on the edge of her gown. Ayan's mother stretched out to her full height and with a long sharp fingernail pushed up Jama's face. 'I want you out of here, or I swear to God I will cut your nasty little thing off.' The courtyard women left the room, leaving behind them a miasma of hair oil and incense.

Jinnow pushed Jama into a crushing grip and kneaded his back, shoulders, and neck violently and soothingly. She told him to go to bed but he didn't, he pulled away and took one last hard look at her. Jinnow's small eyes were framed with short, feathery eyelashes, her skin looked like old paper, moles spread over her cheeks and nose, and three of her front teeth were gold, she was an elderly Ambaro. Jinnow and Isir left their room to soothe Ayan's mother and Jama grabbed his stash of money and snuck out behind them as stealthily as a cat. There was a deep, false silence echoing across the courtyard but he could see twinkling eyes peeking out behind curtains and doors. As he walked out into the sunset, a bitter wind flicked at his threadbare clothes and drew goose pimples from his skin. Stars grew smaller and dimmer above as paraffin lamps were placed on window sills down the street, burning like golden fireflies trapped in cages. Jama heard Jinnow calling him back and glanced over his shoulder, Jinnow stood in the street barefooted, her arm threadlike as she held it aloft. He waved to her, trying desperately to communicate his gratitude and love but he ran on. It fell into Jama's mind that he wasn't a child anymore; he needed to learn how to be a man. Jama reached Naasa Hablood, the Maiden's Bosoms, the conical twin hills overlooking Hargeisa and peered below to see the lamps and lights of the town disappearing into the gauzy brown haze of a dust storm. The wind licked and slapped the cowering wooden nomad huts while the white stone houses stood pompously amidst the flying rubbish but eventually the whole town disappeared as if it was just a mirage from an old Arabic tale. Just as easily Jama was spirited away from family, home and homeland.

Sand scratched his eyes and blurred the path as it danced around the desert in a frenetic whirling ballet. Jama's sarong was nearly pulled off by the mischievous sand jinns hiding within the storm. Jama covered his face with his sarong and managed to make slow progress like that. The dust storm had turned the sun a dark orange, until ashamed at its obscured power it crept away below the horizon to be replaced by an anaemic and fragile-looking moon. Jama stumbled across the hills, kicking rocks away with bare feet, giant thorns poking and prodding danger- ously. Desert animals scurried around looking for refuge, their small furry paws scrambling over Jama's sand-swathed feet. Exhausted, Jama stopped and collapsed onto the sand. With nothing but the howl of the wind around him, he fell asleep, the cold scratch of the storm still assailing his arms and legs. When he opened his inflamed eyes it was the hour before sunrise but he saw a tarred road laid out in front of him as if jinns had prepared it while he slept. It was strewn with sand, leaves and twigs by the departing storm. The wind had calmed and the temperature was mild, he stood up excitedly and scanned the road, left to right, right to left, hoping for the round lights of a lorry to emerge, but there was no light apart from the white of the moon. The tarred road was cool and smooth against his desert-sore feet and he walked slowly as the sun returned joyously to the east, its rays lighting the undulating road until it appeared golden.

A rumbling sound reverberated along the

road and then the 'daru daru daruuu' horn of an invisible lorry pierced the morning air like a cockerel cry. Jama ran down to meet it, and narrowly avoided its gigantic hood as it careered around the bend and raced past. Standing in its sooty trail, Jama wondered how long it would take to get to Sudan, if he had enough money, if he could get food and water on the road. He only knew to walk away from Hargeisa, everything else was a mystery. He walked up the side of a mountain, rocks slipping under his feet. The desert terrified him, the silence, the boulders marking nomad's graves, the emptiness. Jama scampered further up the mountain, hoping to find human company by following the goat droppings left by a passing herd. As he climbed higher, the Maroodi Jeeh valley spread out beneath him, and he scaled the large granite boulders believing that he would be able to see Sudan from the summit. He squinted at the strip of blue on the horizon, unsure whether it was sky or sea. The land looked eerie from this height, dry riverbeds snaked across the earth as far as the eye could see, acacia trees grew bent and stunted in tangled harassed-looking clumps like old widows begging. Massive stony-faced boulders sat squatly amidst nothing. Towering termite mounds, the height of insect architectural genius, stood tall and imposing like bleak apartment blocks. A nomad's house built from branches and straw had a high fence around it, keeping out the emptiness. The skeletons of goats killed by earlier droughts fell apart; their bleached white rib cages jutted out of the sand like teeth and inside them yellow flowers grew from cacti. In the distance shone the rushing, metallic glow of a spontaneous river, fed by rain falling on the mountains. Vultures swooped above the river praying for drowned bodies to feed their families. In the water, opals and emeralds glinted, and above it all flew fluffy white fairy tale clouds in a clear blue sky. Small villages had grown alongside the road, the fragile dwellings placed so close to its edge that it seemed the speed of the racing lorry would blow them away. Here and there forgotten paraffin lamps burned danger-ously in the makeshift homes. The village goats huddled in a group beside camels frozen like statues in their sleep, wooden bells around their necks ringing from the lorry as it flew along. Far off to the north, British colonial officers in khaki rode on galloping horses looking for warthogs to set off their game of pig-sticking. Warthogs were rarely seen in the country any more but the British were even more elusive, preferring to hide from the heat and bloody foreignness of Somaliland by stay-ing in their governmental residences. The sight of the groomed Arabian horses sweating in the scrub, tormenting the poor warthogs, saddened Jama and he climbed back down the mountainside to the road.

Jama walked and walked, no more cars or lorries passed by and he didn't see any camel caravans but he carried on stubbornly. Straight ahead of him the sun got heavier and larger like a hot old lady wobbling before her knees finally buckled and she retired for the night under a red haze. He reached a ruined Oromo town, its once grand buildings fallen down and forgotten, after waiting hundreds of years for their inhabitants to return, the grief-stricken edifices finally fell apart. Jama crept into the old mosque, the wood rotting and clay bricks disintegrating around him. He rested on his haunches and sat there like a madman amid the dirt and debris, bats flitting in out of the silent pulpit and spirits murmuring behind his back. He watched as the wind blew life into an old snake skin and it slithered away to find its old self. Hungry and frightened, he regretted running away and was now sorely tempted to return to Jinnow. He found a well and peered into its gloomy mouth, he suspected it was full of rubbish: twigs, rubble, a dead rat but he was so thirsty he dropped a rock and heard the delicious reply of water. Jama leant further over the lip of the well and the old wall crumbled underneath him, he fell head first into the stinking pit, he spat and blew his nose but the bitter water had already gone down his throat. He scrambled out, terrified the whole thing would collapse on top of him, and went back despondently to the ghost mosque with scratched arms and a vile taste in his mouth. Only when his mother's sleeping body appeared beside him, her ribs rising and falling in peaceful slumber, could he finally close his own eyes. At the darkest hour of night, the sky cracked and revealed a blue and white secret kingdom. The high heavens and low earth were joined by a sheet of conquering raindrops, followed by a thundering marching band that seemed to be playing drums, cymbals, violins, and reedy flutes whose notes fell down and smashed against the gasping desert earth, battering down an angry song of life. Jama was awoken by this miraculous concert heralding the end of the dry season, and sleepily turned onto his back to receive his benediction. Rain splattered against Jama's lips and he opened his mouth to drink it in, he heard happy laughter echoing around him and saw drenched jinns cavorting and dancing as they reclaimed the desert for themselves.

Jama placed his feet in the large footprints

the jinns had left behind. Left leg, right leg, left leg, right leg, he rode high on long thin legs sculpted by each grain of sand, each stone, each dune they touched. All around, large iridescent pools had formed from the night's rainstorm, they looked like mirages in the drifting heat of the day. Jama stopped regularly to marvel at the sudden deluge and examine his face in the water's silky surface, he picked at karir berries and drank rainwater. The mountains had become pyramids of blue and dark purple under the rainclouds and it was with a joyful heart that Jama walked through the downpour, washing away the memory of months of grime, slaughterhouse blood and misery. A caravan of wet camels and nomads went sloshing past him, the young herders casting a quick suspicious look his way as they jumped over puddles. Jama followed the group discreetly; hiding behind the legs of an old camel carrying a sick woman bundled up in hides. The caravan stopped at a saint's tomb and began unloading, the women taking charge of the tents, the children, the sheep while the men wrestled with the camels. The rainy season had finally arrived; bash bash and barwaaqo, the season of splash splash and God's rain. Everyone had a sparkle in their eye; their necks craned towards the clouds for months could finally relax. For a few months life would be a little kinder and people would have the leisure to recite poems and fall in love. Green shoots sprouted everywhere and the camels ate as if they were at a Roman feast, glades appeared beside dusty flats that had magically become rivers. In the mornings the camels would be called by name, and with a heave and a groan they would get up and amble over to their proud owners.

The saint's tomb was a simple structure with a large white-washed dome but it brought together a cosmopolitan mix of travellers, rich men with high turbans and supercilious expressions prayed next to hard working, subjugated Yibirs, Tumals and Midgaans. Ascetic nomads asked for blessings alongside boozy merchant sailors, home for the first time in years. Country women with bare heads and exposed bosoms howled for fertility as did veiled, sheltered townswomen. Jama moved around in the mêlée, praying for a father while the women prayed for children, he observed the fervour of the other worshippers and hoped that God could still hear him through the clamour.

A little distance from the tomb was a hut surrounded by an inquisitive crowd. Jama pushed through and saw a nightmarish scene; an old man had a young boy's head clamped between his knees. The holy man cut open the boy's head; a flap of hairy skin fell to one side and he scored back and forth over the skull with his dagger. Finally, a square of the boy's skull came loose from the soft watery pulp of his brain; the old man carefully picked it out and placed it to his side. A woman explained to the silent audience that the boy had fallen off a mountain, had been asleep since and was not expected to wake up, his father had brought him to the holy man in desperation. The boy lay lifeless throughout the operation, but his father was seated next to him, his eyes wide and white. Jama wished that he was the sleeping boy with his own father bent over in fear and love.

Jama spent the night at the tomb, Allah's name was repeated all night until it echoed everywhere and seemed to emanate from the tomb, the trees, the mountains. From the nomads' camp he could hear drumming and ululations long into the night, the young men and women danced under skies that blazed magenta, jade, silver, violet with lightning. The air sizzled between downpours and the young warriors jumped up as high as fleas, throwing their spears in the air, showing off their martial acrobatics. Jama fell asleep with the stars dancing above his head, whirling dizzyingly to the drums and chants.

The next morning, a man ran around yelling for the people to rise and observe a miracle, the boy had awoken and was speaking again, old and young crowded around the holy man's hut and saw the light of the boy's blinking eyes in the gloom. People shouted out 'Allahu Akbar, Allahu Akbar, God is Great' and brought gifts of incense and dates to the man and his son. The holy man stood aloof from the spectacle, he calmly picked off the beads of his rosary and chewed a wad of qat. When an excited party of worshippers approached him, he waved them away and returned to the cool of the tomb. Jama saw the miracle as proof that of all the tombs in Somaliland, God's attention was on this one. He raced away from the tomb expecting God to deliver his father up to him. Back on the road, within moments a lorry appeared, it was white with BISMALLAH painted in red and yellow on its front, asking for the lord to have mercy on it, from its mirrors dangled withered jasmine chains but their scent still fragranced the morning air as the lorry whizzed past.

Jama chased after the lorry, waving and shouting, 'Wait! Wait! Are you going to Sudan?'

The lorry slowed down with jeers from the cab. 'Of course not. We're going to Djibouti, if you wanna get in just get in! Hurry up!'

shouted one of the men sardined in the cab, the reflection of their bodies in the wing mirror creating the impression of a many-headed hydra.

Jama hauled himself up the ladder, throwing himself into a corner of what was essentially a large wooden crate, containing goats, mangoes, onions, qat, and huddled men. There was a stirring as the child boarded, eyes peeped out and looked him up and down before falling back into sleep. The metal bars around the crate dug into Jama's neck and stopped him sleeping so he turned around and bade farewell to his homeland, a captured prince exiled along with goats and chickens. His country was an afterthought of the empire builders, a small piece on a global monopoly board to be collected to spite the others. His people were seen by the British as a fierce, unruly race, who made a good photograph but were not a modern nation deserving equal status to the adult, civilised states of Europe. His land had been carved up between France, Italy, Britain and Abyssinia. Now the Somalis and British coexisted, usually peacefully, the Mad Mullah had long been crushed but his apocalyptic warnings still floated in Somali minds and gave them intimations of a calamity that awaited the world. Which was hinted at by the peppery, burning, mustard-scented winds blowing in from Abyssinia, the silence of the great League of Nations gossiped about by nomads in the desert.

The British had built the road to ease their passage into and out of their possession, and now Jama trundled along it, making slow progress towards the artificial border between Somaliland and Djibouti. The sun had fully reclaimed sovereignty over the sky and shone her rays down on her subjects, pushing beads of sweat down their temples. The smell of grease, petrol and decay drifted into Jama's nose but he kept his eyes open, willing this journey to come to an end.

Djibouti Town, Djibouti, September 1936

No border or sign alerted Jama to the fact that he was in a new country, it was just a feeling of going under. The lorry moved along with its nose pointing down, down until it straightened out in a plateau of hellish, bewildering heat. Djibouti was low-down and hot, it looked even more barren and fearsome than Somaliland, and the few trees that dared exist held up their arms in defeat. Rocks cracked open in fifty degree heat. The earth was bleached white and the few comforts that the Somali desert shyly held out, blossoming cacti, large matronly bushes, lush candelabra euphorbia, were here maliciously denied. The air had a corruption to it, a mingled scent of sleaze, sweat and goat droppings. Jama could hear people talking in a strange language over the din of road drilling and to his amazement they drove past a knot of reddened European men in tight little shorts. Grown men in shorts so small that they nearly revealed what Allah had commanded be hidden. They stood, hands on hips, thick moustaches bristling under their boxy hats, ordering around a group of sweating Somali workers. Jama's neck craned back to look at these men as the lorry sped past, certain that it was his first glimpse of the dangerous, womanly men of sin he had heard about in Aden. Jama's hands gripped the planks of the crate as he watched the mysterious men retreat into the distance.

A man with moss-green teeth waved him back down, 'Fransiis, Fransiis, settle down, they're just frenchies, country boy, haven't you been out of the wilderness before?' His mocking, bloodshot eyes stayed on Jama as he sat down and self-consciously composed himself.

A breeze blew into Jama's face, the smell of sea salt and the warm wetness of the air gave him an impression of travelling through a town at the bottom of the sea. The lorry slowed down in traffic, and arms and legs grew out of the blankets around him, stretching and straightening. They had reached their destination. Their lorry sat sadly in the traffic, after so many miles of whistling along clear desert roads, it chuggered out sooty smoke from its rattling exhaust pipe. They climbed out of the back, passing a few coins to one of the many arms sticking out of the driver's cab, heads all fixed ahead, cheeks bulging with masticated qat. Jama felt like fainting, the heat from the vehicles pushed up the temperature by a few more unbearable degrees. Cars and lorries were strung in a neat chain while army vehicles tried to weave in and out of the queue, their horns blasting a path through. Muscled pink forearms waved directions at the uninterested crowd, drivers had left their seats to gossip and share water but now they jeered at the pompous legionnaires. Still only on the outskirts of Djibouti Town, Jama could already feel its bustling energy. He approached the beginning of the traffic jam and saw its cause; European soldiers manned a checkpoint, and were nearly taking apart the vehicles in search of smuggled goods. Ignoring the complaints and abuse of drivers, banana crates were jimmied open, livestock were released from their pens, sleeping travellers were searched. Amid all this commotion Jama eased his way around the checkpoint behind the backs of armed legionnaires.

A wide boulevard opened up before him, Jama dawdled along enjoying the novelty of paving slabs under his feet. In Hargeisa the ground was made up of a hundred different types of sand but there was not one paving slab in the whole town. Here, palm trees grew by the side of the street, evenly paced out like guards. Buildings stood in the distance, with a style at odds to Somali or Adeni constructions; they were curvaceous and tall, and built to last much longer than the edifices of the British in Hargeisa. This town was conjured up from the fantasies of its conquerors, a home away from home despite the anti-European climate; a provincial French town picked up and dropped into the hottest place on earth. Stalls were laid out by the street under grass awnings, groups of women sold just watermelons, or just bananas, or just oranges. As Jama walked on, the street came to life, young men argued and fought, young mothers sat outside chatting as their babies slept. Old women shuffled around discreetly begging, suited men came back home for siestas and to await the qat deliveries. A pretty mosque with red and turquoise banners flying from its minarets gave out the aadaan; water was sold from the backs of dozy-looking donkeys like in Hargeisa. No-one paid any notice to the market boy, this was a town accustomed to a constant tide of newcomers; Yemenis, Afars, Somalis, Indians, French colonials, all felt that this town belonged to them. There were clashes, love affairs and friendships between the communities but there was also just plain indifference.

Jama wandered around happy to be back somewhere with the energy of Aden, getting a thrill from the taxis whizzing past, the wet heat wrapped around his body. The shops and stalls, their bright goods laid out for admiration, pulled at him. If it wasn't for his hunger to see his father, he would have disappeared into the market's crowded alleys to find friends amongst the filth and chicanery. Nosy goats peered out from doorways, nibbling delicately on vegetable peels and oily paper wrappers as they silently observed the passing crowd with inquisitive eyes. Their thirsty, frustrated kids jittered around under their feet trying to grab at their hoisted teats, the milk commandeered for human enjoyment by red, blue, or yellow cloth guards tied around their mothers' full dripping udders. The crush of life around Jama was breathtaking, shocking after the space and wide horizons of Somaliland. It seemed bizarre for so many people to be concentrated in one place. And the noise! It was as if he had been deaf for months and his ears had cracked open allowing a cacophony of shouting, swearing, music, arguing to pour in. Men stood around corners in knots, leaning against crumbling walls. Their thin chests sticking out from unbuttoned shirts, sweat cascading down their fine features, qat stalks clamped between their teeth, their eyes followed passing market girls, probing and prodding them as they sashayed past.

Jama sat under a palm tree and scanned around for another lorry; he was at the heart of a vast shanty town and could see no way out. Under the shade of the palm, surrounded by noise and movement, everything started to swim around Jama, donkey carts traversed the sky and birds flew with their backs to the ground. Jama's eyes went black and his head slammed onto the dirt.

* * *

When he woke up, Jama realised he had been moved. He was in a small damp room, facing a peeling blue door that creaked on its hinges with the breeze. Through the dim light he saw a cat with a leopard print coat dart out into the street as clattering footsteps approached. Jama shut his eyes quickly as a man and woman entered, 'What have you done, Idea?' the woman gasped.

'I found him outside, Amina, he had collapsed under the palm tree. I tried to wake him and give him water, but he was dead to the world so I brought him in.'

The woman rushed over to Jama and placed a hand on his head, 'Sweetie, you're burning up, what's wrong?'

Jama mouthed words at her but nothing came out. She put a glass of water to his mouth and it burned as it slid down his parched throat. 'I'll get him some rice.' She rushed off, agile legs like springs beneath her, her uncovered hair flaring out around her in black and grey rivulets. The husband stood over Jama, his mouth was lop-sided and Jama stared at it from the corner of his eye. When he smiled Jama noticed a row of golden teeth peeking out, and a smile inched across Jama's face at the memory of Shidane and his silly tale of smugglers hiding diamonds within their gold teeth. The husband thinking that the boy was smiling at him released his full, droopy, manic-looking smile, his eyes twinkling in the dark room. 'So, who is this strong young man?' the wife called out.

'This boy has come to be my ally, Amina, so I won't be bullied by you and the hags you call friends anymore,' replied her husband in a deep voice.

'Ignore him, my son, he's unemployed,' teased his wife.

'Jama Guure Naaleyeh, I am Jama Guure Naaleyeh,' stated Jama proudly, the man and woman nodded, hiding their amusement.

'And who are your people?' asked Amina.

'Eidegalle.'

'Ah a noble Eidegalle has fallen into our Issa hands,' laughed Idea. Jama was entranced by this eccentric man and his outlandish face.

When he was serious, he cocked his head to one side, his mouth set in a sad slope, but then he would explode with mirth, and his eyes, nose, lips and teeth would fly in different directions. Jama quickly learnt that this man could speak English, French, Afar and Arabic as well as Somali, but spent his time cooking, cleaning and loving his wife, who worked as a cleaner in a colonial office. He spoke to Jama as if he was talking to an old friend. In fact so beguilingly that Jama lost his guarded manner and told him things in return; how he was going to find his father, why he had left Hargeisa and how he had learnt Arabic, and a smattering of Hindi and Hebrew on the streets of Aden. They spoke animatedly in a Somali interlaced with Arabic, attracting Amina's mockery. 'Oh here he goes again! Always showing off, why don't you use that babble babble to get a job, eh? No use knowing those birdy languages if you just sit at home.'

Amina's husband held up a finger. 'Jama, let me tell you one thing, while you stay with us, ignore everything this woman says. I swear she is the most ignorant woman you will ever find, she thinks that you make mules by mating donkeys with dogs.' Amina and her husband both cackled at each other's insults.

Idea was the man's name, or to be more precise, his nickname, but everyone called him Idea, even his wife. He had been a teacher in government schools until disheartened with the uses that the colonial government put that education to, he had put down his chalk and become the only male wife in Djibouti. Idea saw that the schools did not disseminate knowledge but propaganda, fooling the young into not seeing any beauty or good in themselves. Idea prepared that night's dinner and it was the best food Jama had ever tasted, fresh spicy fish served with warm, honeyed roti, a dip made from crushed dates and another sauce of softened banana. It was heavenly. Jama picked at the fish bones until there was nothing left on them. It was a world beyond the slop that the male cooks in eating houses served, and Idea looked delighted at the impact that it made on his guest. 'Jama, I bet you have never eaten fish before, eh? Just rice and a little bit of camel or lamb? We Somalis have such a wide coast but we hate fish, why is this?' asked Idea ruminatively.

'I have eaten it before! We used to steal anything we wanted from the cafés in Aden.'

'Good for you but, Jama, I see nomads — Somali and Afar to be fair — holding their noses! Actually holding their noses as they walk past the fish market, and you can see their stomachs caved in with hunger! By God, it makes no sense!'

Jama, feeling full and content, leant back, his stuffed stomach poking into the air. The paraffin lamp was lit and the adults stayed up talking softly into the amber-lit night. The last thing Jama noticed was a downy cotton sheet being laid over him.

In the morning, piercing white light flooded in from the window. Jama dozed while Idea opened the curtains, swept the floor, prepared pancakes and sang songs in different tongues. He was already dressed in a crumpled European shirt and trousers that swung a little above his ankles, thick strapped, brown leather sandals on his feet. Amina had left for work and Idea bumbled around the room, looking at a loss. 'So, Jama, what are we going to do today?' said Idea. Jama looked around the room, at the stack of dusty books in the corner, torn pages sticking out of them, at the clothes neatly folded on a shelf, at the pretty gilt-edged mirror with black dots on its surface and shrugged his shoulders. They sat looking at each other for a minute before Idea said, 'Come on, get washed up, I'll show you around town.' Jama washed his face, brushed his teeth with his finger and poured some water over his chest and arms.

'The tour will start here from my house,

the centre of my world,' declared Idea in a clear authoritative voice. 'This mosque ahead of us was built by the Ottomans, heard of them? No? the descendants of Usman, those plump Turkish lords of the east and west. The little flags are meant to represent Islam's power in all four corners of the world,' boomed Idea, flicking his hands as if he was scattering his words over Jama.

'This alley leads to Boulevard de Bender where our resourceful women sell everything from green chillies to stuffed cobras, pomegranates and leopard skins, medicines and love potions, absolutely everything. I'm sure there are probably even a few souls to be found, there are definitely bodies, the Arabs here sell little boys your age to their cousins over the sea.'

'Do you miss being a teacher?' Jama asked.

Idea stopped walking and looked down on Jama. 'No, when I was a teacher I was working for people who had no respect for me or anyone like me.'

An old beggar woman leant on a stick by the mosque wall, her raisin-black hand held silently out to them. A young boy sat by her feet, a solitary leg emerging from his dirty shorts, his hair and eyelashes dust-matted, Idea passed a coin to the old woman. 'Come on, I'll show you the Sadhu.' Idea picked up his step, rushing through the alley as its night-time corruption faded into daylight commerce. Bras were removed one by one by languid hands from balconies and curtains were drawn for the women to get some peace. Idea moved around like a sniffer dog, barely looking up as he shuffled along, until they reached an open road with taxis buzzing by. In between a shop called Punjabi fabrics and a scrum of black-market, female money changers, was the strangest sight Jama had ever seen. An Indian man, naked apart from a strip of cloth around his privates, sat on a crate with his feet pressed into his lean thighs. Orange markings were pasted on his forehead and his long white hair was coiled in a snake's nest on his head. The Sadhu's eyes were serenely closed, a fat hand-rolled cigarette burned in his left hand, smelling sweet and herby.

'Come on, Jama, on to Plateau de Serpents,' shouted Idea. Beyond the cafés and offices of Place Menelik were the colonial residences and Idea was keen to walk through this forbidden part of town.

Idea pointed down to the road that suddenly became tarred as it approached the European houses. 'Take note, Jama, take note of all the little differences.'

Jama had had many bad experiences with

bawabs when he had tried to go to the European settlement in Aden but Idea had no fear of them. He raised his arm and shouted 'Hoi Hoi' at the uniformed Africans guarding the grand houses. They did not respond, staves in hand they watched Jama and Idea with hostile eyes.

Idea took a deep breath. 'My boy, this is a sad, sordid place, everything, everyone can be bought here, the poor live above open sewers while the rich frolic in those European hotel pools, gormless, mindless, empty people, the French have us in their palms, feeding us, curing us, beating us, fucking us as they please.'

Jama wasn't sure what Idea wanted to show him but he was getting nervous that the police would come. Idea took Jama's hand and they crossed the road to a fenced garden. 'Look at that, Jama.'

Under the shade of palm trees hung two swings, a wooden slide led into a sand pit, an empty merry-go-round spun with the breeze. Idea picked Jama up under his legs and threw him over the fence, 'Go and play,' he ordered. Jama was caught between childish excitement and adolescent embarrassment, but he obeyed. He tested his weight against the swings then started to push himself a little, worried that he would break the rope and be arrested.

'Go to the other one now,' Idea called out.
Jama slid down into the sand pit and then got into the merry-go-round, he pushed himself uncertainly, not sure what the machine was meant to do. A Somali ayah came along pushing a flame-haired baby in a huge, crow-black carriage, an old Indian ayah led a young boy by the hand. The European children were stopped by neighbours who ruffled their hair and rubbed imaginary marks off their skin. Already the children expected to be fussed over and adored and did not smile at the attention. Jama knew that everywhere they went they would be offered good things even though they wanted for nothing. In the shops in Aden, Indian merchants would not allow Somali children over the threshold while Ferengi children ran in and demanded sweets and toys from Uncle Krishna.

'I've had enough now, Idea.' Jama extricated himself from the merry-go-round and climbed over the fence. Idea seemed satisfied that they'd made their point and he held out his hand for Jama to hold, but Jama didn't take hold of it, he wanted Idea to know that he was a young man not a child.

★ ★ ★

The house was filled with a drowning silence, as if there were things going on far away but the sound of them was submerged under metres of water. Jama got up and walked out of the house, he had slept late; the sun was approaching its zenith. He hoped that Idea had gone to the suq as his stomach was already rumbling. Jama walked absent-mindedly through the gloomy room and stared at his reflection in the mottled tin mirror. His eyes were large and sunken and his brown irises were encircled with broad bands of pale blue; his eyes had a look in them that was at once beseeching and proud. Jama's eyebrows were thick and dramatically arched, his nose wide and flat like a lion's, his lips were full and he held them clenched together so that he looked manly and serious. His hair was fine and had a blond-tinge near the temples from hunger; it had retreated from his forehead leaving little tufts where his hairline used to be. His chest was embarrassingly bony and he could count all of his ribs and if he turned around all of the vertebrae in his spine too, his arms were as thin, with elbows sharp and jutting. Jama put his fists on his waist and puffed out his stomach and cheeks, to see how he would look as a rich fat kid. He turned to the side and laughed at his pregnant silhouette, there was movement at the door and he saw Idea watching with his loopy smile.

'Don't worry, Jama, you will get a fat belly one day, just look at mine,' Idea said, lifting his shirt over his stomach and slapping his sagging belly, 'I could make a fortune dancing for old Yemenis, don't you think?' he chuckled. 'Come, help me cook lunch, there is some meat today.'

Jama trotted over to Idea's side and handed him the ingredients and kept watch over the food as it cooked. While washing the dishes, Jama turned to Idea and asked, 'How can I get to Sudan from here?'

'Sudan? What do you want in Sudan?' laughed Idea.

'My father is working there, I am going to visit him.'

The smile fell from Idea's face. 'Do you know how far it is Jama? Our people have been thrown to the four winds. You will have to pass countries where there are wars being fought, even passing through Djibouti is dangerous. Last year three hundred people were killed in one day when the Somalis and Afars took to their spears again.'

'I'll be fine.'

Idea shook his head. 'What makes you so sure?'

'I can do anything, Idea, I can do anything

at all. I walked across the desert by myself, didn't I?'

'And look at the state you were in! I thought that someone had left their rubbish under the tree and there you were passed out. Look, Jama, stay here and you will be fine, stay in Aden you will be fine, stay in Hargeisa you will be fine, but go through Eritrea or Abyssinia and you will see things you don't want to see. Wait here — let me show you something.'

He returned with a frayed book, the spine dangling apart. 'In this book are pictures of our land drawn by Ferengis.' Idea flicked through the green and blue pages until he found the image he wanted. 'See this horn sticking out the side, this is where Somalis live, next to us are the Oromo, the Afar, Amhara, Swahilis down south, all of our neighbours.'

Jama peered over the map, it made no sense to him, how could mountains, rivers, trees, roads, villages, towns be shrunk onto a tiny little page?

'Sudan is here,' Idea plunged a fingernail into a pink country. 'We are here,' another nail pierced a purple spot. 'Everywhere in between is controlled by Italians.' Idea smoothed over an expanse of yellow. 'All this is an abattoir, the Italians are devils, they might imprison you or put you into their army. I read in the papers every day that ten or fifty Eritreans have been executed. There isn't a town or village without a set of gallows. They kill fortune tellers for predicting their defeat and the troubadours for mocking them. A frail Somali boy will be like a little bite before the midday meal to them.'

'Well then, I will take a knife.'

Idea stifled a laugh. 'And you will kill them all with your knife?'

'If I have to I will.'

'You remind me so much of my son, Jama.'

'You have a son?' said Jama with a pang of jealousy.

'I had a son.'

'What happened to him?'

Idea shrugged. 'I took him to be vaccinated and a few days later he died. He was a healthy, clever boy just like you, there was no reason for him to die.'

Jama could see tears gathering in Idea's eyes, so he put his arms around him, holding him tight in his thin arms.

★ ★ ★

As night fell, the neighbourhood filled with lights and music, drumbeats picked up speed and then stopped abruptly. The strings of a lute were strummed lightly, and men came through the alley carrying larger musical instruments. Children, infected with excitement, came out of their homes giggling and chasing each other, getting hot and dusty before being called in for their baths. Incense burners were placed on the street to repel the smell of rotting waste that overpowered the town as soon as the sun came down. The shacks built above the open sewer seemed to palpate and shift away from the rank churning stench that shimmered beneath them.

'Yallah! Let's go, there's a wedding,' shouted Amina when she returned from work. She poured water into a tin bath for Jama to wash, and he went to work with soap, lathering and rubbing away at his skin, trying to remove the never ending layers of dirt. The red soap was new and hard and Jama played it up and down his ribs as if he was a zither, until his bones jangled and his red skin hummed. He held his mother's amulet far away from the water but dared not take it off in case jinns stole it.

When he came out clothes were strewn everywhere, even on the floor the clothes looked festive and special. There were fabrics shot with silver or gold thread, lacy underskirts, sequinned shawls; dresses cut in daring, flashy, modern ways, deep purples and turquoise, pinks and jade greens, yellows and ruby reds. Amina came into the room looking like a queen, her hair out of its scarf, magnificent gold earrings dripping down from her ears to her neck. A low cut red dress, glittering with red sequins, fell loosely from her body; gold bangles ran up and down as she threw her arms up in delight at Jama's shiny clean face. Amina left the room and came back in wielding eyeliner and a tin with a reclining lady on it, she passed these to Jama to hold.

'Open the kohl for me, my sweet,' Amina said to Jama. He carefully unscrewed the lid to the kohl, passing the ornate tip to Amina, and she painted her eyelids with a sweep of black.

'Now rouge, please,' she said, admiring her work.

Jama had never seen rouge before and fumbled with the tin, eventually snapping it open and holding out the red goo to Amina. She dabbed some on her fingers and rubbed it into the small apples of her cheeks, her mouth thoughtfully open, Jama savoured her soft breath against his face. Amina's skin looked dewy but her bewitching black eyes belonged to a wild woman like Salome.

'Get your sandals on, Jama, quickly,

quickly,' Amina ordered. Jama awoke from his reverie and looked behind him. She had bought him enormous sandals, with brass buckles at the ankles.

'Thank you, aunty,' he said, as he struggled to put the heavy sandals on.

Idea followed them into the night. He wore a beige baggy suit that glowed in the darkness. Amina had put on oily Yemeni perfume that hung sweetly in the air as she sauntered along, greeting her neighbours as they came out of their houses, gossiping and pinning up their hair. The wedding was to be in the centre of the African quarter, at the Hotel de Paradis, and the beat of a drum and the soaring of a female voice could already be heard from the hotel. Young women in high heels tripped up and down the road, ferrying make-up, clothes and rumours to one another. Around the veranda of the hotel, poor people lingered, their clothes dusted off and their faces spit shined, hoping to slip into the banquet unnoticed. They followed the Yemeni, Somali and French guests up a spiral staircase to the roof. The view from the top reminded Jama of the gowned and bejewelled English that he used to see dancing on the rooftops of the expensive hotels in Aden. Those hotels always had African bawabs to shoo away anyone who looked too poor or too black. A band sat in the corner, the drummer chewing qat and the female singer humming softly to herself. They soon realised that the men and boys were drifting towards the back to give the women the prime seats at the front. Idea took Jama's hand and led him to the wall. The women of Djibouti stalked around him with their perfect make-up, wearing layer after layer of glittery clothing in the sweltering heat. They were so wild and free in comparison to Hargeisa women; they were crude, they flirted with men, jeered at their manhoods and their mothers, nothing was safe from them. The food was laid out on tables along the side and the men hung close, pinching small cakes and samosas when the women were not looking. The marriage was between a Somali man and a Yemeni woman, and Idea said that it might be a difficult match as the Yemeni women all seemed to be around three foot tall. Young men clotted into groups, clocking the young women who ambled past. The band got up and played a popular song that got the crowd clapping their hands and ululating, then the couple came up the stairs. The bride was wearing a large European dress that swamped her tiny frame, her husband wore a dark suit and a fantastic smile; both had fragrant garlands of jasmine around their necks. They were led forward by their serious-looking mothers and seated on gold thrones. The bride's friends and female relations rushed up to fuss around with her gown, as guests queued up to kiss, embarrass and place money in the groom's lap. When everyone, apart from Jama and Idea, had gone up to harass the couple, the food was handed out. Whole families had turned up without invitation to partake of the banquet and the families of the bride and groom gave freely so as not to bring any bad luck to the marriage. French men sat together, looking uncomfortable, grasping their expensive presents between their legs.

Idea turned to Jama and took his hand. 'I like having you here, Jama. Why don't you stay with me and Amina? I'll teach you to read and write. You can always find your father when you've got taller and bought yourself a bigger knife.'

Jama set his face against this seduction. 'No Idea, I can't wait, I have been waiting my whole life. I want my father now, what if I wait and he dies?'

Idea understood, he patted Jama's hand. 'Alright Jama, I tried. Let's see tomorrow how we can get you to Sudan without having your head blown off half way there.'

The party carried on late into the night, with the scandalously dancing women, broiling inside their hijabs and expensive dresses, fainting in the furnace-like heat. Market boys occasionally showered them from below with handfuls of gravel and secret lovers took advantage of the crowd and confusion to sneak off together. Amina finally led Jama and Idea back along the dark road to their house, ignoring the illicit susurrations around them. A few sunburnt French legionnaires skulked around in their dirty white shorts, whispering up to their girl-friends' balconies to be let in. Jama looked up at the sky, beside the moon was a bright star he had never noticed before, it flickered and winked at him. As Jama squinted he saw a woman sitting on the star, her small feet swinging under her tobe and her arm waving down at him. Jama waved to his mother and she smiled back, blowing shooting star kisses down on him.

★ ★ ★

Idea walked on ahead to the docks at L'Escale, his arms swinging loosely by his side, absentmindedly patting Jama's head and stroking his hair. Jama tried to keep up with him, all the time wondering if he really did want to leave.

Amina had woken Jama up before she left

for work and passed him a lunch wrapped in cloth. 'Good luck, Jama, I hope you meet your father, but whatever happens, don't lose faith in yourself. You are a clever boy and with a bit of luck you will live a good life,' she had said before smothering his face in kisses. He had not washed his face after and those kisses still burnt red on his skin.

Jama peered up at Idea's face, the lopsided smile was still there but there was no joy in it, his eyes were in pain. Jama grabbed Idea's hand as it swung beside him and held it, thinking secretly that if he didn't already have a father, he would have chosen to be Idea's son.

Idea looked down on Jama. 'When you go to Eritrea, you will see even more clearly, there are Ferengis who think that you don't feel pain like them, have dreams like them, love life as much as them. It's a bad world we live in, you're like a flea riding a dog's back, eventually you will end between its teeth. Be careful.

'Above all, Jama, stay away from the fascists.'

'Fascists? What are fascists?'

'They are disturbed Ferengis who do the work of the devil, in Eritrea they have tried to wipe us out, in Somalia they work people to death on their farms, in Abyssinia they drop poison from their planes onto children like you.'

Jama nodded, but he couldn't comprehend not being alive, not feeling pain or happiness, not feeling the gritty earth beneath his feet. Perhaps these fascists should be avoided, he thought but he didn't really believe that they could hurt him. The very first Ferengi Jama had met had worked at Aden's Steamer Point. The white man had stuck a sharp needle in his arm and worn gloves to handle him but the Somali man accompanying Jama to Aden had said it would protect him from disease. Maybe white doctors couldn't be fascists, Jama thought to himself. They reached the watery expanse of L'Escale, passenger boats and larger merchant ships floated on the surface of the dirty water, loading and unloading. The porters shouted at each other in Somali and Afar and sang work songs to make their loads easier to bear. Idea and Jama stopped at the edge of the concrete platform. Jama bit his lip and his feet wavered in the air before stepping down onto the decking. He thought about telling Idea that he had changed his mind and wanted to stay, but he knew that he could not bear the betrayal of exchanging his real father for another.

Idea conducted Jama through the crowd.

'We need to find out which boat is going to Assab, we have a clansman there, an askari called Talyani. Tell him you are my nephew, he will help you get to Asmara and from Asmara you can take the train.'

Old creaky pilgrims with red beards and white shrouds piled into a small dhow, the boatman filling every square inch of space with penitent flesh. Idea spoke a litany of languages to different officials, trying to find out where the boat to Assab was leaving from. They followed the curve of the harbour around to a quieter area where a small steamship painted yellow waited on the water. 'It's this one I think,' called out Idea, he rushed on ahead, skipping up the wooden gangplank.

Jama watched him accost a couple of bare-chested sailors before stopping a Somali man in a peaked cap. Idea counted out francs from his pocket and pointed out Jama waiting by the ship. The captain waved him over with an expansive sweep of his hand.

Idea waited at the top of the gangplank. 'I wish I could make you stay, but this will have to be goodbye for a while I guess. Learn how to read, Jama. I was hoping to teach you while you stayed with us, but you deserted me. Anyway, come here.'

Idea patted Jama's cheek and put a

handkerchief full of coins into his palm. 'It's not much but it will help.'

Jama held back his tears and hid his face in Idea's paunch, his heart raced and he couldn't say the words he felt inside.

'I wish I could run away with you but that woman has me bewitched, don't forget me, Jama, learn how to read!' were Idea's last words before he turned his back and returned to Amina. Jama found a shady place on the deck and watched Idea's figure recede into the distance, his feet jiggled by the shaking engine underneath. There were a few passengers mingling about, and a couple of crewmen smoking cigarettes beside the railings. Jama approached them, feeling forlorn all of a sudden. He placed an imaginary cigarette between his fingers, tilting his head back and pursing his lips like the sailors, invisible smoke curled up into the sky. When the sailors finished their cigarettes Jama went to investigate the boat. He followed the small steps leading to the lower deck and tiptoed inside, the smell of old fruit and tobacco emanating from behind shut doors. He wondered where the anchor was kept when they were at sea, it must be an ancient, holy looking thing, he thought, silver encrusted with green barnacles. He wandered to the end of the walkway and peered through a hatch in the floor, it was black but Jama could see a figure hunched before a furnace in which a small orange fire blazed. The figure was naked apart from a pair of shorts and was busily piling up chunks of coal, oblivious to the peeping tom behind him. Jama understood that Djibouti was kept so hot by troops of little men like him feeding underground fires. He left the fireman to his sweltering work and crept away to the upper deck.

He dreamt happy dreams, dreams in which he disembarked the ship to find a grand black car crawling to a stop before him. The passenger door was clicked open by a suited arm, a solid gold watch ticking and beaming against the dark skin of the driver. All those promises his mother had made about him being the sweetheart of the stars looked to him as if they would finally come to pass. He was going to be a normal boy with a real father, he wanted his father above anything else in the world, he was becoming a man and needed a father to light the way. Jama had so many questions for Guure. Where did you go? What have you been doing in Sudan? Why did you not come back for me? Jama felt ready to explode; his sentence was finally over.

The boat shook violently then steered away

from the harbour; the wait had been interminable. Jama's mouth tasted sour and his tongue was dry and cottony. He ate the lunch Amina had prepared for him, putting the cloth over his head against the sharp sunlight. The boat cut a clean line through the clear, green-tinged sea, gliding like a rich European dancer on the rooftops of Aden. The boat journey seemed too easy to Jama, he mistrusted ease and comfort, it being so foreign to him. Jama concentrated on the shoreline, hoping to make out some land-mark; something he would recognise from the stories he had heard from Idea, but he recognised nothing. Later, as the sun travelled to the west, painting broad sweeps of pink and orange and red and purple across the sky in its wake, islands appeared on the horizon. Islands ringed in fine white sand, the leaves of lazy-looking palm trees swaying heavily, the gentle coral reefs around them lashed by the duelling waves of the Red Sea and Gulf of Aden. Jama counted seven small islands and realised happily that they were the seven wicked brothers. Idea had told him that they had been evil pirates who God had caught in a raging storm and turned into islands, to be forever whipped by the violent winds of the Bab el Mandab Strait, the Gate of Tears.

Assab, Asmara, Omhajer, Eritrea, October 1936

The passengers gathered their bundles and children while the crew ran around preparing for landing. Jama stood up and walked to the prow of the boat. After docking, a man in a vest announced 'ASSAB, ERITREA'. Jama had to keep pushing back the clamouring bodies behind him, who crushed him as they yelled to be let off. Finally, a gangplank was placed against the vessel and the gate released.

Jama followed the other passengers, they were mainly Afars returning to see family in Dankalia but a few Somalis and Yemenis were mixed in with the crowd. Jama's attention was caught by a gigantic board standing on two poles, a helmeted head was pictured. A menacingly large nose and heavy lantern jaw in a white face were all Jama could make out in the growing darkness, European writing encircled the image. Jama noticed other men raising their right arm to the picture so he did the same, wondering why anyone would go to the effort of painting such an ugly Ferengi. Jama sidled up to a Somali man who looked

142

askance at him. 'Yes, boy?'

'Uncle, I am looking for a clansman, do you know an askari called Talyani?'

'Talyani? I know of one Issa man named Talyani, but the devil knows where he lives. Ask at the police station,' the man replied.

★ ★ ★

'What do you want? It's too late to be begging, isn't it?' shouted a voice behind the door.

'I was sent to you by Idea in Djibouti, I am his nephew, can you help me go to Sudan?' Jama said, his voice higher than normal. The heavy door was unlocked and Jama stepped in.

Talyani's home was immaculately clean. Sitting on the floor was a young woman with a baby suckling at her breast; she gave a polite nod to Jama. 'You can stay for a few nights, the boat to Massawa is due soon. This is my wife, Zainab, and my son, Marco,' Talyani said.

'Get him something to sleep on when you're finished, Zainab, and food too, I'm going to bed.' Talyani disappeared into the dark hallway but then came back. 'You're his nephew huh? On what side?'

Jama thought quickly. 'On both sides, my

mother is Amina's half sister and my father is his brother.'

Talyani twisted up his eyebrows but let it go. 'We'll speak properly in the morning.'

Jama let out a long breath. He was lucky Talyani had not asked him to recite his grandfathers' names. The house was silent, only the baby's sucking disturbed the air, and Jama stood awkwardly near the door. Zainab moved quickly and quietly around the room, arranging blankets on the floor for him.

'Let me help,' Jama offered. Zainab shook her head, her hair falling across her face and casting a shadow, but he could pick out another shadow within it, the purple-black print of a fist around her eye.

While she laid out a plate of rice and stew, Jama gazed at her baby. Marco's round cheeks were shiny and smooth, his little chin resting on the blankets he was coddled in, he slept like a king without a care in the world. Jama ate in silence while Zainab fluttered around, fetching water and straightening furniture that was already straight. They could hear Talyani through the wall, clearing his throat and making himself comfortable, reminding them he was still there. The plates were quickly emptied and Zainab spirited them away, washing them immediately. She returned to pick up her baby and hesitated at the doorway.

144

'Is there anything else you need?' Her small face as she turned around was that of a teenager, with puppy fat and pimples.

'No thank you,' replied Jama, wondering how much older than him Zainab really was.

★ ★ ★

The room looked strange in the early morning sun, bare and shiny, as if it had been licked clean. Black and white photographs of Talyani in the uniform of an Italian askari stood proud in varnished wooden frames. The schoolboy socks pulled high up towards his knees, a strange tall hat on his head, his hair was black and wavy like an Italian's, hence his nickname. He was a smiling colonial mascot in costume and Jama couldn't imagine him pouring sand into the engines of Italian trucks or spitting in their food the way he would. Talyani must be like the ones Idea mentioned, thought Jama looking at the pictures, the ones who gunned down the Abyssinian farmers and children.

Zainab became melancholic as the day of Jama's departure approached. She told him he had been her first guest since she had arrived in Assab and she envisioned a long stretch before anyone else came to visit. Zainab had nearly forgotten what it was like

145

to have someone to talk to and do things with. Her teenager's life with its cast of sisters, aunties, friends and neighbours had come to an abrupt end when she married, a sacrifice she had made without any real knowledge of what she was leaving behind. Her friends had been impressed with her bravery in leaving Somaliland and so had Zainab, until she realised that she was in thrall to a drunken tyrant and would only ever see the four walls around her and the ceiling above her head. Talyani, on the other hand, had freedom and a life in the outside world but he was rude and patronising to their Afar neighbours, families who were largely opposed to the Italian invasion of their country. Talyani sang Italian songs loudly in the backyard and had taken to giving the fascist salute to passers-by. If it wasn't for the baby, Zainab would have stowed away on one of the steam boats and hot-footed it back to Burao.

Jama was woken on his last morning by the clatter of pots and pans crashing to the floor. Talyani's voice rang through the house as he shouted at Zainab in the kitchen.

'Didn't your mother teach you anything, you idiot! Pick these things up, I didn't buy them for you to destroy.'

Jama covered his ears to block out Talyani's

146

viciousness and chased after his sweet dreams. Talyani's boots approached. 'Are you ready? I have places to go,' he said. Jama slunk out of the covers and went to the basin, the water washing away the last vestiges of his dreaminess.

They waited outside while Talyani secured two large locks on the front door. Marco kicked his legs out from his mother's hip and gurgled with excitement at feeling fresh air on his skin. Zainab squinted up at the cerulean sky, her red clothes made her look young and free, but she held on tightly to her son. Jama could not imagine Zainab growing old in this town, there were too few women and too many askaris for him to picture her strolling down these streets as a wispy old lady.

Assab was buffeted by hot, dry winds blowing in from the volcanic black deserts of Dankalia. Maybe Assab was too close to that apocalyptic waste for the Italians to make much effort with, despite it being their first imperial foothold since the Caesars. They had bought Assab for a moderate sum from the Egyptians. Its buildings were ancient and crumbling, stained grey and deformed by the unrelenting wind. The people were a rag bag of wanderers; Abyssinians looking for work, Yemeni fishermen following the shoals of the Red Sea, nomadic Afars with their teeth filed into points, Somalis on their way to somewhere else. Although a busy port like Djibouti Town, most Assabis slept long into the day and those up and about had a pinched, frustrated look on their faces, angry at missing the epoch when this area was one of the richest on earth. As part of the Axumite Empire, Assab had exported rhino horn, hippo hides, apes and lions to Rome, Egypt and Persia.

A cargo boat swayed to the side of them, its paint shedding swathes of metallic leaves. It was the only vessel moored and it seemed to have come in to die, heaving and sighing heavily as it was. Talyani stopped and handed Jama his flimsy two lire ticket, his pass to his father.

'The journey will take about half a day, I will find someone to escort you to Asmara. Wait until you see that place, Wah Wah! The Italians have turned it into one big paradise; there are picture houses, hotels, shops that sell whatever you could want to buy.' With his eyes blazing, Talyani left them to find Jama an escort for the rest of the journey. He returned quickly with two other askaris, young men with smooth skin.

'These boys will put you on a lorry from Massawa to Asmara, it's not far,' said Talyani proudly tapping them on the back. 'You can get a train from Asmara to Agordat, and then a lorry. The roads are fantastic now, the Ferengis have brought progress to this country at last.'

Talyani shook Jama's hand, nearly crushing it. 'Maybe you will become an askari, like your father and I.'

'My father is a driver, not an askari,' corrected Jama, put off by the example Talyani set of them.

Zainab shook Jama's hand and he boarded his second ship. Talyani marched on ahead and Zainab reluctantly followed, turning back to wave intermittently, her smile bright in the morning light.

Underneath his feet Jama could hear the bleating of sheep and their hooves jittering on wooden planks. He crouched down away from the hot wind and peeped through the cracks in the wood. He could make out bony heads and fluffy bodies in the shafts of light cutting through the hold, and their oily scent drifted up in the heat. The young askaris climbed the gangplank, their heavy slow steps belying their age. Look at all those hot clothes thought Jama, he felt faint just looking at them. The ship left the harbour quickly and with little warning, leaving behind hollering stragglers who raced along the quay to catch up with it, holding their sarongs up between their legs. 'Masaakiin, poor men,' muttered Jama as he watched them desperately gesticulate to the laughing crew.

The shriek of seagulls made Jama sit up, and he wiped the drool from his cheek. Ahead of him lay mountains and hills higher than he had ever seen, reaching beyond the clouds. Underneath the mountains nestled a pretty whitewashed town, its jetty reaching welcomingly out into the sea. As Massawa got closer, Jama could see an island of elegant arches and stuccoed white palaces looming over another island crammed with shanty towns of corrugated sheets and wooden planks. The rich town and poor town tied together by a concrete umbilical cord. A sign faced out to the sea, one of the askaris leant forward, trying to pick out the words on the salt-scoured board. 'The pearl of the Red Sea,' he recited slowly. Jama smiled at the glamour the sign promised. Dhows plied the placid sea and birds fluttered, pecking at insects on the mud flats surrounding the causeway. They entered a maze of streets, the askaris leading the way with the long strides of ostriches. They entered dark mysterious alleys that suddenly opened up into light-filled squares and then led back into darkness. Jama looked up. Some of the houses had wooden shutters and intricately carved balconies, one had a mammoth, onion-shaped dome sitting squat on its roof. Ancient mosques, their walls uneven with repeated whitewashing, stood separate from the homes, like dignified grandparents sitting on the street watching the world go by. The silver cross of the Orthodox Church shone a supernatural white on the skyline, behind the star and crescent of a mosque. Jama let out a happy sigh at the covered market, bedecked with bright awnings over the stalls; goods neatly laid out on tables like booty recovered from Aladdin's cave. Despite its antiquity, Massawa was tidy and well kept, with pockets of incredible wealth hidden like pearls inside an oyster shell. Servants piled in and out of the grand homes of Armenian, Arab, Jewish and European merchants. Everywhere there was the sound of quiet and profitable industry. And yet, nearby lay shanty towns where sparsely filled cooking pans burnt easily and Italians in shiny black boots idled about in cheap bars, nursing glasses of beer.

They crossed another longer causeway into mainland Massawa. This part of town seemed plainer, more residential, where everyone went to rest after all the allurements of the old town.

'We'll get a lorry along this main road,' said one of the askaris.

It didn't seem like much of a main road to Jama, it was barely wide enough for one vehicle. Jama stared at the horizon, his father could just appear around the bend, it was more than possible that he drove up and down these roads, he thought. It wasn't a busy road and the sound of anyone approaching made Jama's heart lurch. One of the askaris ran out into the road to hail down a lorry and, seeing the uniforms, the driver stopped. Jama quickly glanced up into the cab, 'not him' he reassured himself and they all piled into the cab. The vast depression in the earth he had entered in Djibouti was now rapidly ascending and the vehicle creaked and screeched to manage the incline. The driver recited the al-fatiha under his breath, while the askaris joked to hide their fear. The lorry nearly lost its balance as it clambered up, scraping its underside as it righted itself.

'It never gets easier,' said the driver through gritted teeth.

Jama, at first terrified by the precarious highway, began to enjoy it, calling out hazards for the driver, 'Look! A pothole! And over there some loose rocks, be careful, driver!'

He could hear the driver's heart pounding near his ear and the gears of the vehicle crunching beneath him. The askaris, relaxed by Jama's vigilance, fell asleep, their heads lolling from left to right in unison.

'Hey, you're good at this, little boy. You wanna work for me?' the driver said, Jama nodded eagerly and they exchanged smiles in the rear view mirror.

They finally reached the manicured avenues of Asmara, everywhere new houses sparkled, the paint on them barely dry. Large Italian villas were painted in mouth-watering reds, corals, pinks, yellows; blossoming purple and white flowers flowed over their walls. It was the tidiest, most fertile place Jama had ever seen. Trees rustled at the side of the road, cleaners swept the rubbish-free pavement, and there was so much paving that everywhere seemed covered in patterned stone tiles. Jama looked around, all the shops were run by Europeans, the town seemed to belong to the fat-bellied men with upturned moustaches sitting outside the shops. Women in dresses that exposed their arms and legs cycled up and down the gentle slopes. The only Africans he could see were the street cleaners.

'It's strange, isn't it? Don't worry they have been generous enough to leave us a scrap of land further down,' said the driver.

Jama leant across the askaris so he could see more clearly through the dirty window. Three-storey buildings with columned fronts towered over the lorry as they passed through the main avenue. A huge cathedral with an iridescent mosaic cross appeared before them and women in black and white gowns stood on the steps picking at their prayer beads as the church bell tolled. Eritrean beggars sat by the wall of the Cathedral, swathed in dirty white shammas.

Jama shouted, 'Look! Gaadhi dameer!' and pointed excitedly as a donkeycart drove past, the donkey cantering and swishing its tail, a little boy holding the reins.

The driver found the way to the African reservation and slowed down. 'Where do you want me to drop you off?' he asked.

'Further down, where the Somalis are,' answered one of the askaris. They drove on and drew to a halt outside a teashop full of Somali men.

Jama let the askaris pay for him. The driver beeped the horn for Jama. 'Nabad gelyo, peace be with you,' he called out before the lorry pulled away.

'Are you going to pay for the food, little man?' one askari asked.

Jama picked out a few coins from Idea's handkerchief. 'Get me a lot, I'm hungry,' he demanded.

The askaris returned with full plates. 'Who are you looking for here?' asked the taller askari.

Jama shrugged, confident that someone would take him in, 'Anyone, an Eidegalle I suppose.'

'I'll go and ask in the tea shop,' the askari said getting up. Jama could see him circulating around, shaking hands, making jokes. The askari came back a while later, trailed by a lame man with a basket full of charcoal in his hand. They exchanged salaams.

'An old Eidegalle woman lives this way, but I warn you that she can be difficult,' said the charcoal seller.

The houses in the reservation were small and packed together, with animals tied to poles outside. 'It's this one,' said the new man stopping at a beehive-shaped tukul with a rush mat serving as a door.

Jama shook the rush mat and the askaris stepped back, an old woman with a hard face and humped back pushed aside the sheet.

'Who are you?' she asked brusquely. Jama recited what he knew of his lineage, skipping over grandfathers and mangling old-fashioned names. He explained that he was en route to Sudan and just needed somewhere to sleep for the night.

'What does a little runt like you want in Sudan?' the old woman challenged.

'I am going to find my father,' Jama shot back.

'Are you sure you have one?'

Jama turned to march away from the old witch. The lame man was laughing with the askaris as they returned to the tea shop.

'Wait, wait! Don't take an old woman's words so seriously. You can stay for a night.'

They sat far apart in the hut, listening to the couple next door fighting until they also fell quiet. Jama, feeling overwhelmed by the silence, cracked, 'How did you get that hump on your back?' he asked.

Awrala cackled. 'Ha! You see, boy . . . my father came here to be a farmer, well that is not completely true, he actually got bored of the hard work very quickly and made us into farmers, I spent all day like this,' she demonstrated the bent over posture, balancing her hands on her thighs.

'From the age of five to eighteen, I ploughed, and sowed and watered and harvested, hard work like you young people would never believe,' Awrala boasted.

Jama wanted to tell her about all the carcass delivering he had done in Hargeisa but he left it. A light in her eyes had switched on.

'Then the Italians came and took over his land, finito! Boof! It was gone, all that hard work wasted, it was beautiful land, so much water and life unlike our own barren country, but I am still bent over, over a broom now.

Do you want to feel it?' she said laughing.

Jama was taken aback but his fear of her had gone. He walked behind Awrala, and she guided his hand over the hump. It was as hard and knobbly as a tortoise's shell, it seemed a heavy thing for such an old woman to be carrying around everywhere. He tried to knead it under his hands but it was too firm.

Awrala chuckled under his fingers. 'Enough now, it's ticklish, get some sleep.'

'Do you want me to tread on your back?' offered Jama, pitying her poor misshapen spine.

'No, no, your weight would break me,' she said, stifling a yawn. She arranged their blankets on the floor and curled up under hers.

'My head is killing me,' Jama whispered.

'Don't worry, sleep it off, you're not used to the altitude here,' she replied sleepily.

Jama unable to sleep tried to keep Awrala awake. 'Don't you have children?' he asked.

'No, after three husbands I accepted I was barren,' replied Awrala, clicking the beads of her tusbah.

'Why don't you go back to Hargeisa then?' Jama asked.

Awrala perked up. 'Why should I? I'm not Somali anymore, the place where you are born is not always the best place for you, boy. There is nothing in our country. I have got too used to the rain, hills, and cool air of Asmara. I'll be buried here.'

Jama listened to Awrala's breath whistling through her teeth until he finally fell asleep.

★ ★ ★

The morning air was frosty and hazy, the grass wet with dew. Everywhere stood mouldy green stumps where trees had been cut down for firewood. A smell of burnt coffee and charcoal emanated from the little dwellings, acrid in the sharp air, and Jama coughed and hawked along with the men emerging from the huts. The heat from Awrala's tea warmed his stomach but his face, fingers and feet were numb. It was as cold as an October morning in Hargeisa, he had always wanted to see the rumoured ice fall from the sky during the dry season, but wondered why God didn't send the ice to Aden where it was needed more. They left the African reservation and walked down a steep hill; they passed women and girls marching sure-footedly uphill, carrying bundles of sticks and firewood bigger than themselves, their torsos bent over with the strain. To Jama they looked like bewitched women taken over by monstrous humps, with tentacles trying to reach out to other victims. A bus sped past and the firewood women jumped quickly out of the way as it skidded dangerously close; the bundles on their backs fell apart. At the front of the bus a few white faces peered out while all the black passengers were squashed in the back. Awrala led the way with a speed that made a mockery of her age, pushing people out of her way. As they got closer to the railway station, Italians appeared, porters trailing behind them with suitcases and large trunks. The station was crammed with workers and travellers milling around like termites. All the men wore hats even though they might be barefoot. On the platform, Jama found the iron beauty that would take him to his father; she had a snub nose and big round eyes, and shone radiantly green through the cloudlike steam.

Jama ran to the train and Awrala pulled him back scared it would hurt him. 'Let me touch it,' he exclaimed.

Wrenching his arm away from her, he stroked the side of the locomotive as if it was a kitten purring beneath his fingers. Watched by the Italian engineer inside the engine car and an Eritrean fireman, the little boy greeted the manmade snake. The inside of the train's head contained shiny brass instruments, glass circles with fluttering needles and a big leather seat. Jama walked enviously away and behind him came the sudden, shrieking call of the train's whistle, he jumped, his feet rising from the ground in shock. He turned back to the engine and the two men waved.

As they walked the length of the train, the carriages got less grand, the number of seats increased, the flowers in vases disappeared, and when Awrala stopped they stood next to the last carriage. Awrala gave Jama his train ticket and waited for him to find a wooden bench before she left, propelling herself through the crowd. The carriage quickly filled up, people sat on the floor, stood wherever they could, held their goats between their knees, stuffed squawking chickens into the overhead storage.

Jama fidgeted, worried that his bladder would get too full and he would end up wetting himself. The final whistle shrieked and the train juddered to a slow start. Jama sat next to the window and watched as Asmara, green and calm, disappeared into the distance. He thought sadly of Awrala resting underneath its earth one day, unable to enjoy her beloved hills. Tall regal trees lined the tracks and little villages flashed by the window, as did shepherds leading fat brown cows through fields and glades. Shimmering streams meandered across fields, birds waded along their banks while women bathed.

School children chased one another on their way to school flanked by massive Italian-owned plantations, the land suddenly dominated by wheat for miles. As the track climbed higher, the land became dustier and drier. Jagged grey mountains pierced the sky, isolated tukuls nestled in their hearts.

The train picked its way along fine, crumbly mountain paths, a dead donkey or camel sometimes lying far beneath them. Everywhere Jama looked there was another giant mountain, rippling with muscular strength, each one competing with the next in attaining proximity to Heaven, as God had enjoined his creation to do. The peaks looked ascetic with heads shaved of greenery, they had long foregone water and the pleasures of life, silently awaiting the day when Allah would bless them for their piety. 'Manshallah, praise the lord,' uttered Jama, awed by God's genius. All around him was paradise, full of what was good in the world as well as bad. Life is just this, Jama thought, a long journey, with lightness and darkness falling over you, companions all around, on their own journeys. Each person sitting passively or impatiently, wondering whether the tracks of their fate will take them on a clattering iron horse to their destination or will sweep them away on an invisible path to another world.

At Keren, many of the passengers got off, eager to get to the great market before it became crowded. The humid sweatiness inside the carriage got off with them and Jama stretched out his legs for the rest of the journey to Agordat. After Keren, the train began a long descent down to the plains and the heat rose again. The train screeched down the escarpment. The wheels against the tracks sounded like knives being sharpened and the metallic hiss put Jama's teeth on edge. A young Eritrean man played idly on a stringed rababa, it sounded like an angel's harp and he turned to watch him play for a while. The rocking of the train made Jama's eyes heavy but he was too excited to sleep.

The train inched into the small station of Agordat, its sleek paint coated in fine brown dust, steam glistening over the black locomotive like perspiration. Jama disembarked at this simple market town. A large mosque dominated the skyline and a bustling market was already in full swing. The turbans and Arabic arches reminded him of Aden. The only people he could see not wearing turbans were selling crocodile skins, dressed in long beautifully colourful shirts with ballooning trousers. Jama approached them, 'As-salamu alaykum, where can I get a bus to Sudan?' he asked in Arabic.

The reply was heavily accented, 'Past the suq, there is a main square where the buses leave from, but it will only take you as far as Omhajer, you will have to get a lorry across the border.'

Jama became curious, 'Where are you from, sahib?'

'I'm Takaruri from a place called Kano, a Muslim place on the other side of Africa. Fifty years ago my grandfather and his people passed through many countries on their walk to Mecca. By the time they reached here, they had run out of food and money so they settled, hoping to make enough money to cross to Arabia, by Allah's command one day we will,' the man laughed.

'How far is it from here to this Kano?' pursued Jama.

'Three years' walk,' said the man, his face sombre.

★　★　★

The square was a dun coloured plot of land, empty of people apart from two Eritrean askaris and a coffee seller. A small rusted bus baked in the sun, two white-eyed gulls watched the scene from a telegraph wire, the red of their beaks looked painted on amidst the ochre and khaki dourness of the square.

The driver turned up after the sun had passed its zenith, his trousers and vest gaping with holes, a peaked hat on his head. He didn't acknowledge anyone but boarded the bus and stretched across the back seat to sleep, covering his face with a handkerchief. Jama felt his head pounding from the sun; sharp pain skewered him from temple to temple, his tongue was parched and swollen. He bought water from a vendor and watched a young woman enter the bus depot a metal suitcase in her hand. A unit of young Italian soldiers marched in behind her. White light reflected violently from the suitcase, panning over him and the Italians like a searchlight. The bus coughed into life and Jama and the woman rushed to be first on; the driver held his arm across the door blocking their way and gestured to the soldiers. Jama didn't comprehend and jumped aboard when the driver's arm dropped. The driver approached, shouting and jabbing his finger in Jama's face, gesticulating to the back seats. Jama turned his face away and blanked him out, the driver grabbed him by the wrist and tried to pull him up, Jama slapped his hands away and spat at him. The Italian soldiers watched the commotion, some laughed, most just stared. The driver led Jama to the door and pushed him out of the bus. He landed squarely on his feet and unleashed a torrent of abuse at the driver and the watching soldiers, 'Baboons, what you looking at? May Allah break your spines, you debauched donkey fuckers.'

The soldiers boarded the bus, an Italian with the long limbs of a spider got on last and spoke to the driver, his dark eyes following Jama as he paced around. The driver shook his head but the Italian continued whispering in his ear. Eventually the driver relented and called over to Jama, reeling him in with his arm. Jama hesitated, his anger seething like a nest of snakes. The driver escorted Jama to the back; the gangly Italian smiled as he walked past, his dark eyes framed by thick black eyelashes. Jama gave him a small smile in return. When he was seated safely in the blacks' seats the driver held out his hand, rubbing his fingers together. Jama counted out a reasonable fare and gave it to him. The driver held up the money to the soldiers and ridiculed him; he started gesturing to the door again so Jama gave him double the amount. Crestfallen, he counted out the remaining money in his lap with hunched shoulders. The sisterfucker had bankrupted him.

The soldiers grew boisterous, shouting and jumping from seat to seat to play fight. Most of them were in their late teens and full of hormonal energy. They lit cigarettes and sang raucous songs; they seemed like holidaymakers rather than an imperial army. Any passing girls were subjected to cat calls and genitals pressed against the bus windows. The older soldier at the front of the bus looked on with fatherly good humour. But they left Jama alone, seeming to forget about his presence completely as the bus followed the course of a wide river west towards Sudan. Despite the hot plains, the river nourished enough earth to feed farms and wild date palms. Cows, rare in Somaliland, here grazed happily in large herds. The end of the trip was quiet; the soldiers had tired themselves out with laughing and now slept on each other's shoulders, trickles of drool staining their uniforms. After passing idyllic riverside villages tilled by dark skinned, brightly clothed people, Jama arrived at a checkpoint outside Omhajer. It was the last stop in Eritrea before crossing to Gedaref in Sudan where armed Italian soldiers came onboard the bus. They made a show of looking over Jama and the woman. Through the dirty window more Italians could be seen waiting behind sandbags, a machine gun aimed at the bus. A checkpoint guard shoved his watch into the gangly young soldier's face and gesticulated to the darkening plains. The young soldiers peered out of the sand-blown windows and reached for their guns. Their officer placed a calming hand on the guard's shoulder, but the guard thrust the hand away, angry cords in his neck protruding as he continued to rage. The young Italians were silent and the Eritrean woman whispered in Jama's ear — patriots had attacked the checkpoint and stolen a truck. Jama stifled a giggle behind his hand.

Omhajer was swamped with military tents and food stalls run by former askaris. The town swung to a military beat and testosterone formed clouds over the men's unshaven faces. The pulse of the town stopped for a moment when the Eritrean woman disembarked the bus, cobblers stopped cobbling, merchants stopped selling, and jaws paused mid-sentence. Men who had got used to the hard angles of male bodies, now fixed their eyes on womanly undulating curves, and nearly died of delight. The woman felt the heat of their eyes burning away her clothes and rushed off to her village. Jama saw Somali, Eritrean and Libyan askaris but none looked friendly, their faces were contorted and imbecilic with lust.

Behind the straw back of a stall, Jama counted his abattoir money and let out a desperate sigh, it was barely enough to buy food. Jama sprinted out into the streets, cheetah-fast, hunting for groups of Somali askaris, running close to a clump before realising they were Eritrean and skidding on his heels. Askaris turned and watched the strange boy run in and out of alleys. A Somali askari yelled out, 'Hey, what are you looking for, kid?'

'A clansman, an Eidegalle askari!' shouted Jama.

The askari laughed. 'Well, you can stop running, you've found one!' Jama ran to him, the soldier had a kind face, he put a thin hand on Jama's head.

'Why are you looking for me then?'

Jama cleared his throat and began, 'I need help finding my father, he lives in Sudan but he used to be an askari.'

'Who is your father?' interrupted the soldier, a cigarette in his hand.

'He is Guure Mohamed Naaleyeh,' panted Jama.

The soldier exploded in laughter, coughing out a dark haze of smoke. 'You're Guure's son?' he said eyes round in delight.

Jama nodded, folding his arms around his bare chest.

'Waryaa! Everyone come and look! It's Guure's son!' More laughing men approached Jama, they slapped him on the back and manhandled his shoulders.

Jama stayed silent as they poked him and pointed out his father's nose, or argued over whether Jama had the same slouched posture as his father. They were close enough for Jama to smell the wood smoke and sweat on their uniforms. The first askari broke through the crowd and pulled Jama away. 'Where have you come from?'

'Hargeisa.'

'By all the saints, do not lie to me.'

'Wallaahi, I swear and I came from Hargeisa.'

The askari was silent and Jama could hear the others throwing his father's name around as if he was a long lost brother.

The askari held Jama's hand, his dark skin matched Jama's exactly. 'Your father is a good friend of mine, of us all, he was always telling me about his son, his strong little warrior, he would threaten us with your vengeance, but look at you! You're nothing but a few bones strung together.'

'I would kill for my father,' Jama protested, 'anything he wants I would do! How can I get to him?'

'There are no buses to Gedaref, only military vehicles, and the Italians do not allow passengers, but you can get a ride with one of the Sudanese merchants here. It is only a few hours' drive, but they leave only once a week and they charge a hefty sum,' the askari explained. Jama's heart was racing, he didn't want to spend any time in this garrison town but it was dawning on him that he would be forced to.

The askari read the dejection in his face. 'We can get a message out to him though, tell him you're coming,' the other askaris mumbled their assent.

Jama's eyes reddened. All the fatigue and strain and misery of the journey had reached a crescendo at its near end, and came pouring out. He turned to hide his face and the soldiers looked to one another for solutions to the little boy's problem.

'Don't worry, while you are here, you are my guest, you will sleep in my tent, eat my food, learn how to be an askari, this is the least I could do for Guure,' proposed the first askari.

The askari led him to a long row of identical canvas tents, stopping at one of them to pull aside the flap. 'This is it, have a rest. If you need me I will be five tents down on the left, I will bring you a bite to eat soon.' Jama entered the gloomy tent and collapsed onto the dirt floor.

After a night on a sweaty borrowed mat,

with soldier food lying badly digested in his guts, his skin red and swollen from the attacks of mosquito hordes, Jama decided to get up. His arms and legs ached but he needed to find out more about his father. He shook the flap of the tent the askari had directed him to the previous night and a man's voice shouted, 'If you are not the devil, come in!'

Jama went inside; five men were on the floor, bundled over one another in the cramped space. 'Hello, Guure's son,' the askari said, other askaris groaned, placed their arms over their heads to block out the sound disturbing their sleep.

'Hello,' said Jama, looking around the Spartan tent, pleased he was finally someone's son.

'What brings you here so early?' asked the askari. He reached in his trouser pocket for his toothstick, a thin twig with a fibrous, splayed end.

'I want to know more about my father,' replied Jama, as if it was his due. He squatted in the corner and waited as the man eased the toothstick over each tooth, spitting out its fibres.

'You don't even know my name yet, you little bulabasha! I'm Jibreel. Guure is a great friend of mine, he is a happy, generous man, and the best company you can find. When we marched, we used to jostle each other to be close to Guure, so we could hear his jokes and impressions. He mimicked everyone to perfection, especially the Italian bulabashas — time would just fly by. He was always first to start off the marching songs. Do you have a beautiful voice like him?'

Jama shook his head regretfully.

'He talked about you a lot, you know. He would sometimes get word of you from askaris who had lived in Aden and knew your mother. He was proud of you.'

'Isn't he a driver?' interrupted Jama.

'Maybe, you need identity papers and money and other things, we all left home with only the clothes on our backs, maybe in Gedaref it's easier. A group of them disguised themselves as Sudanese traders and snuck off in a truck, pissed off with the Italians and their stupid white man black man laws. They want you to step into the gutter when they approach, say master this and master that. I think Guure left just after he saw an Italian sergeant make two askaris drink his piss as a punishment. That's the way here, it's not a life but it's better than death, but good on Guure for getting out . . . the longer you stay, the less of a man you become.' A sleepy soldier repeated this dozily after Jibreel.

Jama's appetite for information grew as it

172

was fed. 'What does he like look?' he asked with bright eyes.

'He is smallish, stocky, looks young for his age, your kind of brown, he has a big head, strange yellowish hair, strong arms, big teeth like you.'

Jama's face contorted as he tried to picture his father but it was too sketchy to be satisfying, and not as handsome as the man in his fantasies.

'Don't tax yourself, you'll soon be able to see him with your own eyes,' laughed Jibreel. 'Your presence here is big news, so it won't take long for someone to reach Guure and tell him you're on your way, it's unlikely he will be able to get back here, they don't take kindly to deserters, but we will have a collection and see if we can help,' he said with a wink.

Jibreel put a cigarette to his mouth and Jama watched the way he held it between his lips, struck a match and let tendrils of smoke escape from his nose as he inhaled.

'Let me have a try.'

Jibreel handed the cigarette over with an amused smile; Jama put it to his mouth and sucked too hard, smoke shot up his nose, singeing all the soft membranes. His eyes watered terrifically and his lungs burned, it was as if he had shoved his face into a thick fire. Jama stifled his coughs and shamefacedly handed back the cigarette.

Jibreel continued to laugh at him so he returned to his tent and chewed over everything Jibreel had said.

★ ★ ★

As a frontier town, nestled between the borders of Abyssinia, British Sudan and Eritrea, there was wildness to Omhajer. Every day some askaris would arrive while just as many deserted, it was the wild west of Eritrea. Jibreel told Jama of the suffering he had seen. Refugee women and children picking undigested grain from cow dung, emaciated men with bodies like mobile skeletons sitting on the road and expiring, their eyes wide open. Gunfire occasionally rang out from the checkpoint and the prison before it was drowned out by market trader calls and donkey brays.

One day, a week after Jama had arrived, Jibreel appeared dusty and panting, but the herald of good news. 'I have just received a message from Guure passed on by a returning Somali merchant. He has become a lorry driver for Ilkacas, a Haber Yunis man in Sudan. The merchant told Guure that you were here in Omhajer.'

Jibreel took Jama's shaking hands in his. 'Your father is coming to pick you up.'

Jama floated to the seventh heaven, his heart fluttered around his ribcage as he drank in this blissful news. He grabbed hold of Jibreel's waist and squeezed him tight, unable to communicate his joy in another way.

'Let go, Jama, I can't breathe,' laughed Jibreel.

Jama loosened his grip but held on, imagining Jibreel's lean body was his father's.

Finally Jibreel prised Jama off him and together they looked for askaris to tell the good news to. They handed over celebratory cigarettes and shook his small hand, Jama could not sit still, could not eat, he laughed hysterically at the askaris' jokes and grasped them in suffocating embraces. Jama thought about the gifts his father might bring, the stories he would tell, the songs he would teach him, and stayed awake all night.

Lorries came and went regularly from Sudan, with supplies of cigarettes and other necessities, but still his father did not appear. Each day was an ordeal of waiting, each minute, every hour was not fully lived because his heart was suspended between hope and despair. He hung about the main thoroughfare, teetering around on tiptoe, staring into the cabs of arriving lorries.

Jama scrutinised the place his father had tarried for so long. It was a khaki kingdom, with absolutely no women to be seen anywhere. Italians stomped around, their skins tanned to nearly the same colour as those they professed to be civilising, whips made from hippopotamus hide hanging from their belts. Somali soldiers, some young, some approaching middle age, some polite, some rough, greeted him as he passed. Nearby, black veterans from the Italian defeat at Adwa sat begging, an arm and a leg amputated by the Abyssinians to punish their disloyalty. Jama walked all over the small busy town, avoiding the more secluded alleys and lanes, before returning to the tent with a handful of sultanas and peanuts pilfered from a Sudanese merchant. He got up at dawn and followed askaris around until sunset. His clansmen made him a communal little brother, patting his head and giving him puffs of their cigarettes. They all knew his father and could recount memories of him. He would be passed on from one askari to another like a pack of cards, only returning to his mat at night, when the booze came out and the soldiers favoured more adult conversation.

★ ★ ★

Jibreel entered the tent, his dark face ashy and drawn. He stared at Jama for a moment, 'There is someone here to see you, Jama,' he said.

Jama trotted by Jibreel's side, kicking pebbles out of the way and waving to his friends, his face burning with white-hot joy. Jibreel was stiff and silent beside him. Jama tidied himself up, spat onto his dry white elbows and knees and fluffed up his hair with his fingers. Jibreel's eyes were wide and shiny; Jama saw the reflection of a flock of crows taking flight in them. A man spilt a basket of lentils as Jama passed and crouched down to scoop them up, while a group of Somali askaris stood nearby smoking.

'Wait here, he's coming,' mumbled Jibreel, before joining the other askaris. The minutes ticked by as long as days, the sun's heat felt like a heavy weight on his head, Jama prayed for his father to hurry up, the Arabic words muddling in his mind as mosquitoes buzzed beside his ears. A man came over the horizon, a small cardboard suitcase hung from his fingers. Jama took tiny steps forward. As the man approached, Jama's heart sank as he looked up and saw a middle-aged, grey bearded man staring down at him. His skin was a creamy light brown and he wore a red fez perched on the side of his head, his stomach hung a few inches away from Jama's face; this was not the man he had imagined.

'As-salamu alaykum Jama, forgive me but I come with unfortunate news. Guure's life has ended. He was on the road from Gedaref when he ran into a military roadblock, they opened fire and killed everyone. We buried him yesterday in Gedaref. We all live on borrowed time and by the decree of Allah-Kareem, Guure's time on earth has passed. It was not his fate to see you, here are his belongings. May Allah have mercy on you.'

The man's words swam around Jama without meaning. They sounded like the crashing of waves or the gurgle of blood to him, their substance broken up and diluted. Jama crouched down on the floor, covered his ears, he needed to vomit, he couldn't breathe, grief had stolen the air from his lungs, drained the blood from his veins, he clawed at the earth to bury himself.

Jibreel pulled at Jama's arm but he refused to rise, to open his eyes, and Jibreel withdrew to stand by the wall and wait. At last, Jama inhaled a deep breath and took hold of his father's flimsy suitcase. The touch of the handle, its shape moulded to his grip, its colour stained with his sweat, set Jama's hand aflame. He stared into the stranger's eyes, and the man nodded and walked away, back over the horizon.

Jama crouched down, bent over the suitcase, his body taking the shape of the boulders placed above nomads' graves. He untied the string holding the case shut and delicately opened it. He hoped to find his father's head inside, just so that he would finally know what he looked like. He wanted to press his hand against his father's stubble, to trace the face that contained the only likeness of his own. Instead, he found a threadbare mauve ma'awis, a few notes and coins, an amber tusbah, a worn down toothstick, a stringed musical instrument and a rusted toy car.

Jama pressed his face against the grit of the Eritrean waste-ground, his journey at a bitter end. The moon hid in shame and left Omhajer in mourning black. One by one, the planets Jama's life orbited around had spun away and left him in a universe where he was just debris floating in starless obscurity.

Omhajer, Eritrea, December 1936

A plaintive song creaked out of the wind-up gramophone, a soaring soprano backed by a full orchestra battling against the din of the teahouse. The turntable wobbled with every revolution, its handle turned by a piece of human furniture. The tassel of Jama's fez fell over his eyes as his body lurched back and forth behind his arm. A group of Italian soldiers sang along to the gramophone, holding their Melotti beers aloft and rocking on broken chairs. Already giddy with power, they sang into Jama's face, spittle flew from a booze-slackened mouth into his eyes. Askaris walked past and laughed at their inebriated officers intoxicatedly celebrating their saviour's birth. Jama didn't laugh or pay notice to the Italians, he was counting, he was up to six hundred and eighteen turns and would start counting again when he reached a thousand. His arm ached but he carried on. Counting occupied the parts of his mind that were becoming unruly and wild, the parts of him that wanted to break off the arm of the gramophone and slit necks with the sharp needle. He swapped arms without losing count and wiped the spittle on his face against his shoulder. The fez had been placed on his head by one of the drunken men to manic laughter as Jama's head disappeared into it. Even these Italians had probably known his father, had known and owned him more than Jama ever would. A cockerel pranced out onto the terrace, pecking at fragments of roasted corn on the floor. Its long red neck worked up and down like a piston as it made its stately progress between the men's feet. The bird's yellow claws pitter-pattered against the concrete in the crackling moments between songs. Eventually the voice of a bombastic tenor filled the air and covered up the squawks of the proud bird as he was carried back to the kitchen by the cook, a tight grip around his wrinkled old neck, his scrawny feet feeling impotently for the ground. Jama watched the cockerel's exit and his ear followed the cook's footsteps, waiting for the scraping of knife against feathers, muscle, tendons. It came and Jama swallowed hard, death seemed so inescapable to him now, he wondered at how he had never taken heed of it before. He felt his heartbeat race and skip and tumble over itself but he continued working the gramophone, the resultant music assuring him that he wasn't dead but real live flesh and blood. The

Italians slid off their chairs, one of them left a lira on the table, plucking his trophy fez off Jama's head. The fascist eagle's beady eyes and outstretched wings threatened Jama from the coin and Jama stared back, his sore arm still needlessly turning the gramophone crank.

Every day a cockerel heralded dawn with all the urgency of an angel blowing the last trumpet. Jibreel crouched over a short broom, sweeping dust and dirt out of the tent opening, his figure throwing Jama back into darkness each time he passed the doorway. Dust blew up Jama's nostrils and into his mouth and eyes, gritty and salty. Jama threw his arm across his face but Jibreel continued sweeping around him, motes of dust dancing around his head in the weak tea-coloured morning light. In grief, Jama felt cut off from life, as if there was cotton wool in his ears, in his mouth, in his mind, around his heart. His surroundings seemed muted and distant, even his dreams came to him in dull monochrome. Behind him Jama could hear the daily massacre of cockroaches and dung beetles. The unfortunate creatures did not understand the demarcation of their land and Jibreel's, so were doomed to be bludgeoned by Jibreel's broom every morning. The black shells were smooth iridescent gems in the dusty tent, they tinkled like jewels when with a flick of the wrist Jibreel threw them onto the hard soil outside. Jama waited for Jibreel's shadow to disappear before retrieving his aday toothbrush, he was in his thirteenth year but already his limbs were being stretched on an invisible rack, lengthening drastically and painfully each night. His mother's amulet hung around his neck, a dull weight like those around the necks of half-Italian babies thrown into wells by Eritrean girls. Jama massaged his limbs, pulled himself to his feet and stalked off towards the teahouse, his head and eyes down to avoid his neighbours' verbose greetings.

With a tray of dirty glasses in his hands Jama surfed over the lunchtime wave of diners. The Italians ate first and only after the last European had his fill could Africans be served. Plenty of saliva and dirt went into those first batches of spaghetti bolognese. Jama scooted back to the kitchen, the tray balanced carefully in his hands, and tripped over a headless goat that lay sprawled across the floor.

The glasses flew into the air and smashed into the wall. 'Bravo Jama! There go your day's wages,' laughed the Eritrean cook.

'Why did you leave the bloody goat in front of the door?' snapped Jama as he brushed dirt off his scraped knees.

'I need some entertainment don't I? Stuck in this smelly hot kitchen all day,' replied the cook, laughing harder at Jama's peeved face.

'I'll get you back you dameer, just you wait and see,' threatened Jama, taking the hot plates outside. Pain and irritation scrambled Jama's usually perfect memory, and he handed the plates to the soldiers who shouted loudest for them. A young Italian on a table of officers took them out of Jama's singed fingers, his dark olive hands passed lightly over Jama's, and his dark eyes fixed on the boy's face. Jama looked back at him, the soldier had a thin goat face, his nose was long and hooked and his eyebrows unruly. His lower lip was fuller than the top and he chewed it ruminatively.

'You're that boy from the bus, aren't you? Who nearly got thrown off?' the soldier asked in Arabic. Jama stayed silent.

'You don't remember me, do you?' he continued. Jama didn't reply.

'Stop talking to the Africans,' interrupted the Italian's companion. He slapped Jama hard on his bony rear and shouted, 'Move it, Move it.'

Jama stole a glance at the first Italian before running back to the kitchen, he had recognised him, it was the gangly one who had persuaded the thieving bus driver in Agordat to let him on.

'What's the matter, Jama? You look like you've been bitten by a devil,' said the cook.

'One of the Italians keeps staring and talking to me.'

Cook laughed. 'Shayddaans! Here, give me that glass on the side.' Jama handed it to him. Cook turned his back and slowly dribbled urine into the glass, mixing it with tea and sugar and handing the whole concoction back to Jama.

'Tell him it is free, our special drink for special customers.'

Jama laughed with sadistic mirth. He took the glass and placed it gently, deferentially in front of the gangly Italian. 'For you signore.'

The Italian raised an eyebrow, 'Well, I guess he does recognise me after all.' He drained the amber filth down his throat in a few long gulps and Jama felt a pang of unexpected guilt at the sight.

The last few Italians were clearing out of the teahouse and hungry askaris waited under the shade of a dying acacia, Jama kept away from the gangly Italian after handing him the dirty drink, he hadn't even told the other boys what he had done. Jama felt a hand on his shoulder and jumped when he saw the man looming over him. 'Thank you for the drink, it was kind of you,' the Italian began.

His lips were wet and Jama turned his face to the side fearing his pissy breath. 'Look, I've been watching you. We need an office boy, someone honest and hardworking like you, I am sure you could get paid more with us than here.'

Jama shook his head and carried on looking towards the side, he had seen and heard from askaris the value of keeping your distance from the Italians.

'Suit yourself, but the offer is open if you want it,' said the Italian with a shrug. Then his black-haired, long fingers felt in his breast pocket and emerged holding delicate, wire-framed glasses. Jama watched from the corner of his eye as the long, large fingers fumbled and placed the beautiful glasses on his too-long nose. Jama coveted them. It looked as if a metal and glass butterfly had decided to spread its translucent wings across the hard, bony face, giving the Italian a kinder, more thoughtful appearance. With his second pair of eyes in place the Italian strolled off, acknowledging the salutes of the askaris with a loose salute of his own.

After that day Jama watched the Italian, the bluey-brown eyes in the sea of brown skin and the brown pools in the Mediterranean olive face regarded each other with curious interest. The fascist legs splayed open in languorous authority, the booted feet playing with each other, crushing beetles underfoot with a satisfying crunch. Jama's legs were stiff tired poles compelled to keep moving, his feet so dry, grey, hard he could barely feel the ground underneath them. The Italian raised a beer bottle and clinked it against his friend's, Jama collected glasses from the broken tables. More and more fascists and askaris were being sent to fight the guerrillas and the teahouse had a portentous melancholy atmosphere. The Ethiopian patriots with their powerful afros were a menace to the Italians; forts were overrun, checkpoints ambushed, garrisons invaded. The army of ghosts in white shammas were impossible to fight; with the mournful faces of Coptic saints, the patriots skewered Italians on homemade bayonets. They materialised and vanished as if they had wings under their homespun cotton. Dukes, lords, barons, peasants banded together despite poison gas, gallows, machine guns and flame throwers. Near Omhajer, the famous Abyssinian patriot Abraha and his men in their lionskins stalked the Italians, and like lions they picked off the last man or the last vehicle in a convoy. The trees hid them, the leopards warned them, the wind swept away their footprints.

A few askaris returned to Omhajer to report back on the front where the Italians had turned against their own askaris when they could not catch the spectral Abyssinians. One man had seen the Italians force askaris to lie down in the muddy water of a narrow river so they could cross along their backs. Underfoot, black bodies were mounted on top of each other, the men at the bottom drowning, murky water gurgling down their throats.

In this dangerous climate, a few of the lazier boys had been let go, but Jama had held onto his job. The gangly Italian and his stumpy friend got up and stretched out their arms, yawning loudly with afternoon ennui as they picked up their rifles. The other Italian had large, dark patches of sweat growing out of his armpits, groin and back.

'Waryaa! Hey you,' shouted the tall Italian at Jama in mangled Somali. 'We are going hunting, come and collect what we shoot, there will be a few coins in it for you.'

Jama walked over to the veranda and piled all of the glasses at the cook's feet.

'I'm off now, I might earn some real money with these Italians,' said Jama as the glasses tumbled against each other with a soft tinkling. The cook took a deep drag on his cigarette and smoke drifted from his nostrils.

'Keep your wits about you, Jama. Run away if they start behaving strangely, or you might return as one of their wives.' The cook pursed his lips and blew out a long plume of smoke.

'Seriously, be careful, Jama.' The cook winked before putting out the cigarette with his bare calloused foot and padding back to the kitchen.

They walked in line across the Eritrean plains, Jama slowing down to maintain the requisite distance behind them. The shorter Italian was breathing heavily and going red in the heat, a black swipe of hair was plastered to his forehead. His legs were like hairy sausages in woollen socks, his heavy bulbous torso balanced precariously on top of them.

'This little boy reminds me of my greyhound, both long, lean, black. God I miss that dog, he knew more about me than anyone,' puffed the shorter Italian. 'Might be dead by the time we get home. Poor Alfredo, he had problems pissing when I left. I'll never find a dog like him again.'

The tall one didn't respond, but took off his glasses to wipe the steam off them.

'Are you a dog man, Lorenzo? City boys never truly understand animals like we do, it's about understanding what their eyes are telling you, you have to know what an animal needs better than he does. Look at this little darkie with us, if we told him to walk over there, he would do it, because he knows that we know better than him,' he stopped to take a swig from his water flask.

Lorenzo stopped ahead of him and took a gulp as well, Jama looked away to hide his thirst but the tall Italian walked over to him and thrust his flask into his hand.

'Oh Lorenzo! What did you do that for?' exclaimed the short Italian. 'He's probably crawling with diseases. Why put yourself at risk, they're used to this heat, it doesn't affect them like us.' Jama drank a little, holding the flask away from his lips, the short Italian's face was contracted in disgust, his mouth open to reveal yellow and pink.

Jama wiped the top of the flask with his sarong and handed it back to the tall Italian with a small nod of thanks. Jama's grasp of Italian was sketchy but he understood that these two soldiers were fighting their own private battle. Their arms moved violently about and they threw words at each other as if they were grenades.

They carried on marching. The grass was high and rustled against their legs as they passed, crickets made small talk within it, birds sunbathed stock still on branches. Jama noticed a coven of vultures flying overhead following an imperceptible trail of death. The

Italians were after big game, zebras, leopards, maybe one of the few elephants still left in Eritrea, anything to boast about back home. They walked and walked unable to see anything bigger than a rat.

The short Italian drenched in sweat and frustration threw his hands up. 'Enough! Enough walking! Let's stop here. We'll just shoot what we find.'

Lorenzo looked around, there was nothing, just yellow grass and blue sky. 'We've walked this far, Silvio. Why stop now? Near a stream there would be better game,' reasoned Lorenzo, still walking on ahead with Jama a respectful distance behind him.

'No, no, absolutely not, I am stopping here, my legs will not move an inch further, tell Alfredo to scare up the birds or something,' panted Silvio. Lorenzo sighed and gave Jama his instructions.

Jama gingerly walked up to a spindly tree and gave its trunk a gentle shake. Nothing stirred. 'What's he doing? Tell him to make some noise, to scare the goddamn things,' barked Silvio with growing irritation.

'Make noise, run around,' said the tall Italian in Somali. Jama felt stupid but he ran around, yelled out, kicked at the grass and trees, beat the scrubby bushes with a stick. A few sleepy birds rose drowsily off their nests and flew straight into a volley of rifle shots, their proud chests blown into a cloud of feathers.

'More, more!' shouted the tall Italian, Jama ran to another tree and whooped and swooped, more birds flew out. Some fell straight to the ground in shock, their wings outstretched.

'That big tree over there now, throw stones at it,' said the tall Italian. Jama ran over to it and did as he was told, a leopard came scrambling down its trunk, its muscular back gold and black.

'Get it, Alfredo, get it!' shouted the short Italian, beside himself with excitement. Jama looked on as the leopard ran past him and away into the dark tangle of thorn bushes and aloes.

Jama chucked the last few stones in his hand at the leopard's back.

'For fuck's sake, chase it, Alfredo, tell him, Lorenzo, don't let it escape!' the short Italian jabbered.

'It's gone Silvio, leave it,' said Lorenzo lowering his rifle.

'Goddamn it,' exploded Silvio, throwing his hands in the air. 'A leopard! And that stupid little nigger lets it escape, I said if there was one thing I would bring back from Africa it would be a leopard that I had shot myself, and look! This imbecile just lets it run right away. I'm tired of blacks, I really am, I have had it up to here with them,' Silvio raised his podgy fingers up to his neck.

'Calm down, Silvio, it wasn't his fault, we weren't fast enough.' Lorenzo pulled out a handkerchief and wiped his face and hands. Gun shots still rang in the air with an electric effervescence.

'Come let's collect what we've got and go back,' said Lorenzo softly. But Silvio still had adrenaline pumping through his veins, 'Tell him to collect any birds that are still alive.'

Lorenzo gave a long sigh and told Jama to collect them. Jama poked around the grass. A few birds were still moving and he guiltily picked them up by their wings and piled them in front of the Italians.

'Grab one by its feet and hold your arm out to the side,' said Lorenzo as he lit a cigarette. Jama did as he was told, the bird was nearly half his size and it hung heavily, flapping its wings and struggling forcefully for its life, digging its claws into his palm.

The short Italian was a few paces away, he brought his rifle up. One of his blue eyes scrunched up into a white and pink fist, he moved his shoulders around and steadied his aim. Jama looked at the rifle barrel pointed right into his face, flared like the angry nostrils of a charging bull, Jama bit down on his tongue as he realised what the Italian was about to do. The gun blasted and Jama saw the bullet that was intended for him burst from the gun's left nostril in a red and orange explosion and soar over his head. The tall Italian had pushed the nose of the rifle into the air just as the short one had fired.

Now the short one shoved the taller one in the chest. 'What's your problem, I haven't come all this way to let little black bastards lose me my quarry.'

The tall one gave him a few sharp slaps in the face. 'Calm down! You're behaving like a fucking animal. If you're not careful I'll send you home with a bullet in your fat peasant behind.' Jama watched in shock, holding his bladder tight, as the short Italian spat in the other's face and roared in Italian at him.

'Come on, you son of a bitch, Jew, Jew, you fucking Jews think you are so much better than everyone else, I'll teach you a lesson.'

Lorenzo grabbed him by the testicles and wrenched them down until Silvio's knees buckled, and he cried out, tears streaming down his red, porcine face. Lorenzo released his grip and snarled, 'Stay the fuck away from me, Silvio, or I will turn you into a Jew with my fucking teeth.'

The tall Italian's glasses were twisted

across his face and his teeth were bared like an angry dog's. 'Hey, boy! Come on! Let's go!' he shouted at Jama, his voice strained and hoarse.

Jama walked after him, his knees weak, the blast of the gun still ricocheting in his skull. He stepped around the short Italian as he lay on his side in the dry grass, clutching his groin.

★ ★ ★

The office was inside a khaki tent. A table sat in the middle of the dirt floor with brown files and papers neatly piled on top, a typewriter sitting silently to the left. Maggiore Lorenzo Leon pinched dried tobacco between his fingers and dropped it into the mouth of his pipe. A cup of coffee steamed beside him. Jama waited in front of the desk.

'Welcome, Jama, what can I do for you?' asked Lorenzo, the pipe wobbling in his mouth as he spoke.

'I wanted to know if you still need an office boy,' replied Jama in his best Italian.

'Yes of course, one second.' Lorenzo took matches from his shirt pocket and lit the pipe. 'Ahh, that's better! Start today, I'm very busy and need someone to help me.'

'Si, Signore' said Jama. He stood waiting

195

for an instruction, Lorenzo carried on smoking his pipe.

'Well?' laughed Maggiore Leon.

'What do you want me to do, sir? And, sir . . . how much will you give me?'

'Good question. Let's start you on five liras a week, you are only a small thing, I don't expect to get much work out of you.'

Jama's heart fell. Five liras! It wasn't worth leaving the café for five liras and at least he got fed there, but Maggiore Leon seemed to be an important man, and in a place like Omhajer proximity to importance mattered a great deal.

'Start by sweeping the floor, and then I'll find something else for you,' continued the Maggiore. So you're not so busy after all, thought Jama, his suspicion rising.

Lorenzo watched Jama's clumsy sweeping, the broom slipping from his grip, the Italian laughed to himself; If only his friends could see him sweating in a fascist uniform watching a native boy cleaning up for him. He found everything amusing now, fascism, communism, anarchism, he could only trust in the patently idiotic. The pantomime Duce's bombastic radio pronouncements had him nearly wetting himself with laughter. As had the Blackshirts marching in front of his balcony in Rome deliriously howling for an

Italian Abyssinia, senile housewives offering their wedding rings to pay for the civilisation of a country they could not place on a map. He had joined the army late enough to miss most of the fighting but early enough to benefit from the generous officers' allowances. To his delight he had also found a few Abyssinian maids to enjoy before the others had infected them with unpleasant diseases but Omhajer was still a hardship posting after the leisure of Libya. It was a dusty, impoverished town full of the dregs of the Italian army, and a battalion full of ex-prisoners, alcoholics and lunatics, few of whom had even finished their elementary schooling. They hated Lorenzo's books, glasses, rumoured Jewishness and bullied him the way only soldiers can their officers. Lorenzo intended to study anthropology back in Italy so took photographs of the local villagers and notes on their lifestyles and societies; he had learnt a smattering of Somali from the Somali askaris and he had even been invited home for a meal by a well-to-do Sudanese merchant. The other officers were shocked and disgusted at this intimacy with the natives and one had threatened to report his crimes against racial hygiene to the commander.

Lorenzo had been struck by Jama's

self-possession the day he had been thrown off the bus. Lorenzo sometimes caught Jama muttering to himself in the teahouse and saw him loitering around town late at night and began to feel sympathy for him. When his mother's letters had first arrived, describing in her unsteady, spidery hand her anxiety that Italy would go the same way as Germany in its treatment of Jews, Lorenzo had first brushed aside her concerns, reminding her that she had also trundled off to the synagogue the day Italy had invaded Abyssinia to sing the fascist anthem 'Giovinezza' with the other neighbourhood crones. 'Not in Italy, mama,' had been his final word on the subject. Now that he had spent time with rough, country Italians, and heard their anti-semitic jokes and rants, he grew more circumspect and advised his mother to get her savings out of the bank and be prepared to leave. Soldiers idle in their barracks said incredible things, even Lorenzo was shocked out of his cynicism when a soldier said the most exhilarating experience he'd had in the army was firing into a civilian crowd at Gondar. He had seen children, cripples, old women in the crowd but had pumped away with his machine gun until they all lay on the ground.

'Sir, I am finished. How much will I get as

a soldier? Can I become a soldier for you instead?' asked Jama leaning on the broom.

Maggiore Lorenzo looked at Jama. 'Why would you want to be a soldier? You're so young, you haven't even stopped growing yet.'

'Well, give me lot of macaroni and I will grow quickly,' argued Jama.

Maggiore Leon laughed. 'With teeth as big as yours, I am sure you could get through a lot of macaroni, but no, Jama, you have to be fifteen to sign up and then they treat you like dirt anyway, don't bother yourself with soldiering. Here, go buy me some cigarettes, you can keep the change.'

Jama went to the Sudanese tobacconist and bought the cheapest cigarettes on offer. When he returned to the office Maggiore Leon had gone. Jama placed the cigarettes on the table and sat on a chair against the wall to wait. The sun rose to its zenith and flies buzzed lazily in the heat, Jama scratched his bites and paced the room, driven to madness by the flies, he left the office to search for the Maggiore.

Maggiore Leon and the other officers were sitting around in the teahouse, Melottis in hand. 'Ah Jama, I thought you would find me, do you have the cigarettes on you?'

Jama shook his head and scratched his bites violently.

'Go and collect them for me, then go home, I am not going back in this afternoon. The mosquitoes are vicious here, they'll eat you alive. When you get to the office open the desk drawer, there is balm for your bites that you can take.'

'Si, signore' said Jama.

Back in the office, Jama opened the drawer. It was full of scrunched up papers, forms, letters and a small pile of black and white photographs, Jama checked the door and pulled out the photographs. They were mainly head and profile shots of local Bilen peasants. There was a photograph of a Takaruri man holding up the skin of a baby crocodile and a Sudanese merchant smiling, his hands held out over his goods. The last picture was of a teenage Bilen girl, topless, her arms wrapped around her waist, her expression hidden by ornate gold chains that draped down her forehead and from nose to ear. Jama's eyes scanned the incredible image. He had only ever seen his mother naked but this girl looked like a mythical creature, unearthly, he could not tell where or when it had been taken.

'Sta'frullah, God forgive us,' he said under his breath, he felt his hands burn as he held it, so he stuffed the photos back into the drawer. Jama retrieved the twisted tube of balm and put the cigarettes in the waist band of his sarong. These Italians were becoming more and more perverse to him, he felt that they would corrupt his soul, no wonder his father, God have mercy on his soul, had fled them. He thumped the cigarette packet on the table and stomped off as Maggiore Leon shouted 'See you tomorrow,' at his back.

Jama slept in whichever tent had spare ground, not that he managed to sleep much. Millions of mosquitoes congregated in the camp, moving in battalions from body to body, they colonised the bloodstreams of men while they innocently slept but Jama seemed the only one driven to distraction by them. He constantly shifted around, rubbed his legs together, scratched his bites and slapped his skin, irritating the men whose dreams he punctured. He used the Italian's medicine but it just seemed to attract the beasts.

'Allah, you look like something pulled from the earth, what happened to you?' said Jibreel.

'What do you think happened?'

Jibreel felt guilty about Jama, the boy's soul seemed dimmed. 'I'll get you some aloe, why don't you rest for a while,' he offered.

The aloe soothed his skin but Jama felt like something evil had entered him, as if a jinn was pounding his head with a club, alternately roasting him on a spit and plunging him into ice cold water. He shivered and sweated, sweated and shivered until his mat felt like a bucket of water had been sluiced over it. Jibreel watched over him and Jama heard his muffled voice through the pounding in his skull but couldn't even turn his eyes towards him.

Jibreel folded his arms, and unfolded them, took a heavy breath and bent down over Jama. 'You have mosquito fever, I don't know what I can do for you but I will go to the Italian clinic and see if they will give us anything.'

Jama, his head spinning and whirring, couldn't remember entering the tent or imagine ever leaving.

The medic refused to give Jibreel anything, the quinine for the askaris had run out and the more expensive medicines were reserved for Italian soldiers. Malaria pounded at Jama's body and made him feel like he had been attacked by a madman, without painkillers or quinine, he had to wait and see if this unseen madman would manage to cause enough harm to kill him. Far above him his mother realigned the stars, bartered incense and beads with the angels so that they would spare her son, and browbeaten they reluctantly complied.

Jama opened his eyes and instantly closed them again as a scorching wind blew across the plains and threw sand and grit into the tent, he shivered in the heat and rubbed his starved stomach. His skin buzzed with bites, red and angry like fire ants. With his leaden limbs too heavy to move, Jama raised his head and saw a pot on the fire. 'Jibreel get me some food.'

'Well done, Jama, you're a clever boy, I thought you were gone,' Jibreel said.

'Get me food,' Jama growled, unable to remember anything, he was in no mood for melodrama. While Jama slept and his antibodies chased the malaria virus out of town, Maggiore Leon was being chased out of Abyssinia by the antibodies of nationalism, the anti-Italian bodies of Abyssinian patriots. Before his descent into delirium, Jama had agreed to travel with the Maggiore into Abyssinia, to a place called K'eftya, five days' journey from Omhajer through deserted land, the people had been cleared away to provide Lebensraum for the Italian colonists. Maggiore Leon took with him four Italian officers, thirteen Somali askaris, and twenty Eritreans in a convoy of speeding trucks. The Italians slept in one truck, the Africans in the other two. Hyenas laughed all night, leopards roared, and watching Arbegnoch held back and waited for the fascists to drop their guard. Maggiore Leon had a bad feeling about this trip, the emptiness of the landscape depressed him and he wondered if Jama had disappeared because he had heard something was looming. Lorenzo slept badly, so he was the first to hear the soft footsteps in the dark, he reached for his gun and clambered up to his feet, whereupon Abraha the Fierce cut his throat from ear to ear. Abraha and his gang, hidden by the colluding clouds, worked their way through the fascist necks and then started on the Africans. They showed no mercy to the traitors, killing even the young Eritrean boy who had replaced Jama. A few men ran screaming for their lives into the dark bush; only two returned to Omhajer to report the attack. When a second convoy went to reclaim the Italian corpses, they found them black with flies and the precious white skin had been sliced clean off their faces.

Jama heard about the knifing and slicing from Jibreel and didn't know how to feel. Jama's clansmen had been killed in one of the trucks and they discussed how the Italians had buried them in mass graves without any prayers. Jama had escaped two deaths in a matter of days but he still felt pursued by death, he stayed in the tent longer than he needed to, scared of the dangers that lurked outside. The image of the Maggiore's skinned face haunted Jama's dreams, as did Abraha's dagger. Only when he heard the other askaris complaining to Jibreel about the boy holed up in their tent, eating their food, did he rise and stagger to the office.

★ ★ ★

'It's you is it? Well, your Hebrew friend has gone to meet Jehovah, so if you want to keep working here you better do exactly as I say and never even so much as look at me in the wrong way, got that, Alfredo?'

Jama's heart sank as he listened to his new superior, he could barely make out the rapid Italian but the cold gaze of the Italian who had shot at him was as clear as glass. Jama had a strong urge to flee but he lacked the courage or energy.

'Things are hotting up around here, and I need a disciplined, efficient team, the Duce has plans for a great Empire and the responsibility for creating it depends on men like me. I will take insubordination in this office as a form of treason against the empire,' the Italian bellowed into the air.

The office now teemed with soldiers and Eritrean askaris coming and going, and Jama couldn't imagine a place for him in this industrious beehive. The Italian grabbed him roughly by the shoulder and placed him by the desk. 'Take this and keep the flies off me,' he demanded, thrusting a fly whisk into Jama's hand.

Jama nearly laughed as he held the long, blond whisk limply in the air. Jama could smell the man's sweat oozing from him, a dirty feral scent washed over Jama with every swish of the whisk. Beside the thick arm of the Italian, a coiled hippopotamus-hide karbaash whip waited. Jama knew that despite the pain in his malaria-weak muscles he must continue or risk having his own skin whisked away. Unfortunate civilians and askaris carried the livid geography of lashes on their backs. The Italians used hippopotamus skin because the tough hide cut through human skin like a razor. One hundred lashes were enough to kill a strong, healthy man, and they were generous with the blows. Jama felt that one stroke of the whip would probably send him to jannah in his delicate state. Standing so close, Jama could count the thin strands of hair greased over the Italian's bald pate. He scrutinised the thick line of dirt under the man's fingernails, the colour of old blood.

Jama stood in the busy street after work. He felt strange and dirty, and he hoped he might find familiar company to lose himself in. Dust kicked up by pedestrians and donkeycarts glittered in the setting sun. A crowd came up the dirt road, in its midst a local Takaruri crocodile hunter carried a large drum. He was as-saayih, a town-crier, and he marched sombrely and ceremoniously.

He addressed the by-standers in a sad voice: 'Fighters of the land, the seas and the air, blackshirts of the revolution and the legions, men and women of Italy, of the Empire — listen, by decree of Emperor Vittorio Emanuele, all possessions held by the natives of Italian East Africa are deemed to be held only in trust and their true ownership will be adjudicated by colonial legislators. All hunting, fishing and trapping is prohibited without permission from colonial authorities. Oh people, hear me, they are telling us we own nothing, and we can not kill a thing for our mouths without asking them first.' The crowd laughed uncertainly.

'Oh no, this is no joke, people! They are saying they own everything that lives. These locusts will take the food out of our children's mouths,' roared the town crier. Jama walked alongside him as he made the announcement at every corner, his voice getting more hoarse and more tragic with every declaration.

Jama pulled at the man's sleeve as they

walked. 'What will you do? Will you still catch crocodiles?' he asked.

'No son, not around here. When a jackal is shitting, the ants give it space. I will find some other work for the moment.'

Jama was surprised by the hunter. He could wrestle with man-eating crocodiles but like everyone else had been beaten by the arrogance and violence of the fascists.

★ ★ ★

'You're late, Alfredo!' barked the Italian as Jama ran in one morning, he avoided looking at the angry red face. He had developed a terrible fear of one day invoking someone's unrestrained anger, he knew what some people were capable of and hated being around reckless fury. He didn't try to explain that his sickness had still not left his body. 'Scusami signore,' muttered Jama as he reached for the fly whisk. Jama caught his breath as the Italian grabbed the karbaash and struck him on the palm. Tears shot out of Jama's eyes and his hand curled up like a leaf in a fire. The Italian stared into Jama's eyes and Jama stared back waiting for a glimmer of remorse.

The Italian slowly sat back down. 'You dare be late once more and see what happens to you,' he threatened, his face calm and unworried.

Jama looked down at his palm, the skin was churned up like a freshly dug field, he could see the meat of his hand and the sight made him retch.

'You filthy brat! Get some sand and clean that up,' yelled his master. Jama staggered out. A Somali clansman stopped him in the street and washed his cut clean and wrapped a cloth around it, Jama was sobbing in pain and the clansman tried to calm him.

'Ilaahey ha ku barakeeyo, May God bless you, May he stop you hitting the ground, May he keep your head up,' chanted the clansman. 'Go right back inside, Jama, and show him that you are a man, we will get our time, that stupid man doesn't realise how vindictive we Somalis are,' he smiled and held Jama loosely against him.

'Go now, life is long.'

Jama returned to the office with a scoop of sand and threw it carelessly over the curdling vomit. He refused to make eye contact but picked up the whisk with his good hand. He felt proud and brave as he endured the stinging in his hand, he kept his chin up like a soldier.

It is hard to avenge yourself on someone you fear, when everything about them, their height, power, possessions, confidence, imposes a sense of your own inferiority. Even a child's imagination shrinks in the presence of terror. Jama returned every day to be bullied and shamed despite the humming sickness in his bones, he was like a moth drawn to the harsh light of the Italian's omnipotence. Every day askaris were brought in, and Jama would watch over Silvio's shoulder as he sentenced them to hanging or flogging or some original torture that he had devised. The Somalis, Eritreans and Arabs were like dumb little children in front of him. Jama studied the way the Italian operated; he learnt that neither physical ugliness nor moral weakness mattered in the world of men. A man was respected if other men feared him, and the Italian had somehow cracked the mystery of manufacturing fear in people. He was unpredictable and uninterested in the camaraderie of his peers, he reminded Jama of a wild boar, always on the verge of attack. There had been boys like that in Aden and they were the most dangerous, drowning smaller children while pretending to play or dropping rocks onto their sleeping heads. There were times when the Italian would try to show his gentility and he would put delicate music on the gramophone as he wrote letters home. With the floating up and down of the high pitched music, he would close his eyes and a greasy smile would spread across his face like animal fat over a griddle. He never said please or thank you like the dead Italian had done but he would moderate the usual viciousness in his voice while the music played. Soon after, he would return to his usual brutality with a slap or a thrown pen. Jama invented new insults silently in his head that made him smile patronisingly at the Italian: 'Son of a thousand donkeys,' 'Son of your sister and grandfather', 'Dirty-bottomed infidel,' 'Pig-eating pig', 'Molester of goats and chickens'. But Jama also began to unconsciously emulate Silvio. He stood up straight and stuck his nose in the air, he avoided eye contact, he slicked his hair down with water, swear words began to pepper his speech.

Today Silvio was excited and energetic; he had made Jama polish his shoes until Jama could see the hairs in his nose clearly in the leather. The commanders had visited Omhajer and expressed their satisfacion with Silvio's work. The office was full of Italians playing cards and drinking. One of them had found the Maggiore's camera somewhere and was trying to operate it, fumbling around with its delicate mechanisms. The flash popped like a flash of lightning in the man's eyes and he threw it back on the table. Jama's boss picked it up and began to arrange the drunk men in rows for photographs, he demanded someone take portraits of him alone, and he posed with his chin jutting out like Mussolini. He ordered askaris in from outside and with great happiness told them to hold him up in the air, four emaciated Eritreans and a Somali manoeuvred him onto their shoulders and grimaced under his weight.

'Take a picture quickly, take it!' shouted the Italian, as giddy as a schoolgirl; the askaris looked down as their shame was memorialised. The Italian's buttocks reeked of too much rich food, and his monstrous thighs felt like pythons around their necks. The other Italians applauded and wolf whistled at him, and as soon as he came down, they all wanted to take a similar photograph to send to their brothers, fathers, wives.

★ ★ ★

Jama staggered to work the next day, his head pounded and his legs felt as if they had died beneath him. He looked up at the hazy sky; he had to approximate the time from the sun and the events around him, he did not understand the Italian's insistence on arriving at a particular minute. He thought it stupid of the white man to place so much importance on portioning up time into little meaningless fragments rather than following the fluid movement of the sun as rational people did. He hurried as fast as he could and saw the Italian waiting at the entrance of the tent, his hands on his hips, his whip curled up in his fist. Jama turned to run away but his legs were too slow, Silvio grabbed him by the back of the neck and dragged him away.

Jama called out 'Help me! Help me!' to the Somali askaris but they stood in fearful silence. Jama was brought to a wooden pen, where chickens had been kept. It was empty now apart from floating downy feathers and streaks of chicken shit. The Italian stopped and kicked Jama ferociously into the dirty pen.

'Stay in there you! How many chances do I have to give you? You should all be wiped out, you good for nothings. Do not dare get up or I'll hunt you down and whip that black skin of yours clean off.'

Jama clutched at his side, fearing his ribs had been broken. He cried out in his mother tongue, 'To hell with you! You miserable mother-fucking pig,' but the Italian strode away, not deigning to turn his head.

Jama studied the jagged wound on his palm and felt his bruised ribs and demanded that God kill his offender. The clouds dissolved as the sun rose higher and higher. Jama waited to be let out but no-one came for him. He stared longingly at the low gate but was too afraid to let himself out. Shooting pains ran through his body when he tried to lie down. An Eritrean askari he did not know gave him a sip of water, hurrying away before anyone could chastise him. The pain in his side, the scalding sun over his head, the twisting hunger in his gut wrenched out pitiful, hesitant tears from him. He wanted his mother badly, to salve his wounds and hold him to her breast; she would have fought anyone for him, even the Italian, but without her Jama was a nobody. He felt old and hopeless. If his life ended here in this animal pen there would be no prayers, no tears, nothing to mark his life as being worth more than that of a chicken. His stars had failed him and if his mother was still watching from heaven she could feel nothing but shame. Jama watched a figure approach the pen; it was the crocodile catcher with a young tortoise wriggling in his hands.

'What are you doing in here, boy?' asked the crocodile catcher incredulously.

'That swine put me in here,' replied Jama, gesturing towards the tent with his chin. 'Where are you taking that tortoise?' he asked back.

'I thought I would take these madmen at

their word. I found this little tortoise in my plot eating my crops so considering we don't own anything anymore, I thought I would give it to them to deal with,' and with that the crocodile man spat out a wad of tobacco and marched over to the tent.

The crocodile catcher returned with two askaris and they were all laughing uproariously. The Italian had charged the tortoise with theft and given it a seven day custodial sentence. Jama was to be its cellmate and guard. They placed the tortoise in the pen more gently than Jama had been thrown in, and the crocodile catcher gave Jama a handful of roasted peanuts from his deep pockets.

'Did he say how long I have to be in here?' Jama called after them.

The crocodile catcher turned back to him. 'I don't know, son, but he is a very strange man, his soul stinks. Don't worry we will look out for you. I will bring you food later.'

The crocodile catcher kept his promise, he brought Jama food and water and even grass for the tortoise, and kept Jama company as the sun set and the hyenas laughed their way into town. Jama was frightened and tried to stop the crocodile catcher departing by telling story after story, but in the end the crocodile catcher stretched with a loud yawn and went home. Jama was left alone with the wild animals, ghosts and mosquitoes, wondering what the repercussions would be if he went home for the night. Askaris were known to report on each other to earn rewards from the Italians. Jama stayed awake all night, shivering with cold and jumping at every rustle and crack in the darkness surrounding him, he had images of a lion leaping over the fence and carrying him away by the throat. He had just fallen asleep when the first askaris arrived at daybreak. The next day he was still not pardoned and he spent the day turning the tortoise over and studying its head, limbs and shell. It was a beautiful thing, one of the most perfect of God's creations, it moved around ruminatively, picking at stray weeds without a care in the world. Its hard shell was a source of envy to Jama with his fragile, damaged flesh.

Only on the third day, with his skin bitten to smithereens, did the Italian call Jama out of the pen. He stood humiliated and furious in front of his tormentor; the Italian chuckled at the sight of Jama covered in dust then cleared his throat for the satisfaction of a lecture.

'Alfredo, you have been a nightmare for me. I sometimes felt that you were not all bad and had a few brains, but you have disappointed me at every turn. You have been

216

a total, total disaster as an office boy. I don't know what that communist Jew boy was talking about when he praised you, maybe he had needs that you satisfied, but I am made of better stock and I have seen your worthlessness. Get out and don't come back.'

Jama walked out with huge relief, but the Italian yelled after him. 'Hey! Hey! Come back here, never turn your back to your superior, boy! Come here and salute me now!'

Jama ignored him and ran back to the tent. He picked up his aday and his little savings, put them in his father's suitcase and left Omhajer.

Keren, Eritrea, 1941

Jama met a group of white-robed and turbaned traders by the road out of Omhajer. A young Sudanese man among them saw the poor state Jama was in and offered him food. They rode a lorry together towards Abyssinia. Before long the trader had agreed to employ Jama as a tea boy in his stalls in K'eftya and Adi Remoz, towns in the vast highlands of the Gondar region. They travelled for five days in the back of the lorry, marvelling at the paradise they passed through; the landscape was a juicy emerald green, with wild mango trees full of frolicking, singing birds, herds of giraffe and zebra gathered around blue watering holes. Jama would have been happy to jump off the lorry and stay in this small heaven but shiftas and patriots lurked amongst the trees and long grass. It was unsettling to see a place so lush, so full of promise without one tukul or any kind of human dwelling. They did not see a soul until they reached the outskirts of K'eftya, where Jama and the Sudanese trader jumped off. Jama spent listless days walking around K'eftya selling tea to the few people who could afford it; loneliness and boredom filled his days. He didn't want to even remember his mother or father, a new bitterness was infecting the way he thought about them; their mistakes had left him in this destitute state. When it rained he waited under a tree, when the sun returned he would walk, he rarely talked to anyone, just eavesdropped on conversations and stared at the women under their colourful umbrellas. The months crawled past until, far away to crowds of millions, by radio and by special appearances, Benito Mussolini — hands clasping his belt and chin pushed into the air — declared tribal war on Britain and France with proclamations of 'Vincere! Vincere! Vincere!'

Jama and the other teaboys gathered in the market to hear the digested and translated version.

'Should I plant more tomatoes? Will the Ferengis be buying from here or Adi Remoz?' one woman asked.

'Will we get a railway station now?' asked another.

All the young men were hushed; some wondered whether this war would be as ruinous as the invasion of their country, while others wondered if it would be more profitable to become askaris now or later. In Rome, Mussolini the opportunist, the failed primary school teacher, that syphilitic seller of ideas fallen from the back of a lorry, that gurning midget, calculated how many hundreds or even thousands he would need to claim dead before Hitler would deign to cut him a slice of the victory cake. A few thousand, he told his aides, that's all. Fascist officers toured Italian East Africa touting for the upcoming attraction and young Somalis, Abyssinians and Eritreans were tricked, cajoled and forced into signing up.

Two enlistment officers finally arrived in K'eftya and set up a table outside the new police station. A long line of men and boys waited to enlist; Jama passed brightfaced twelve year-olds running away from home, starving rheumy-eyed farmers, shiftas who had betrayed their fellow thieves, strong village men who could not afford dowries. Jama waited in the midday sun until his turn came. The Italians behind the wooden table laughed at the battered cardboard suitcase clenched in his hand, they seemed amused by most of the Africans. They asked his name, age and told him to give them a twirl. Jama was exactly the kind of illiterate boy they were looking for and he put his thumbprint where they told him, for once neither knowing nor caring where they sent him. They issued him a rifle, a shirt, a pair of shorts, a blanket, a kit bag with all kinds of toys, knife, tin bowls, field dressing, a water flask, more possessions than he had ever owned, and in exchange all they wanted was for him to join something called the 4th Company. They even gave him a flour ration and an adult wage of fifty lira a month. With this he was meant to buy sandals, which the Italians thought were an optional extra for their askaris. At his tender age he could not imagine grown men sending him to his death; neither could he imagine the kind of mechanised, faceless slaughter the Italians would bring to Africa.

Jama had never seen war; the only battles he could imagine were the sporadic feuds that nomadic Somalis engaged in, played according to a strict set of courtly rules that forbade the killing of women, children, old men, preachers and poets. He could feel the money being thrown into this conflict and it thrilled him, it felt like a festival was being prepared. Everywhere he looked, lorries filled to bursting zoomed past. More and more Italians appeared and then disappeared back into Eritrea. Tanks and all sorts of strange vehicles trundled along roads feverishly built ahead of them by tired African labourers. Installed in his Company with a quiet, well-behaved Commander by the name of Matteo Ginelli, Jama awaited orders. The

Italian war machine decided that Jama 'Goode' Guure Mohamed Naaleyeh Gatteh Eddoy Sahel Beneen Samatar Rooble Mattan would be most useful as a Signaller. He crossed the little Eden in between K'eftya and Omhajer once again, this time in a military convoy, and began his training. He fell in love with his first task: he was to write out messages on the ground to planes flying overhead. With huge strips of white cotton Jama spelt out words, memorising the squiggles and lines of the Italian alphabet by giving them nicknames. A was the house, B was the backside, C was the crescent moon, D was the bow, his favourite was M which looked like two boys holding hands. Commander Ginelli called Jama 'Al Furbo', the clever one, for his quick grasp of Italian and the other askaris adopted this as his nickname. While the other boys asked to see the card again and again to replicate the strange symbols written on it, one look and Jama could copy out perfect messages. Even though planes never flew overhead to read these messages, working in the sun, running about, wrangling with the huge sheets in the breeze with other boys shouting for his help made Jama feel capable for the first time in his life. He practised writing letters in the sand, mastering 'Jama', 'ciao', and his mother and father's names.

When Commander Ginelli brought two new boys to join the Signallers, Jama was too engrossed in his messages to bother looking up, but a sharp slap on his shoulder brought him to attention. It took him a second to recognise the face but there stood Shidane, taller than him now and with a shaven head, chewing on a matchstick. Shidane grabbed hold of him and over his shoulder Jama saw little Abdi looking on with a big smile.

'So walaalo, fate has brought us together again,' said Shidane, his voice incongruously deep.

'Looks like it,' Jama said uncertainly.

'We thought you were dead! People said that you had been taken to Hargeisa, shitting your guts out, but looks like you're made of stronger stuff. You would not believe the life I have been living, I found a gold coin in Suq al-Yahud and there are Suldaans who have not enjoyed the luxury it bought me,' brayed Shidane.

'So what are you doing here?'

'It was a coin, not a goldmine.'

They set to work. Abdi told him they had enlisted only a few weeks earlier when the Italians had invaded British Somaliland.

'You should have seen the British pack up their things and run to the coast, my God! It was as if their trousers were on fire,' laughed Shidane, impersonating the British dash out of Somaliland.

Jama laughed happily and remembered how much fun Shidane could be; he had no respect for anyone or anything. Abdi was still quiet and calm, with a serene face caught somewhere between childhood and maturity. Shidane had persuaded him to sign up so that they could earn enough money to travel to Egypt and join the British Navy. Joining the navy was all Shidane wanted to talk about.

'Man, you will never believe how much they are paying Somalis to load coal onto the British ships, we are going to be rolling in money, Suldaans will want to borrow from us, Ferengis will be jealous of our cars, houses and women. I'm telling you Jama Guure, with one month's pay you could buy more camels than any toothless Garaad.'

Jama was taken aback by the torrent of words that came out of Shidane's mouth; he didn't even stop to breathe. 'What do you think of these Italians?' Shidane finally asked of Jama.

'Not much. They hate Somalis, and Eritreans or any black people.' Jama thought about telling them about the Italian who had kept him locked up in the chicken pen but realised Shidane would only laugh at him.

'So they're like the British?' piped up Abdi.

'Yes but they use more hair oil. One askari told me that after two Eritreans tried to kill an important Italian in Addis Ababa, the Italians killed thirty thousand Habashis in a few days, and it wasn't just the soldiers either. Shopkeepers, barbers, all of them went out with clubs and knives and killed in revenge.'

The boys were silent as they tried to imagine thirty thousand dead people. 'It would be like a whole desert worth of people,' said Abdi.

'No, it would be like Al 'Aidarous mosque filled ten times over,' corrected Shidane. 'Maybe we can shoot some of these Italians in the back of the head when they're not looking, even up the score.' Shidane made a rifle out of his hands.

Jama held his finger to his lips. 'Don't say things like that, you never know who is listening,' he admonished. With Shidane out of earshot, Abdi whispered, 'Did you ever find your father?'

'Nearly. He's buried over the border in Sudan.'

Abdi grabbed Jama's shoulder. 'I will pray for him, and one day you will do hajj for him, agreed?'

Jama nodded.

'Good, inshallah we can get rich here and

travel to Egypt, or at least steal that aeroplane you always wanted,' smiled Abdi.

Abdi and Shidane brought joy back into Jama's life. They worked together, ate together, slept together. As a team they spelled out messages for planes that never came near enough to read them. Jama taught them to recognise the letters and they spelt out swear words when they ran out of official messages. Their Commander was relaxed and preferred visiting other Italians to supervising the playful young askaris. Every day more Somalis appeared in clouds of dust along the road, some of them joining the Signallers, some travelling to other battalions.

As their messages became more ordered and professional, boredom set in, they were stuck on the outskirts of Omhajer swallowing dust, so the Commander decided to set them on a march. In double file, their packs on their backs, rifles slung over their shoulders, they marched to K'eftya and Adi Remoz, then back again. Shidane carried Abdi's pack and askaris from Jama's clan looked after him, carrying his rifle when he dragged it along the ground on the long thirsty marches. The Somali and Eritrean askaris sang songs in their own languages, jokingly taunting each other, and Commander Ginelli taught them songs. Jama's favourite was about a Habashi girl taken to Italy after being freed by a fascist from slavery. 'Faccetta Nera, bell'abissina, aspetta e spera che già l'ora si avvicina! Little black face, beautiful Abyssinian, she waits and hopes that the hour is already approaching!' Jama sang loudly. It seemed that many languorous Italians had only made the arduous journey to East Africa because they had been promised that they would find there Abyssinian lovelies, it was fascistic sex tourism, all sun, sex and slaughter. Eritrean girls trailed behind many Italian Battalions; some of the camp followers had barely reached puberty but had already been mistresses to many soldiers. The infants they carried on their backs were not recognised by the Italians and would forever be known as bastards or, as the officials described it, children of X. Jama felt sorry for the thin bundles on the girls' backs. Despite everything, he had his father's and grandfather's names and that made him someone. When he recited his abtiris he felt important, as if he was meant to exist to keep that melodic line going.

Once the Signallers had completed the unnecessary marching, the Italian commanders decided to invade Sudan. Jama was part of the second Roman Empire that would conquer this vast antique land. They set off from Omhajer early one morning, their flour rations safely packed, water in their flasks, bullets in their rifles. Shidane had pilfered a few tins of unknown goods and promised to make a delicious meal for the three of them.

'Do you think there will be serious fighting over there?' asked Jama, a ball of fear gathering in his gut. He was crossing an invisible mountain in his mind, from the land he knew into the unknown territory that had claimed his father.

'I doubt it. The British can't fight anyone armed with more than a sharpened banana,' Shidane replied. He was fearless. His name meant 'alight' and he was on fire with intelligence and courage, he could burn with a look, warm with a touch. They passed through plains where grass grew higher than the tallest man, and the singing and dancing quietened as they approached the border with Sudan. Two Eidegalle men were dragging a Howitzer and Jama, Shidane and Abdi hung back with them, smoking and talking.

'Have you had any girlfriends, Ascaro Jama?' Shidane smiled.

'Yes Ascaro Shidane, women love me.'

'Yeah, yeah, in your dreams they do. I've got eight girlfriends.'

'What! You think there are eight days in a week?' Jama scoffed.

'No, I know exactly how many days there are in a week, but you need an extra girl for those special times when you've worn one out.'

'Dirty bastard,' laughed Jama. 'What about you Ascaro Abdi, got any girlfriends?'

'No,' cut in Shidane. 'He's already had enough trouble with women. He made us leave Aden when he was caught with an Arab girl. I saw her with a baby just before we left, and guess what, even from far away I could see the light bouncing off that baby's big forehead.'

'Ya salam!' laughed Jama. 'What really made you leave Aden?'

Shidane and Abdi giggled. 'We were caught stealing shoes from outside the mosque, we had new shoes every Friday! Sometimes we even sold the idiots back their shoes saying we had found them in an alley. It was working well until we stole the shoes of a detective, then we were put on the first ship back to the homeland.'

* * *

The Italians rode on horseback far ahead, trying to hide their fear from their charges, but many of them kept ducking into bushes to ease their loosened bowels. When they finally reached the border, panic and jubilation took hold of the hundred men and they charged in all directions searching for something to conquer. There was only desolation; deserted homes, burnt cooking pots and the paraphernalia of refugees, forgotten shoes and sheets. The invaders passed along dirt tracks, their guns and artillery useless against the oppressive susurrations of cicadas. Just as Jama was about to fall asleep on his feet, he heard shooting and clambered up a date palm to get a better look. With a pounding heart he saw two white-robed Sudanese policemen on horseback fleeing from the Italians. Their black stallions evaded the bullets and Jama could see puffs of dust where the bullets landed. Askaris fired into the air in excitement and it felt like a genuine battle was taking place rather than a routing of two sleeping policemen by a hundred soldiers. Italian officers chased each other to the saddles that the Sudanese policemen had abandoned in their haste, and held them aloft as if they had found the Ark of the Covenant. Everyone cheered and whistled. 'We are part of a victorious army,' the Italians said, 'every man should be proud of what they have achieved here today.'

Shidane, Jama and Abdi laughed deliriously at the sight of the Italians fighting over the busted old saddles. Pushing and shoving each other for the glory of taking home a souvenir from the day they conquered the mighty British Empire. Eventually, some agreement was reached and the saddles were handed over to the askaris to carry back to Omhajer. Four askaris proudly carried the saddles on their shoulders and even Jama and Abdi reached over to touch the old leather for remembrance's sake.

'We are the testicles of the Ferengis,' sang the askaris but Shidane frowned at them. 'We have thrown our balls away,' he grumbled.

Despite their victorious foray into Sudan, the war was not going well for the Italians. British Hurricanes made raids on Asmara and Gura, shooting to pieces fifty Italian aircraft before they could ever leave the ground and read Jama's messages. Although the Italian army in East Africa outnumbered the British by four to one and Jama had yet to see the enemy, the Italians were fighting a losing battle. Agordat fell even though the Italians had inflicted heavy losses on the small contingent of Indian and Scottish troops. All it took was for a turbaned sepoy to get too close and yell 'Raja Ram Chander Ki Jai' and Italian officers would drop their guns and head for the hills. Barentu was left to the British without so much as a fist fight while the generals in Rome and Asmara desperately tried to find a town for their last stand.

They chose Keren, a Muslim town of whitewashed buildings, camel merchants and silversmiths; it was nestled like a medieval fort in the bosom of a severe mountain range, with only a small gorge for access. The Italians bombed this gorge with more energy and vitality than they brought to any other activity in the war. They pulled up their imaginary drawbridge and awaited the Scots, Indians, French, Senegalese, Arabs and Jews who made up the Allied effort against them. Jama and the Signallers were called to Keren along with ninety thousand other askaris. Jama was one of the last to arrive, it took days of marching with blistered feet and nauseating lorry rides to get to Keren.

On the fifteenth of March 1941, the battle began. Ten thousand shells an hour were fired by the British and Italian guns, and even a mile behind the front, Jama's bones were rattled by explosions. Jama, Shidane, and Abdi trembled as they watched over the valley where Indian and Italian killed each other over African soil. 'Ya salam!' exclaimed Shidane every time a British bomb hit the askaris. Everything became more serious. They were finally taught how to shoot, using tin cans as targets and Shidane the fearless, as he started to call himself, became the best shooter among them. The askaris were constantly scrutinised and observed. The British were said to be using northern Somalis as spies so the Italians kept them away from the fighting while they still could. Trains regularly brought up supplies to the Italians, and Shidane used his friendships with Somali cooks to obtain delicacies such as chocolate, tinned chicken, tinned peaches, and his new addiction, condensed milk. His pack always rattled with tins of sweet, thick milk and he charged askaris for the pleasure of a drop in their tea. While 4th Company guarded a munitions store near town, caravans of refugees trundled past, some on camels, some on mules and the poorest on foot weighed down by their children, fleeing as their country was destroyed. Shidane's enlistment pay was burning a hole in his pocket so he frittered it away buying refreshing camel's milk from the wealthier refugees. As the battle raged on over the hills, Jama made binoculars of his hands and watched explosions that gave the mountains the appearance of erupting volcanoes, blood lava pouring down their slopes. It seemed to him that the mountains would crumble under the bombardment. Occasionally, 4th Company would have to desert the munitions as the RAF flew ominously over them, but the British planes sought out more substantial targets, they scored a perfect, deafening hit on a train bringing ammunition to the Italian front line. The train flew off the tracks as the mortars, grenades and magazines blew up. The driver in the steam engine tried to race away from the burning carriages but was eventually engulfed in a white-hot inferno. The boys were attracted to the valiant British forces, they waited impatiently for the next humiliation to be meted out against the Italians. On the one day it seemed that their signalling would be finally put to use, they looked up eagerly to the sky to see eight Italian planes in formation above them; but they were quickly attacked by three British Hurricanes. In the ensuing dogfight three of the Italian planes crashed into a valley and the other five limped away. It was so exciting that the Commander pulled out his whip to quieten the boys. Jama was the first to become afraid of the bombers and began to tie twigs onto his head so the planes could not see him from above. Shidane and Abdi humoured him, competitively adding to the foliage on their heads until they resembled walking bushes, their faces lost behind veils of leaves.

Every night the British would halt their

bombardment for ten minutes to play caterwauling Italian opera on their loud speakers followed by summaries of all the defeats the Italians had suffered that day. After the Italian segment, Eritreans and Somalis working for the British would translate the news and exhort the askaris to desert, offering them rewards and medals if they did so. The askaris did not need much encouragement, every night under the cover of darkness, thousands of askaris crept away, never to be seen again. All the Amhara disappeared when the British reported that Haile Selassie had returned from exile and Abyssinian patriots were pressing onto Addis Ababa. Ogadeni Somalis returned to their families and camels when leaflets were dropped down on their heads reporting that rebellion was brewing in Hararghe. Saturn and Mars had slid into conjunction and the nomadic Somalis saw that a great defeat lay before the Italians and left before the stars punished them too. That left a hodgepodge of Eritreans and young urban Somalis who used the leaflets to wipe their bottoms. From the ninety thousand askaris who had been present at the start of the battle for Keren, sixty thousand remained. The Italians tried to keep these obedient by shooting deserters or tying hands and feet behind backs and throwing insubordinate men into mountain gullies where jackals waited for them. The Italians also reprised one of their special forms of execution, they tied mutinous askaris, usually Somalis, to the backs of lorries and accelerated along the rough road until there was nothing left on the end of the rope apart from a pair of manacled hands. One askari had a postcard he had bought from a hawker in Mogadishu and he showed it to Jama and the boys. They squinted at the picture of the lorry unable to see anything of interest. 'Allah,' shouted Abdi and he pointed to the shackled hands that hung off the back of the lorry. The hands were piously cupped as if in prayer but the wrists were angry shredded stumps, inscribing their curses in bloody script onto the dusty road.

'Where's the rest of them?' asked Jama.

'Probably still along the roadside,' said the askari taking back his postcard.

Every askari returned from the frontline with a horror story, the daily carnage, the lack of sleep, dead bodies exploding in the heat, men going mad with shellshock, the evil ways in which the Italians humiliated their black comrades.

'The bulabasha told me to bury the white bodies but to leave the black to rot, I couldn't believe it, we had all just sacrificed our fucking lives for them,' raged one Eritrean askari, 'when I said I would bury them all together, he raised his pistol to me.'

Jama, Abdi and Shidane listened to these stories at night around the campfire. 'Let's stay until we have earned enough money to travel to Egypt,' they agreed. They hadn't yet seen the violence and savagery of the war close up and still believed they could escape it altogether. At night, the askaris pooled their flour rations and cooked together. Shidane usually commandeered the pots and pans to make bread and surprisingly delicious stews with stolen cooking oil and spices.

'My mother is the best cook in Aden, she doesn't make the sloppy bowls of grease you people are used to,' he boasted.

They crouched down around the fire and burnt their fingers trying to get to the stew before the others, even if bombing sorties flew overhead the men would rather stay put in the open than risk missing out on Shidane's cooking. Some jittery men would be half standing up, half crouched, nibbling the sour bread between shaking fingers. A man jumped out of his skin as a munitions store exploded and put his foot right into the boiling pot. The askaris jumped up in a rage.

'Waryaa fulay! Hey coward! Look where you're stepping, get your dirty feet out of our food,' the boys shouted at him with no concern for the red, scalded foot he pulled painfully out of the cauldron.

Jama and the boys angrily returned to the food as the man shuffled away. They slept huddled together behind a boulder, Shidane as always slept with one eye open like a caiman, keeping guard over his charges. When it was too loud to sleep, Shidane told ghost stories that made Jama's hair stand up. Backlit by the bombs, he would describe all the kinds of evil that he had seen.

'Wallaahi, may God strike me down this moment if even one word is untrue, one night when you two were snoring away, I saw something hunched moving down the mountain, it had white, white skin and long claws that scratched against the rock. I closed my eyes thinking I was hallucinating, but when I opened them again, the thing was stood up like a man. Its red eyes were looking right at me so I ducked down behind a rock, praying for my life. The English had stopped bombing and everything was totally black, I lit a match thinking the beast was coming for me but it had already found a victim. It had an askari by the throat, and it was carrying the limp man back up the mountain, it disappeared but all night I could hear bones breaking and flesh being ripped apart. There are cannibals

238

here, I am sure of it.'

Jama could believe anything Shidane reported. He hated the strange noises that carried on the air on quiet nights, growls, howls, screams, prayers. The wounded askari's pleas of 'Brothers, help me' would turn into 'May you all be damned to hell' before there was just silence.

As the stench of bodies grew, Jama was separated from Shidane and Abdi; he was sent with a small unit to defend a munitions store close to the frontline, while they were ordered to Keren to collect replacement binoculars for the Italian commanders.

Shidane embraced Jama. 'Don't worry, walaalo, I will have a mouth watering meal waiting for you, but if it gets too bad up there, desert and leave a message with one of your clansmen, we will come and find you, Al Furbo,' said Shidane.

Jama didn't dare speak, his voice would betray him. Shidane stood proud in his uniform as he waved goodbye. From a distance the dirt on it was invisible and Shidane looked more elegant than any other askari, with his handsome brown face, bright eyes and long limbs.

Some things Jama would learn with time, some things he would not, but askaris described seeing Abdi and Shidane in Keren, their papers scrunched up in Shidane's hand. The town teemed with deserters and men separated from their battalions and military police herded them to camps before sending them back into battle. Abdi tightly held Shidane's hand as they manoeuvred around the mad drunken men. They arrived at the huge tent that housed the supply depot and had to suppress gasps when they ran in. It was like Ali Baba's cave, glinting with hundreds of treasures, tins of food, coffee, bags of sugar, sacks of tea, weapons, shoes, binoculars and other gadgets.

They were the only askaris in the depot and they instantly drew the attention of the white men. 'Ascaro, what are you doing here?' shouted over one middle-aged man.

Shidane held out the flimsy requisition order and waited for the man to come and get it.

'Come here, boy, it's not your place to be waiting for me to walk over to you,' the man shouted.

Shidane handed him the note, the clerk put on spectacles to peruse the order. While he read Shidane and Abdi looked around to see if they could sneak anything into their pockets. At the top of a sack lay chocolate bars in brown wrappers and Shidane wrapped his fingers around one and snuck it into his shorts.

'Put that down now,' demanded the supply clerk.

Shidane returned the chocolate bar and smiled.

'That is a serious crime, ascaro, count your lucky stars I don't walk you straight back to your commanding officer and report you.'

Shidane listened with a smile on his face, he only picked out the words 'ascaro', 'officer' and 'report' but could understand the gist of what the clerk was getting at.

'Get out and wait outside while we prepare the order,' said the supply clerk pointing to the exit. The boys left looking all around them.

'Don't worry, I will get something, I wanna get Jama a surprise for when he returns, inshallah.'

'Don't bother, Shidane, it's a bad idea,' pleaded Abdi, trying to give his voice an avuncular authority but whispering with fear.

The supply depot was within an Italians-only area, although a few German soldiers worked there, flying about like Nazi flags, their hair bleached white and their skin red. Abdi and Shidane were the only non-whites within the wire perimeter and they could feel their skin tightly wrapped around them.

Meanwhile Jama had reached the munitions store high in the mountains, the cave was packed high with guns and mortars and there was a heavy metal door built across its entrance. All around the satanic guns roared and clattered. An Eritrean askari joined them and he and Jama stood guard at the door while the Italians observed the scene below them. The British were getting closer and closer and most Italians were hoping their defeat would be swift and painless. Jama could see only stick figures running about through the smoke, when he crept closer to the footpath he saw askaris fleeing the bombardment, feebly holding onto their heads as if that would stop them getting blown off. Somalis usually said that holding your head would bring calamity but in the askaris' case the calamity was already upon them. Jama had a terrible feeling about this day, it would bring death for sure; he knew by the blood red sky, all churned up like the entrails of a dead beast, and the burning men who rolled desperately on the ground unable to put themselves out. Jama was ordered back to the cave by an Italian and he dragged his feet, he wanted to stay as far away from the dark oily munitions as possible, his skin itched with the fear of being blown up. Hardened Indian and Scottish soldiers were close to breaking through to the peak that Jama and a thousand other askaris were guarding; and these shaking, illiterate boys, their stomachs tight with fear, their pants wet with terror, waited to be overwhelmed.

One calm little boy waited for his chance to line his pockets at the Keren supply depot.

'Come here and get it then,' barked out the clerk to Shidane.

They returned to the cavern of treasures, the clerk handed Abdi a heavy crate of binoculars and Shidane reached up to help his uncle carry it out. The clerk laughed at them, 'You skinny Somalis, you're no use to anyone.'

Shidane and Abdi shuffled towards the exit and the clerk returned whistling to his paperwork.

'Psst keep a look out,' Shidane whispered to Abdi, before placing the crate down next to open sacks of spaghetti and rice.

Shidane pretended to fix his sandal as he stuffed handfuls of rice into his pockets and the crate, Abdi kicked him sharply in the ribs but Shidane had already seen shadows and smelt their sulphuric fumes. Three Satans had walked into Shidane's life: Privates Antonio Alessi, Cristiano Fiorelli and Stefano Tucci emerged from the shadows looking as if they had just sailed out from the underworld. They were stocky young men who had spent their time in Africa stacking boxes and cleaning spillages in the depot, they were as pale as worms but their hands and hearts thirsted for blood.

'What do we have here?' exclaimed Cristiano.

Shidane stood up and went to pick up his crate, Cristiano kicked it away forcefully and the binoculars and rice spilled out with a clatter. The clerk ran over shouting obscenities. Antonio and the clerk had a quick discussion and with a shrug the clerk walked away. Antonio ordered Abdi to clear up the mess, then the soldiers surrounded Shidane and led him away. Shidane turned around to look at Abdi before he disappeared into the bright sun.

The depot clerks led Shidane to a tin shack in a corner of the compound, the corrugated metal had buckled and cracked in the heat, the door resisted but eventually admitted them with a shriek. The hut stank of urine and the only light came from the chinks in the metal, but Stefano lost no time in getting wire from his pocket and tying Shidane's hands behind his back. It was only then Shidane's bravado faltered and he let the smile leave his face. His hands were firmly tied when Cristiano kicked Shidane's feet away from under him, and the others laughed and Shidane could smell alcohol on their breaths.

'You shouldn't have stolen from us, little nigger,' slurred Cristiano. 'We are trained killers.'

Shidane stared up at them, his face tense, repulsion shooting from his eyes. Antonio kicked Shidane in the eye and his eyeball was ripped from its socket, Shidane stumbled to his feet, blood pouring out of his eye socket.

Stefano had left the shack and returned with a short metal pole and a small tin. 'Musulmano, I thought your religion forbade theft, don't they cut off your arms for that?' he said, twisting Shidane's hands as if to tear them off. 'I guess if you're so hungry we should feed you. I've got something you'll love so much you will be licking those lips for days.'

He handed the pole to Cristiano. Shidane, blind in one eye, rocked back and forth and squirmed about like a snake cut in two. Stefano pulled out slimy, gristled slices of pork and shoved them down Shidane's throat like a demented mother. Shidane choked on the dirty meat and the oily thick fingers in his mouth. Cristiano smacked the pole over Shidane's head and the boy keeled over onto his side. Antonio took hold of the pole and hit Shidane's kneecaps until he heard the loud cracks he was looking for. At this Shidane soiled his pants and began to beg.

'Por favore, buoni Italiani, smettere,' he pleaded, and for that Antonio bludgeoned his mouth until all Shidane's beautiful teeth were obliterated.

'Are you frightened now, don't you wish you had never stolen from us?' whispered Antonio, as he prised Shidane's mouth open with the pole into a ghastly smile, the pain made Shidane swoon.

'Let's strip him,' suggested Stefano tentatively.

'Yeah, look at him squirming around like a bitch on heat,' agreed Cristiano.

As they stripped Shidane, Abdi was marched out of the compound by the clerk. 'Ascaro, where is the other ascaro, signore?' asked Abdi desperately.

'Get out,' shouted the clerk, 'I am going to make sure you get your punishment too.' He kicked Abdi in the behind. Abdi skirted around the wire perimeter trying to catch sight of Shidane, he saw the clerk enter a rusted shack and then walk back to the depot.

When the clerk peered into the gloom and saw the naked young askari, sliding around in his faeces, raw flesh where his eye and mouth should be, he nodded to his colleagues but he didn't know why. Many would pass by the shack when they heard what was happening in there. Some hung around to watch but most drank in the sight and then scampered away like little boys who had seen up their teacher's skirt but didn't want to be caught staring. Abdi heard the rasping, gurgling grunts along with the rest of the compound but he thought it was an animal in the shack not his beloved nephew. Shidane floated in between consciousness and a watery dream world that glided around him, pulling him into a narcotic stupor before it evaporated and he fell back into his flesh, his eyes like two glowing coals in a dying fire. He could feel his shin bones splintering with each strike and then his innards were raped with the pole, at this his soul died and he waited for his body to follow it. They were relentless; they toiled over him, like mechanics pulling a car apart for scrap, vandals destroying a masterpiece, they dissected Shidane. They needed to see how his strange, beautiful, black body operated so they tore it up, raided it, it took hours but they were dedicated labourers and this was perhaps the last chance they would get to kill. Cristiano delivered Shidane back to his pagan God with a blow to the back of the head that sent mosaic pieces of skull into Shidane's brain, ripping his sixteen years of dreams, memories, and thoughts into bloody shreds. Once Shidane had stopped twitching and the

Italians realised the fun had ended, they looked at the dull, cumbersome cadaver lying at their feet and left the shack aroused but unsatisfied. They washed their hands at the tap near the latrines and agreed to meet later at the army brothel. Cristiano saw the little askari waiting by the fence and spat in disgust at him. It was left to two anonymous Italians to drag out the corpse and dump it outside the perimeter fence. Abdi, waiting there, saw the crumpled naked body laying face down in the dirt but didn't approach it. He had prayed all night so he did not believe that it could be Shidane. Only after a group of Eritrean askaris kicked it over and he could hear them saying 'Somali, Somali' did he approach. It was a version of Shidane, a clumsy approximation, a crumpled facsimile that he saw, a human stain, not the boy he had loved and grown up with. This was something a hyena had chewed up and spat out. Abdi tried to understand what he was seeing but he couldn't.

While Shidane was stolen from this world, Jama too was battling with Izra'il, the angel of death. His time came in a dark mountain cave; British rockets lanced through the black sky to seek him out, lighting up the clouds with lethal white arcs of death. The rockets chased each other, hurtling with indecent speed to fertilise the ovum of extermination within Jama, until finally one snub-nosed spermatozoa found his hiding place. It smashed into the door of the cave just as Jama tried to slam the door shut on it. Jama got up, eyes blinded by the light and heat, he was covered in what felt like blood, his arms and torso were slick with it, he believed he was dead, and his first thought was one of disappointment. The soul was pulled away from the body just to be dumped in a dark echoing void. He stumbled and felt a hand underneath his foot, he kicked it away in panic.

'Audu billahi min ash-shaidani rajeem, I seek refuge with Allah from the Shayddaan,' he stammered. The heat and sulphur in the cave was infernal, and Jama cursed himself for not having prayed or fasted throughout his short life.

Fresh air blew in through the gash in the door, and he put his mouth to it, sucking the sweet air into his burnt throat. When his legs and arms stopped trembling he pulled himself weakly through the shredded door. Outside, everything remained the same, rockets still cascaded down, fulminating angrily, striking men and mules. Jama looked behind him and in the phosphoric light saw the bulabasha's shaved head blown away, lying at rest by the blackened, shredded leg of an Eritrean askari. They were all dead, but they looked like they were playing, their legs splayed in dynamic poses, their shirts ripped open, their limbs entangled without care of rank or race. 'Lazy dogs,' Jama thought, 'why don't they get up and walk like me,' but then he realised they were not Muslim, God would leave them where they fell because they had denied him, while he could wander until Judgement Day consigned him to his rightful place. So he wandered, fearless, aimless, with the power of a zombie, back down the narrow pathway to Keren. As the cowering sun peeped over the horizon and slowly crept out of its bunker, Jama realised that it was sweat soaking his clothes not blood, he carried on walking.

He reached Keren and attracted jeers and laughter, he looked like a cartoon character, his face was blackened with ash, his shirt was blown open and his wavy hair, thick with dust, stood on end. Jama kept his head down and wanted to walk straight through town but was stopped.

'Ascaro, where have you come from looking like that?' asked the sergeant blocking his path.

Jama's clothes stank and still appeared to be smouldering. He looked up into the sergeant's blue eyes. 'From guarding arms store number fifteen, the rest are dead.'

The sergeant looked up towards the mountain and tutted, 'Go back then, you can't leave your position unless you have been told to, when will you askaris learn some fucking discipline, it's because of you people that we're losing this war.' He took a long breath. 'Take another uniform and some food from the supply depot, get the men at the depot to arrange a few other askaris to go with you.' He ripped off an order sheet and thrust it into Jama's hand. Jama's eyes bore into the sergeant's back.

Askaris shuffled past Jama with shifty glances in his direction as if he would spontaneously combust, but he had fought off death and inside he was triumphant. His life took form around him again, his heart beating, warmth returning to his skin, and all around Italians bellowing commands and insults. He tried to imagine the expressions on Shidane's and Abdi's faces when he told them that he had miraculously survived while all the others had been turned into mincemeat.

He smoothed down his hair and approached an angry-looking Somali. 'Uncle, where is this depot place?'

'Waryaa, look at the state of you, tollai, what have they done to us, fuck the depot, get away from here, I'm warning you to stay away from that hellhole. They killed one of us there last night, in cold blood, a young boy like you, run now if you know what's good for you,' the man raged.

The man seemed crazy, he was wearing an army shirt with a ma'awis wrapped around his waist, and he kept clutching at his groin. Jama wandered all over town, until he found the depot, it was calm, businesslike and sated after the night's bloodletting. The soldiers served Jama quickly and politely, even dropping a couple of out-of-date chocolates into his bag as a treat. Jama filled his flask over and over at the tap and then went into the daylight, ready to find Shidane and Abdi and show them the carnage at the cave.

Abdi was close by, crouched down by the perimeter fence. Jama raced up to him, trying to form the story in his mind, he knew that his mother had placed a shield of the coolest air between him and the rocket but the boys would never believe him. He looked around, he needed Shidane to hear the first telling of it too, when it was still spicy and dramatic.

'Ascaro Abdi, you will never guess what happened to me, look at me, Abdi, look at me,' Jama pulled Abdi's chin up so that he faced him.

Abdi was muttering and rocking on his

heels, covered in dust, his jaw was trembling and he pulled his face away. Jama saw a stain of rust-red blood on Abdi's shirt and collapsed next to him. He tried to put an arm around Abdi and gather him closer but Abdi shot to his feet and started screaming, he picked up rocks and threw them with all his might at the compound, a rock bounced off a tin roof before Jama dragged him away.

'Where's Shidane? What's happened, Abdi?'

'Come with me, Jama, you want to see, come with me,' shouted Abdi and abruptly leapt to his feet, Jama chasing after him.

Abdi led him to a clearing beside the road, before stopping abruptly and turning towards Jama. It was the first time Jama could look into Abdi's eyes. Under Abdi's furrowed eyebrows they were unfocused, wide and lost, behind them nothing, a bare ruin. His mind had been startled from its temple and had circled above before flying away. Jama took a step back, but Abdi grabbed his hand in a clumsy hard grip and pulled him forward.

Abdi's face was ripped open by a smile. 'Look there was nothing here when I buried him, and now this bush,' Abdi pointed at a huge sprawling shrub, its grasping leaves violently green and alive.

'Who did you bury here?' asked Jama.

'Shidane of course. They killed him, and I

buried him. Where were you, Jama? We could have saved him.'

Jama started to tremble and Abdi stared at him before pulling a disgusted face and turning back to the bush. 'When I left, nothing, and now this,' he said as he brushed its leaves with his fingertips.

The bush frightened Jama, it seemed to grow in front of his eyes, and it shone independently of the fading light.

'Who killed him, Abdi? What happened?' said Jama through his tears.

'Who do you think, idiot? The people I saw you with at the depot, they tore him apart, they ate him, and threw out what they didn't want.'

'Let's go, Abdi, come with me, let's go to Egypt, I have enough food on me, come, get up, let's go, enough,' coaxed Jama. He felt cold and dead again.

'I would rather die than eat their food. I'm staying here with my nephew, you can go where you like.'

Jama's sobs became louder and louder but Abdi just snarled at him, 'Leave me alone, take your stupid noise somewhere else.'

'I'm not leaving you,' cried Jama, 'what happened? You just went on an errand, Abdi, what happened?'

In a monotone, Abdi told him about the

rice, the three Italians, the shack, the noises, and by the end Jama understood and he could look into Abdi's eyes without flinching. As evening fell, a large full moon sat imperially in the sky, glaring down at them, and as Jama collected firewood, Abdi picked up rocks and threw them at its white, pockmarked face. His feet kicked up fine dust as like a dancer he leapt up at the moon. Jama turned his back on him and got the fire blazing with a box of matches Shidane had given him, afterwards he held the box tight in his hand and prayed for Shidane's soul. They both slept without eating, as if in sympathy with Shidane, who would never eat again or boast about his cooking again, who was now a meal himself, a feast for maggots. Jama wrapped Abdi in his new shirt and lay down, nearly on top of the fire, afraid that the chill inside him would freeze his heart. He could not sleep. Morbid thoughts ran through his mind; life was tenuous, there was no value to it, each day brought the threat of annihilation, or the loss of those you loved. He eventually fell into a sleep-like state amongst the smouldering heap of the burntout fire, his teeth chattering, and his icy feet tied up in the ever-growing tendrils of Shidane's grave.

At dawn, Jama woke up, as cold as death, his feet were in the tight grip of the bush, he tore at the thick, reptilian tendrils and they bled red, Shidane was vengeful even in reincarnation thought Jama. As he paced around waiting for Abdi to wake up, his feet gained feeling, they were like the hooves of a racehorse, like Guure's feet, they were not happy unless they could feel miles of earth passing underneath them every day. Ambaro always said, 'The only thing that comes to you if you sit around is death.' This was his family's only philosophy. Jama felt an urgent need to empty his bowels, and walked away to relieve himself. From where he crouched Abdi was completely hidden by the bush, like a fly in a Venus flytrap, he was utterly consumed. Jama quickly finished and ran to wake him up.

'I told you I was staying here,' Abdi thundered. His eyes were still vacant, but now he hit and pinched himself, muttered prayers under his breath, he seemed embarrassed by Jama's presence.

'You can't stay here, they will throw us down the mountain as deserters. You can't do anything for Shidane now, let's go,' Jama begged.

'You go, I will catch up with you,' stuttered Abdi agitatedly, Jama was keeping him from something and he was growing impatient. Jama looked around him, at the grey mountains echoing with the distant din of guns, the dusty road snaking away, he gave half of his food ration to Abdi, held onto his skinny body for an awkward embrace and then walked away.

* * *

Jama took off his mutilated army shirt and stalked away from Keren; he jumped into bushes when he heard convoys approaching and chased after traders who fled on their camels when they saw the half-naked mad boy pursuing them. At nightfall he stopped, lost and hungry, he made gloopy tasteless pancakes, threw them down his throat and ate berries he had picked along the way. Unable to lie still, he started walking by moonlight as well. He had long left the straight slave-built road and now just followed the magnetic pull of the stars. As the sun came up, he saw more evil, corpses crushed by British tanks rushing to victory, dusty white tracks still visible on the black men. Jama broke out into a cold sweat and fled in the opposite direction. By a ravine he stopped to rest, and fell asleep, lullabyed by the gurgling water and smooth caress of the sun. For a long time Jama heard whistling, but in the no man's land between sleep and wakefulness, he ignored it, hoping it was just his imagination. When the whistling turned into humming and laughing, he shot up. He scanned around, nobody, just scrub and silence, he laid down again, only for the whistling to start as his head touched the ground.

He stood up with a roar. 'Soobah! Come out,' he yelled, only a child would play like this, he thought. He stood stiffly, chest out ready to fight. A hand waved out from behind a tree but Jama didn't move.

A man in white Somali robes came out into the open, he smiled, he looked familiar. Jama squinted at the face, trying to place it.

'What do you want?' Jama shouted over.

'Don't you recognise me?' With a sad smile the dark figure beckoned for Jama to follow. Jama picked up a jagged rock and followed the apparition; they didn't talk.

It took Jama a long time before he accepted who had that dancing stride, those long fingers that clicked gently with every step, that face that carried the blueprint of his own. 'Father, it's too late,' Jama said.

Guure led Jama away from soldiers, crocodiles, leopards, to sanctuary; it was all he ever would do for his son. Jama cried when the apparition disappeared near a burnt out village, he searched amid the scorched tukuls, stepped over cold ashes, spilt pots and lost shoes. He entered the skeleton of a hut, only to jerk back at the sight of a young child cowering in the corner. Jama turned to run away from this village of ghosts but the young boy ran after him, grasping at his shorts. Jama stopped and looked at the boy, his ribs hung out, the skin on his old man face was loose and his eyes were like two large moons but he was definitely alive. Jama opened his knapsack, retrieved flour and his water flask, stoked up a fire and began to prepare bread. While he worked the child stuck to his side. He had finished the water in the flask, and now silently watched the bread take form, Jama felt no warmth emanate from him. As soon as the bread cooked, the boy grabbed it from the fire.

Jama towered over him, he could not have been older than seven. Jama shook his head and asked him, 'Why are you here?' the boy was still laboriously eating.

'I am waiting for my family to come back,' he sobbed.

Jama had not seen civilians for days. 'They won't come back,' Jama said flatly, holding out his hand for the boy.

'What is your name?' Jama asked as the boy put his small cold hand in his grip.

'Awate,' he replied.

'Come with me, Awate, I'll take you somewhere safe,' Jama said, unable to leave this small human spirit in the dead village that his father had led him to. Awate knew of a town nearby and directed Jama as he carried him on his back, holding him too tightly around the neck. Awate had been playing in the woods when bombs had fallen on the village and had run back to his tukul to find his mother and brothers gone; he had been alone for days and he clung now like a leech to Jama's skin.

Jama and Awate fled into the lowlands around the Gash river. By the time they reached the date palms of Tessenei and stopped their trek, the British had taken control of Italian East Africa. The Italian jackal had shed its fur and teeth but left many dead Africans in its wake. Jama went to the river, bathed his feet, closed his eyes and rested on the quiet bank, he tied weights to the images of corpses, burning men and lost eyes lodged in his mind, and plunged them to the bottom of the river.

Gerset, Eritrea, July 1941

Jama waited a long time for Abdi, hoping that
he would come around the bend one day, a
little dusty, a little thirsty but otherwise well.
Sometimes casualties were brought to Tessenei on stretchers after stepping on mines or
triggering a booby trap. Jama would rush out
of the shop to see the victim's face but they
were always Eritreans. Jama wanted to search
for Abdi but the countryside was now a
battleground for militias and shifta. Shidane's
grave was a meeting place for bandits who
gathered under his shade to share their loot.
Jama wondered if Shidane's ghost had called
them to him, his spirit sitting beside them in
delight as they counted and plotted. After
shifta attacked Hakim's shop, shoving their
pistols into Jama's face and grabbing sacks of
grain and money, Jama remonstrated with
Shidane and they never returned. Ordinary
Eritreans were also in a warlike mood now
that Italian power had been revealed as
nothing more than a magician's trick, every
man and boy had a pistol, rifle or grenade.
When Italian prisoners of war passed through
Tessenei they hid their faces from the men

they had tortured and the women they had raped. Even after the carnage at Keren, the ascendancy of the European was jealously guarded by the British, who protected the Italians from any vengeance. When bandits attacked Italian villas or shops, British troops conducted house to house searches until weapons and suspects were handed over.

Jama lived a simple existence in Hakim's shop, quietly watching the world pass by, everyday routines, miracles and tragedies turning the machinery of his life. He felt no joy or misery just a deep yearning for all the things he had lost. The war was over but it had taken everything with it, and reduced his world to an island of peace surrounded by a sea of blood. Former askaris came to the store and made chit chat with him, some drank too much, some pretended to have forgotten all about the war but still there was the never-ending inventory of lost souls. 'So and so died of shrapnel wounds', 'Tall Mohamed was hung', 'Hassan was ambushed by shifta', 'Samatar went missing'. Jama could not stop listening even though he was sick of death; he wanted life in its purest form, like birds had, not this stunted thing that the askaris endured. Jama asked the men to look out for Abdi and to tell him that Jama Guure was waiting for him in Tessenei, but Abdi had disappeared, flown away on invisible wings.

Jama listened to the neighbour's cockerel sound its alarm, its crowing muffled by the other morning sounds, buckets of water sloshing, fires crackling, men and women greeting each other, mules braying, babies crying. Hawa came limping into the store, an old woman wrapped in red cotton. She heaved and panted her way in. On her back was a sack of chickpeas and her muscular arms threw the heavy load at Jama's feet.

'Good peas, the best I've grown in a while, I'll want a special gift from you, my little Somali,' she said holding out her hand.

'If I was the boss, you could have anything in the shop, auntie.'

Hawa waited for Jama to weigh the sack and hand over her payment of sugar. He was always generous, giving an extra spoonful to his regulars. Hawa tweaked his cheek and placed the packet of sugar under her arm. It would take another hour for her to walk back to Gerset, and her home in the Kunama settlement. The sky was clouded over, threatening a downpour.

'Stay here, Hawa, wait for it to come and go,' said Jama lighting a cigarette, phosphorus and tobacco sharp in his nose.

Hawa trundled back to him, closing her eyes to breathe in the smoke. 'Give us one, you naughty Somali, or I will report you to the boss.'

Jama broke the cigarette in half and gave her the lit end. 'It's the last one,' he said apologetically.

He thrust the other half behind his ear and checked for rotten fruit in the piles delivered by local farmers that morning. Most of the bananas and oranges were stunted little specimens, bruised and misshapen. He removed the ones that were overripe and shared them with Hawa. As they ate, the rain began, the first real downpour of the rainy season, and the wind blew in spraying them with water. Awate came running in, on his way home from the schoolhouse. He was drenched, his thin clothes plastered to his body.

'Jama, I came top in my class today, teacher said if I carry on like this, he will send me to his brother's big school in Kassala.'

Hawa ululated and smoke escaped in spirals from her mouth.

'Manshallah Awate, you will go to Kassala but dry yourself, you don't want to get sick,' Jama admonished.

Awate lived near the shop with an adoptive Tigre family but he visited Jama every day to grab sweets and share his achievements. His face had filled out and he looked nothing like the wraith Jama had found.

Hakim, the shopkeeper, at first kept a close eye on Jama, 'I've had boys work for me and rob me blind, my rule is any thieves get a taste of my switch.' But he never had to use his switch on Jama and soon left him in charge when he went to buy stock in Kassala. Although he had the largest store for miles, with villages nearby producing all kinds of crops, Hakim was not a natural capitalist, constantly giving his spoilt children money from the day's takings and keeping the best meat for his family. Jama sometimes thought that Hakim only had a shop so that he could have an endless supply of delicacies to shove into his small, wet mouth. Tessenei was a hub of international trade, loot from the homes of Italian colonists was traded for goods from Egypt, and askaris sold their Italian weapons to Abyssinian shifta. Kunama farmers and taciturn Takaruri hunters exchanged their produce for cloth, coffee and sugar, the Sudanese presiding over this mercantile frenzy like referees at a wrestling match. They opened caravanserai and bazaars and sold their sizzling kebabs at every corner. Jama was known to them and everyone else as the little Somali who could speak many languages. Jama picked up Kunama in the shop and would translate for the rural women in disputes over the quality of their vegetables or their debts. All kinds of people came to the shop. Once a man burst in, carrying a spear and shield, wearing the lionskin of an Amhara warrior, only to shout 'Waryaa inanyow!' to Jama. He was no Amhara but a full-blooded Somali, a Haber Yunis man from around Hargeisa who had ended up in Abyssinia and fought against the Italians. He took off the sweaty lion pelt and chatted with Jama about the desert, camels, and his plan to join the British navy in Egypt. Before sunset he picked up his mane, spear and shield and disappeared towards Sudan.

Jama spent two years working for Hakim without pay; he traded his labour for something to eat and somewhere to sleep. On that coffee-scented floor he became a man, his arms and legs no longer able to fit comfortably in the nook, he felt like an elephant trapped in a goat pen. Jama wanted to try his luck somewhere else, Hakim tried to persuade him to stay but Jama had made up his mind. Hakim reached into his pocket and gave Jama exactly two pounds for his seven hundred and thirty days of toil. Awate cried when Jama told him he would be leaving and held onto his long legs to slow him down but Jama prised him off. 'I'll be back, Awate, you can be my coolie when I open a store,' he promised.

Jama explored the local villages looking for one isolated and poor enough not to already have a Sudanese stall. It was a bleak journey. Roads were still blocked by burnt out tanks, minefields were hidden under weeds and bones thrust out from shallow graves. Finally, Jama found Focka concealed in a lush valley; it was a tiny village with barely twenty families who trekked to Tessenei for the merest of things. When the little Somali came to visit and spoke of his plans, they nearly nailed him to a stake to stop him escaping. Amongst the matriarchal Kunamas, women like Ambaro, Jinnow and Awrala were everywhere, bossing him about, giving him unwanted advice on how to build his stall, teasing him about his strong muscles and exotic looks. The villagers were excited to have a foreigner in their midst and Jama's palm frond-covered stall became the talking shop, tavern, and in the evenings, dancehall. Tired and sweaty, young men would come in from the fields and untangle their muscles in wacky dances they named the pissing dog, the hungry chicken, the rutting ram, all the while getting limp on honey mead and running up large debts at Jama's stall. The elders would occasionally perform epic sagas from Kunama history. To satisfy his customers' desires and avoid the high taxes, Jama would hire a camel and take the risky night route through the desert to Kassala. He cherished these expeditions, his pale clothes glowed in the moonshine and sand grains glinted like diamonds in his path. The white-hot stars were so bright they nearly burnt him, and the moonlit dunes would undulate and swim as he was rocked into somnolence on the camel's back. Jama would be jolted awake when he heard the laughs of hyenas following him, the snap of their jaws as they bit at the camels' long thin legs. Smugglers were a delicacy to local hyenas and on this long isolated stretch if a smuggler was thrown off his startled camel he would have no hope of rescue; they would pounce and leave nothing behind.

With smuggled Sudanese cigarettes hidden under his clothes, Jama would return triumphantly to the village. He was never caught by the Sudanese police and doubled his takings with the cigarettes. He expanded the stall until second-hand shoes hung from their laces above his head, paraffin lamps glowered like squat policemen at his side and homemade perfumes wafted out of scavenged glass bottles, oily love potions in dirty green and blue bubbled vessels. Everything Jama sold brought the glamour of the outside world to Focka. Under the eternal woods of overgrown Baobabs and fragrant Tamarinds, a village was being shaken out of a daydream, the magic of oil and coal made life easier, faster, dirtier and Jama's stall offered as much of the outside world as he could carry. When the harvest was brought in, people gasped at the lewd fecundity of the earth. Carrots long and rampant jumped out of the earth, red saucy tomatoes pouted and beckoned from their vines. Emerald citrine, and ruby peppers shone from dowdy wicker baskets, and the lambs, the lambs, shouted and boasted all the way to market. Women carried baskets full of eggs as big as fists on their heads to Tessenei. Focka, only Focka had been blessed, the rest of the villages in Kunama country revealed sullen sacks of gnarled vegetables and sour fruit at market. The people were angry, the farmers of Focka were keeping the lucky Somali to themselves. Women met in all the villages, hushed secret midnight conferences took place.

'Poison him with cobra spit and then bring him here for the cure,' counselled one old woman.

In another village a woman offered herself as the honey trap, but in Gerset Hawa told them to offer Jama land in return for his sorcery.

Jama accepted Hawa's offer of two acres,

but promised the people of Focka that he would keep his stall there. He borrowed a mule from a neighbour and with his blanket, tools and cooking utensils on the mule's back he headed for Gerset. The women had cleared the ground for him, rich soil, damp to the touch, combed through like his mother's black hair. It was a beautiful sight to behold, the first real wealth of his life and he paced along the perimeter, measuring the distance from one corner to another. It was a large open-handed gift from the women and he kissed Hawa's hands in gratitude. The women built him a hut, singing 'Akoran oshomaney' as they worked, 'Don't let your friend down'. They finally left him alone to work his sorcery, but he didn't know what to do. Protected from view by exuberant banana trees, he bent down and picked up handfuls of soil and rubbed it against his arms and legs, it was cool and soothed his hot skin, he brought it to his nose, it smelt of trees and their breath, he tasted it, iron and blood. In his revelry he walked around Gerset, the women smiled and waved as he wandered, he felt wonderful amongst these trusting Amazons, their beautiful village untouched by war, hidden from Ferengi maps. They stopped to welcome him. There were no titles in Gerset, no masters, or lords, not even misses; respect was given freely, equally, generously, all were descendants of Queen Kuname. The men were out with the cows and there was quiet apart from the shout of dogs, coughs of goats and the chuckling of lambs. Tired and thirsty he reached the village shop. He pushed the curtain aside, his footsteps soft, padded by unswept dust. A girl sat behind a crooked wooden counter, her head on her arm, snoring with fat flies buzzing around her head. He approached and she jumped, quickly wiping the drool from her chin. She was beautiful, two sloe-black eyes and red ripe lips atop the long neck of a gerenuk, her pure brown skin set off by yards of carnelian and amber beadery, she had been polished with butter and cream. Meeting her startled antelope gaze, Jama shuffled up to her and asked for a cup of milk and with swift, dancing steps, she went to the old cow in the back yard and milked a cupful.

'Good afternoon,' said Jama, his heartbeat skitting.

The girl nodded to him, she emanated light like a Coptic saint on a church wall but her expression was more suspicious than beatific.

'Where have you come from?' she finally asked, her voice deeper than he expected. He could smell honey on her breath.

'You name it, I've been there,' he smiled, she smiled back, that was it.

★ ★ ★

Bethlehem Bighead was a mule, a Tigra father and a Kunama mother, Muslim and Christian, born in a cowshed, a shepherdess in the morning, a farmer in the afternoon and shop girl in the evening. With a head full of dreams and fantasies, she would pluck lavender and jasmine and come home with blooms in her braids but minus a goat, only to be beaten and sent back out into the darkening hills until she had found it. Her giant, black thicket of hair earned her the name Bighead, and she wore it like a crown of thorns, pulling at it throughout the day, plucking strands from her eyes, from her mouth, from her food. When her sisters jumped her, they used her hair as a weapon, forcing her head back with it and dragging her across the dirt by it. Her mother would sometimes put an afternoon aside to laboriously braid it, laying it down into manageable rows like their crops, before like a rainforest it burst out of its manmade boundaries and reclaimed its territory. She was a true village girl in that she wanted nothing more than to live in a town. Already sixteen, she had to wait for her five older sisters to marry before she could escape. Jama's face came to her now before she fell asleep, his deep, hypnotising eyes saddened her, and there was something about his lost and lonely bearing that made her want to suffocate him in her bosom.

From her perch on the hills, amidst the bleating goats, Bethlehem could see Jama in his turban planting seeds. He was clumsy with his tools and to her amusement he would pull seedlings out of the earth to see how much they had grown. He was trying to stare them into life, she thought.

When she brought the goats back down, Bethlehem sidled past his field. 'You're not doing that very well you know, you shouldn't plant them so deep, they need to see the sun through the earth.'

'Why don't you come and help me then,' Jama said, stopping to stare as she walked past.

'Eeeee! You wish!' she squealed before striding away.

Jama studied the cycles of her day, he loved to watch her make her yawning advance up the hill in the dappled dawn light. She was a spot of red climbing up the grey green horizon, her faithful retinue of stinking goats shouting after her. At midday, as the sun rose she would descend and begin work on her mother's fields, he could smell the flowers in her hair long after she had passed, her ramrod-straight back holding up that black flag of hair. Jama would wait until she was in the shop in the evenings before going to buy his eggs and milk, they talked by paraffin lamp while her family ate dinner.

'What did you do before coming here?' she asked once.

'I was an askari.'

'How stupid you must have been,' she taunted, holding a blade of grass between her fingers in imitation of his cigarette.

The womb light of the lamp made them both braver, able to talk about things that bright daylight or deep darkness would have prohibited, Jama told Bethlehem about his parents and she listened with the attention of a sphinx. In return, to cement their intimacy, Bethlehem described to Jama how her father kicked her for daydreaming and losing goats, how she had never been bought anything her whole life but only given her sister's hand-me-downs.

'Not one thing, Jama, can you believe that, never one thing for me only.'

Jama shook his head in sympathy and touched her hand; she let him for a second before pulling away.

Since Jama had arrived in Gerset, Bethlehem never went out with dusty, chapped feet but massaged them with oil every morning. She pilfered her eldest sister Maria Theresa's coin necklace, earrings and silver anklets, hiding them until she got near Jama's farm, when she would put them on. Scintillating past until he was out of sight and they could disappear back into her pockets. One day her hair was in agrarian rows, another day in two bunches, on yet another she would plait the front and leave the back out, Jama enjoyed the coiffures which gave her face different shapes and moods. As they became closer, Jama rose before the sun to wait for her in the hills where they could spend a few hours together, before the village came to life and began its watch. He waited happily in the cold holding fresh sprigs and blossoms for her, a shiver running through his body when she stepped out of his infatuated mind and became flesh again. He was awkward and giddy around her but she did not complain, she watched him intently and pulled straw out of his hair.

'I have never felt like this before, I feel possessed,' he told her, and she glowed in pleasure.

One dawn, as they sat talking, a deep murmuring came from the skies, a torrent of rain and hailstones fell upon them, bhesh, bhesh, bhesh, land slid down the hillside.

'Mary protect me,' screamed Bethlehem, desperately trying to gather her terrified goats, the earth tore away her anklets and submerged her knee deep in mud.

Jama climbed a fig tree and pulled her out, she was so close he could feel her heartbeat thumping against him, Bethlehem buried her head in his neck while he tugged her free.

'Come, let's get into that cave,' he commanded, she ignored him and ran after the goats, Jama chased them towards the cave and only then did she follow him. The mammoth granite hillside split into a cavern that had all the elegance and delicacy of a cathedral, stalactites fell down like censors and the light playing on puddles dappled against the high dome. Bethlehem said a prayer and kissed her rosary.

'Don't worry it will be over soon,' reassured Jama.

'Will you marry me?' Bethlehem asked, cold and shivering.

'Yes,' replied Jama putting an arm around her shoulder.

They made a loveseat out of the living rock and imagined their new life together as rain washed the old world away. Overlooking, however, was Rumour, she that flits between sky and earth, who never declines her head in gentle sleep, and with swift wings she took flight to disturb the peaceful repose of the villagers.

Jama, Bethlehem and the goats returned to Gerset, to stares and whispers. Bethlehem kept her head high, believing herself to be practically married. She left Jama by his field and went home. Her mother was sweeping goat droppings away from their door.

'What took you so long, Bighead? You should have come home before the rain started.'

'Mama, Jama and I are going to get married,' Bethlehem announced.

Her mother screeched and threw away the broom. 'What is this! What will people say? What have you done?'

'Nothing, mama, we just agreed,' Bethlehem stuttered.

'You will decide nothing without consulting me. I don't want that little Somali sniffing around you, people are already talking, you don't know anything about him so just stay away.'

Bethlehem didn't stay away. She went to Jama's fields and helped him, picking out weeds and checking for blights. The earth was pregnant with so much produce that, come harvest time, Jama employed two more female labourers, offering them a share of the crop in return. Bethlehem's mother walked her to the field and collected her at dusk, but all day the lovebirds could witter as much as they wanted, he described Aden, Hargeisa, Asmara. He did not have to describe Keren to her, the silver markets still glinted in her mind from her trips there as a child. Jama spoke about places but he didn't speak about people, all of the places he described were ghost towns which he traversed alone. He never mentioned Shidane or Abdi, but they were there in his stories, imperceptible shadows that walked beside him. There was a moment at dusk when a cool breeze blew, the leaves shook and rustled, and Bethlehem stretched her back in front of a golden sky, that made Jama melt; but within moments Bethlehem's mother would arrive and march her away, leaving him to return to his cold hut alone.

The women of Gerset brought gifts to Jama's hut, his sorghum plants had towered so high and so strong that twenty women were brought in to help cut them down. The women's harvests were also greater than they had ever been and they showed exuberant gratitude, they brought him a goat, blankets, sweetmeats, figs, all of life's little luxuries. Even Bethlehem's mother came to him bearing eggs, and she smiled tentatively, appraising him all the time. Jama surreptitiously kissed the amulet around his neck; the magic the women saw in him was nothing more than what his mother would scatter on him from above.

The harvest was so abundant that Jama could pay Awate to look after the store in Focka, saving him the back-breaking donkey ride every day. The smuggling trips to Sudan continued but now he could pay for more expensive items, petrol, silver, gold. He was the wealthiest man in Focka, and the second wealthiest and arrogant after Bethlehem's father in Gerset, he was given more land and kept on his female workers. Jama was almost complacent about his talents now. He thought all he needed to do was throw a few seeds in the earth and he would be richly rewarded. Bethlehem became the lady of the manor, watching over the women, overseeing their work, tutting and clucking around them until they complained to Jama. Everything went perfectly, the sorghum grew high and straight and shivered and sang in the breeze. Young men came to admire his fields and store because he was the boy their mothers told them to emulate.

Amidst all the flattery Jama could not hear the whispers of locusts flying towards Gerset. Millions upon billions traversing the miles with a blind hunger fell upon the village without warning. The ugly warriors came from the Nile valley to ravage the rest of Africa. The farmers lunged at them with torches as they ate crops, the roofs of tukuls, through baskets to get at hidden grains and pulses, even the food out of children's mouths. What they didn't eat they maliciously defecated on, poisoning everything. Jama tried to throw cloths over his crops but they ate the sheets as he laid them down and his workers ran away to save their own fields. Within minutes all that was left of his farm were stiff stubs where the sorghum once stood and piles of locusts that had died in the frenzy. Jama ran through the ravaged village, staring dumbfounded as he went from bare field to empty field. The women screamed and rent their clothes, it was too late to pray, to do anything. Children would go unfed, debts unpaid, animals would have to be slaughtered before they starved to death. In his mind, Jama cancelled the debts that the distraught women owed him.

He went to find Bethlehem in the hills. She ran to him, she had been crying. 'I saw them from here, I was so frightened I thought they had eaten everyone! They blotted out the sun, Jama!'

'They have destroyed everything we worked for,' Jama said, taking her hand. He walked her back to Gerset to see the damage.

It was a backwards miracle, instead of God creating something from nothing, he made something into nothing and the suddenness of the destruction kept women wailing in shock. They believed in discipline and patience but all of a sudden that didn't seem to matter anymore. Bounty could be reduced to penury in the blink of an eye.

Jama and the women of Gerset put their shoulders to the plough, they pooled their resources and worked from dawn to dusk collectively. Bethlehem was relieved of her shepherdess duties and she and her mother worked side by side, in Jama's field as well as the others. There was no joy in the work, only furrowed eyebrows and dirty hands. Jama had lost most of his appeal to the local women but a modicum of magic glittered around him; they kept him around as a totem of former hope. Bethlehem became desperate and fearful, worried that the man she loved would fail again. The month of the long rains was late coming, but then came a sickly, squalid deluge that formed stagnant pools in which mosquitoes copulated and multiplied.

Jama's malaria had come back every year since he had been infected in Omhajer but this year he was as weak as an old man. Bethlehem's mother advised putting a cup of sugar in water, leaving the mixture in moonlight and drinking it in the morning, but it just gave him nausea and sore teeth. Many people were falling sick, Bethlehem collapsed at the farm and was carried home; when she returned to work, she told Jama that a medicine man had been sent for. He had asked her where the pain was, she pointed to her stomach and he bit it so hard that he had drawn blood which he spat out and read for clues. To her shame he diagnosed love-sickness and said he had no cure for that. Fortunately, the people were agitated and distracted from everyday gossip. Heavy rains brought locusts, they consulted oracles, sacrificed livestock, prayed to their goddess, but they were not heeded. Like a curse, locusts again darkened the sky. In one day the harvest was destroyed and Gerset beggared, the life and soul of the village, the proud giant sorghum, reduced to yellow stumps.

Jama felt ashamed. The high hopes invested in him now seemed misjudged and he took the locust plagues as a personal punishment. He remembered the story his mother used to tell him about a king who had become insane and was thrown out from his palace to wander the desert, telling insects and scorpions of the sumptuous life he had once lived. Gerset was a different place now, all the men had left to find labouring work in Kassala, and the women called him the eunuch in the harem. He was nothing but a sickly eighteen year old with a fluffy moustache, they laughed. Bethlehem was abused for the airs and graces she had assumed as his betrothed and the only solution she saw to this disparagement was a swift wedding.

Everyday Bethlehem cornered him. 'Well, Jama, go and find work so you can pay for my dowry.'

Jama began to fear her, her desperate eyes burning into him, her tongue sharper with each hesitation on his part.

'I should have known you wouldn't understand anything about how real families work,' she shouted, 'do you understand how you've made me look? Chasing after you, working on your accursed farm for nothing, you have made a fool of me, you stupid foreigner.'

As Bethlehem tried to tie Jama to her, the urge to escape grew stronger and stronger; despite his love for her he resented the way she had laid claim to him, as if he didn't have a past or a future without her.

In the calm solitude of his tukul, he opened his father's cardboard suitcase for the first time since leaving Omhajer. The musical instrument he now recognised as a Sudanese rababa, the toy car was covered in orange rust that made the tiny wheels squeak against his fingertips, and the other paltry detritus of his father's life seared his heart. His loss came sharply back to him and that night he stayed awake in the dark, pinned to the dirt floor by grief for everyone he had lost. Surrounded by his father's belongings, Jama began to imagine himself as his father's sole legacy, everything that once had been his father was now contained in him. It was up to him to live the life his father should have lived, to enjoy the sun and rivers, the fruit and honey that life offered. He picked up the rababa and strummed its five strings, imagining the tunes his father had played to his army friends on their long marches. Jama couldn't put the rababa down, it sat against his thigh and played him, it sang to him and brought memories back. Memories that had lain dormant since infancy, his father's hair, eyelashes, the glint of his startling teeth all came to him in detail, he could feel his father's stubble tickling his breastmilk-fat stomach and the head-rush of being held upside down.

Jama's revelry was broken by Bethlehem pushing her way into the tukul. 'What are you doing? You've been in here for two days,' she demanded, he had lost all measure of time playing the rababa.

'I've brought you some food.' She shoved a dish of sorghum porridge into his hand and then began her lecture. 'The women want their farm back, they need the land. You are going to have to find labouring work, Jama, the Italians are back in Tessenei, you know their language, go get a job.'

'They're not back, it's the other ones, the British,' Jama said patiently.

'You go ask anyone, the British put the Italians back in charge,' persisted Bethlehem vehemently. Jama stayed silent, unable to believe the news.

After eating, Jama picked up the rababa and played for Bethlehem. 'What if I became a troubadour?'

Bethlehem snorted. 'Don't you dare!'

'You don't think people in other villages would pay to listen to my music?'

'If you want to live a low class life like that, I can't stop you, Jama.'

'But you would like to stop me wouldn't you?'

285

'You're a free man, I know that, I just can't see why you would want to do such things, but I forget that you have been brought up in the gutter.'

'Shut up!' he snapped. 'I don't know what's wrong with you, Bethlehem. However good I am to you, you still feel you can wipe your dirty feet on me.'

Bethlehem grabbed her basket and stormed out, Jama could hear her tears but was too angry to pursue her.

Jama carried the rababa with him everywhere he went, he was penniless but not unhappy. In Tessenei were a group of Tigre youths who spent their day roaming around, singing, drinking honey mead and watching the world go by. They spied Jama with his rababa and asked him to join them. With a drum and now a rababa, they roamed the villages around Tessenei, busking at weddings and circumcisions. Jama grew his hair long like them, and it fell to his shoulders in wide black curls. They were wild boys who stripped off and jumped into waterfalls, and gorged themselves on the bounty of nature, wild berries, birds they caught with bow and arrow. Awate admired the new rebellious Jama and waited for him after school, Jama would pick him up at Hakim's shop and carry him on his shoulders to the villages. During daylight they all sat on the granite boulders by the river and tried to sweet talk the washer-girls away from their fiancés.

'Oh, you are beating my heart against that rock,' called out Sulaiman, as he grasped at his heart in front of a giggling girl.

As the day ended they were chased away by brothers and fathers. Jama was carefree for the first time in his life. He had just enough food in his stomach and each day brought adventure and laughter, the boys accepted him the way that only layabouts can, without judgement or demand. He mastered the rababa, making it whine, holler, and pulsate with such a passion that his fingertips swelled and hardened. Awate danced with his shoulders while the other boys sang and played jokes on the audience.

Bethlehem observed Jama's new life silently from her hilltop and brooded over how to reclaim him from the troubadours, but she stomped away from him when he tried to serenade her on the hillside. 'Eeesh! I do not speak to vagrants!' she called.

As Jama walked back from the hills to Gerset, Bethlehem's words followed him. He remembered the rich dapper-clothed seamen in Aden and looked down at himself, at the dirty white cloth wrapped around him and his beaten-up sandals and he was suddenly ashamed of his poverty. Jama remembered the certainty with which Shidane spoke about becoming rich. Unlike Jama, his faith in himself had never wavered, and even as a streetboy he had thought himself a prince whose kingdom had been temporarily lost.

Inside his tukul hidden from the dewy night, Jama listened to rain falling on the straw roof. It beat out a rhythm that pulsed all over the village. He lit the last of Bethlehem's frankincense, its fragrant smoke warming the hut, and stretched out his tired limbs. He was somewhere between sleep and consciousness when in the dim light he saw tendrils shifting and dancing. A man took shape from the arabesques of smoke, extricating himself from the urn like a jinn from a lamp. First his hand appeared, then a thin torso and legs wrapped in ashy robes. He stepped delicately out of the hot coals and approached Jama.

Jama felt a rush of cold blood in his veins as the man touched his face and left a streak of black on his cheek. The man was beautiful, every eyelash, every wrinkle was perfectly formed from blue, black and grey smoke, within his dark eyes was a pinprick of light, like the lamp of a lighthouse seen through a midnight fog.

'Jama.'

Jama didn't reply, his tongue lay dead in his mouth.

'Goode, speak to me.'

Jama looked into his father's eyes, felt the wave of the lighthouse lamp wash over him.

'Goode, this life is a sliver of light between two great darknesses.' Guure's voice was raspy, whispers of smoke were breaking away from him. 'You can not remain here while your fate awaits you in Egypt.'

'Egypt?'

'The world has been broken open for you like a ripe pomegranate and you must swallow its seeds.'

'What of my life here?' Jama asked frantically.

'You will be married with children and grandchildren but you will ride the waves of all the seas and leave your footprints on every corner of the earth.'

Rain came down in broad sheets and battered at the door, cold air blew into the tukul and ripped at Guure.

'Father, why did you leave me and hooyo?'

'I thought my life would be long. I expected so much from it and wanted to come back when I could lay it at your feet, but I was merely a puppet with fine strings holding me up.'

Jama stared into his father's eyes.

'But from the stars I watch you, your mother watches you, we have been beside you during every trial. You have wrestled with misfortune, have fought fate with your small body and our hearts are swollen with pride.'

Another gust of wind threw open the door. 'My time is up,' gasped Guure, his spectral body was torn apart and the lamps of his eyes extinguished, leaving Jama in darkness once again.

★　★　★

The tukul was overwhelmed by the scent of frankincense in the morning and the coal in the white urn was still red hot. Jama put his few possessions over the fire until everything was full of his father's smell. He had no English, no idea how to get to Egypt, but this was not enough to stop him; he finally knew what to do with the small fortune his mother had tied around his neck. He tracked Bethlehem down where she sat forlornly on a rock half-heartedly watching the goats. She gave Jama an evil look as he approached. 'What do you want?'

'I want to tell you something.'

'Well, keep it to yourself, I'm not interested in you anymore,' she lied.

Jama sat down next to her but she moved

away. 'I have been given a message by my father. I'm going to find work like you want me to.' Bethlehem's eyes lit up. 'But it will mean that I have to go to Egypt and spend some time away.'

Bethlehem looked at him as if he had lost his mind. 'What? What foolishness has come over you?' Bethlehem had no idea where Egypt was but she knew it was far from home.

'I'm going to join the British ships and get rich and come home to you,' Jama cajoled.

'Home, home, you won't come home! You will be killed, the hyenas will eat you, you madman!' she hollered.

'Calm down, Bethlehem, one minute you tell me to find work and now this.'

'I want you to get a real job, near here, not disappear to another world because you have been speaking to ghosts! You don't even know where you're going,' she cried. Jama wasn't sure if she was worried for him or was simply angry that he was doing something she hadn't prescribed.

'I could come back a rich man, richer than anyone here, twice as rich as your father, don't you want that?'

Bethlehem's face was wet with tears.

'Why are you getting so crazy, Bethlehem? In the name of God, I'm only trying to do the right thing,' Jama said exasperated.

'No you're not! You want to run away! Just like my mother said you would,' she shouted back. 'You have made a fool of me,' she sobbed.

'If you want to make every decision for me, what's the point of me being alive? You might as well live both of our lives for us. I'm going now, Bethlehem, you will see what I do. Judge me by my actions, that's all I ask, I will come later to say goodbye.' Jama went to kiss her cheek. Bethlehem shook her head violently and pushed him away.

Jama's shoulders sagged as he dragged his dusty feet to Hakim's store. Awate was waiting gleefully for another day with the bad boys but he was to be disappointed. Jama picked him up. 'You know, Awate, when I came to Eritrea I was the same size as you, I was a skinny, desperate little thing, I was never sent to school like you and I learnt everything the hard way. While I am away I want you to finish this school, pick every last bit of knowledge out of that teacher's brain and then go to Kassala. When I come back you will write my letters and read books to me. I will promote you from number one coolie to number one ma'alim.' Jama kissed Awate on both cheeks and set him on the ground, Awate stifled his tears and turned away dragging his school bag along the dirt.

Jama whistled at him. 'Awate, pick up your bag, a ma'alim cannot misbehave in front of his pupil.' Awate held it to his chest and gave Jama a sullen smile.

★ ★ ★

Jama heard a knock on his tukul and found Bethlehem, her mother and many sisters waiting outside for him. Bethlehem had dressed up for the occasion in bright clothes, beads in her hair, silver jewellery hanging from her ears and neck. Her face was angry and red-eyed.

'Greetings,' Jama said hesitantly.

'Greetings' the women replied sourly.

'Little Somali, you have made Bethlehem even crazier than she was. She won't stop crying, she tells me you promised to marry her but are now going back to your own country because a ghost has told you to! She will not eat, work, talk, what can I do with a child like this?' Bethlehem's mother shouted, wagging a finger in his face.

'I'm not going back to my country, I am going to Egypt so that I can return with enough money to pay for her dowry. I'm leaving tomorrow morning,' said Jama, humiliated and unable to look at Bethlehem.

'Forget the dowry, a sane child will be enough. Marry her now, before you leave, it's the only thing that will bring my child back to her senses.'

Bethlehem wiped her nose and eyes, looked pleadingly at Jama.

'I'll marry you, Bethlehem, you are all I have in this world,' Jama said, his heart racing.

The marriage was performed by a group of old women who had some knowledge of the Qu'ran, but everything felt rushed, ramshackle, a goat was dragged over and slaughtered to feed the well wishing gossips trickling in from the fields. Jama and Bethlehem huddled together in awe of what they had just done. The scorn, anger and misery had been wiped from Bethlehem's face and Jama could see her beauty in full luminosity again. She was the most beautiful girl he had ever seen, he surreptitiously held her hand, unable to believe they would now be treated like grown ups, able to do what they liked together.

Jama laughed. 'What's so funny?' smiled Bethlehem.

'I can't believe you've done this,' Jama cackled.

'You can't mess a Kunama girl around, little Somali, let this be a lesson to you,'

Bethlehem said squeezing his hand.

When the women had eaten, they began clapping and singing and Bethlehem taught Jama the dances, flinging her beaded hair from side to side.

'Wah! Wah! Dance, little Somali!' the women exclaimed, surprised that a foreigner could dance so well.

Jama lost himself to the rhythm, Bethlehem's flushed face right next to his, her breath all over him, he danced with his girl until the hyenas started howling.

A procession of sisters, cousins and aunts led Bethlehem to Jama's tukul. She would live there until he came back, a woman of her own. Bethlehem had brought a bundle from her home and as soon as her crying relatives had left, she unpacked and began to redecorate Jama's dusty room. She made the tukul beautiful with bright embroidered cloths covering the floor, straw baskets on the walls and amber and silver necklaces hung from a hook next to a chipped mirror. Jama watched his wife and wondered if she would also be taken from him.

'What are you thinking about, husband?' Bethlehem asked, holding his face between her palms.

'If you will ever leave me,' Jama replied.

'No, never, and I will never let you leave

me either.' Bethlehem put her hand on his heart. 'This is mine now, your heart is my dowry, understand?'

Bethlehem held Jama to her, and he rested his head against her shoulder. He had not been embraced in so long, his flesh had become accustomed only to pain, but now she stroked his scars, kissed his face, brought life and heat back to his cold body.

'Why don't I cut this too long hair of yours? I am meant to be the one with the big hair, aren't I?' Bethlehem asked.

Jama nodded and grabbed his rababa, singing wedding songs while she scrambled around in her bag. Bethlehem had come prepared with a large pair of scissors and she hacked away at his hair until he looked like the young man who had stolen her heart in her father's shop.

'There, you are beautiful again,' sighed Bethlehem.

'You think I'm beautiful?' laughed Jama.

'You are the most beautiful man in Gerset! And maybe even in all of Eritrea. My sisters are so jealous that I captured you.'

'Ya salam! What flattery!'

'By Mary it is the truth, I will never let you escape from me.'

'And I will never let you escape from me, I will bury my heart under your feet. Come let me show you something.'

Jama led Bethlehem outside the tukul, the landscape was lit by a full moon, Gerset was serene and hopeful, a night breeze rustling through the trees. 'You see that star up there, the flickering one, every night before you go to sleep I want you to look up at it and send me a kiss, and wherever I am I will also look for it and send you a kiss. Don't forget, Bethlehem, don't stop until I get back.'

'I won't forget,' said Bethlehem squeezing his waist.

Sudan, Egypt and Palestine, December, 1946

The train cut through nowhere, hurtling past virgin desert. It was British made and inferior to the gliding railway from Asmara. Jama had hitched a ride on the back of a camel to Kassala train station, quiet and morose the whole way. Leaving the tukul at dawn, Bethlehem's hair sprawled over his old mat, he had knelt down and stroked her sleeping face, trying to burn her features into his memory. He could only put his faith in the stars that they would bring him back to her.

Jama had never paid attention to the route Somalis took to Egypt. They were broke, hungry men that passed through Tessenei on their way to Sudan, most could not speak Arabic and were perpetually lost, but he now strained to remember what the more mature ones had said. 'Iskandriya? Sandriya? What was the name of that place?'

He spoke to his neighbours on the train but they were all Sudanese traders returning home to Khartoum who knew nothing of Egypt, they cut him off as he tried to make

298

conversation and talked amongst themselves. Jama looked through the wire mesh that covered the windows and stared at the barren, treeless wilderness beyond the tracks. He bought roasted sesame from hawkers at a small station and, embarrassed by the arcs of sweat growing under his arms, on his back and in his groin, he remained by the train's exit. When his legs grew tired he returned to his carriage, the leather stuck to his skin and he discreetly undid the buttons on his shirt as he nestled back into his seat.

At every stop he stuck his head out of the door, looked around and asked boarding passengers 'Egypt?' Most sullenly shook their heads and hurried past him to find a seat. Hours later after people had performed afternoon, sunset and evening prayers in the cramped carriage, a man who had journeyed with Jama from Kassala called out, 'You need to get off here for the train to Egypt.' Jama thanked him and raced off, holding his father's suitcase tightly under his arm. Crowds were walking towards the station where uniformed policemen stopped and searched them. Jama had never needed identification before, he had no paper saying who he was and where he belonged but from this point on, it would become a priority for him. In this society you were nobody unless

299

you had been anointed with an identity by a bureaucrat. Jama, fearful of the policemen, skipped down from the train as it pulled into Wadi Halfa, ran around the station and followed the curve of a great lake into Egypt. There were no policemen on the border and when he reached Aswan station he bought another ticket to take him north. The train from Aswan terminated in Cairo, and after a three-day journey on hard wooden benches he was dismayed to learn that he needed another train to take him to the great port of Al-Iskanderiya.

Nausea crawled up his throat as the train trundled past the tanneries on the fringes of Alexandria, the smell of dead flesh hanging in the air was exactly like that of the battlefields of Keren. Jama suddenly felt certain that the train would be bombed and go up in a terrible conflagration like the Italian supply trains. Sweat poured down his face and neck, while his heart pounded in irregular beats. Even after the train had slid along the bright blue sea and screeched into the station, Jama sat slumped in the seat like a feverish man, waiting for the panic to subside. Jama began to regret the distance he had put between himself and Bethlehem, he had thrown himself headlong into an intimidating, alien land.

With days of sweat, sand and dirt on him,

Jama first went to the washroom and cleaned himself, washing his shirt in a porcelain sink, the first he had ever used. The wet shirt clinging to him, Jama drifted out into the city, his slight body pushed around by the crushing mass of people outside the station. Jama gazed bedu-like at the beautiful buildings, at their fancy glass windows and colourful tiled façades and floated along with the cool sea breeze to enter the port. Huge cargo ships were gathered together, sounding their deep-throated horns again and again, he would later find out they were celebrating the Ferengi Christmas, earlier and shorter than Bethlehem's. As Jama sat on a bench, tired beyond the point of sleep, a Somali boy sauntered past and sat next to him. Jama could barely make out what he was saying, he hadn't heard Somali for months, but he followed him deliriously. Liban took him back to the fifth floor apartment he shared with seventeen other Somali migrants. The only furniture in the two rooms were stained mattresses piled up in corners, Liban offered Jama a mattress and showed him the damp washroom. From the windows Jama could see over a swath of Alexandria and as dusk fell, lights appeared magically as far as the eye could see. Buzzing in the hot dark like a swarm of fireflies, he finally found Bethlehem's star and discreetly sent a kiss to it. He fell onto the mattress, pushed the suitcase under his head and kept hold of it as he slept.

In the morning Liban took Jama around their neighbourhood. The apartment was in the street of seven girls, a street of rioters and pimps, infamous for the men, women and children on sale behind its doors. They passed sailors, policemen and local Ferengi merchants lurking lustfully in doorways. Alexandria was like the ancient harlot mother of Aden and Djibouti, she had grown rich and now put on airs and graces but in dank, cobwebbed corners her truest colours were revealed. Jama watched the Arabs smoking shishas, the French women, the African waiters and doormen, Greek merchants, Jewish rabbis all moving in their orbits, creating a twentieth-century Babel. A tram scuttled past and Liban pulled Jama on. From the tram they saw the heights and depths of Alexandria. Ships were lined up along the dock, more ships than Jama could remember ever seeing in Aden. They went to a seaman's store on the eastern harbour where Liban pretended to be a sailor to buy a five-penny box of cigarettes and encouraged Jama to do the same.

'We can sell these for six pennies,' Liban whispered, 'enough to buy bread and pay for the room.'

Although small and immature-looking,

Liban was a wily, knowledgeable guide. He had been in Alexandria for a year waiting to join the British navy and was cynical about Jama's chances.

'The British army are based in Port Said, why don't you come with me and see if we can find work there?' Liban asked. Jama was adamant he would stay and try his luck with the merchant navy.

'You don't have a chance, brother, it's nearly impossible to get a passport, and you can't get a navy job without a passport,' said Liban, shaking his head.

As they spent the day together, Jama learnt that Liban was Yibir but in Alexandria, Somalis of all clans fell upon each other for news, companionship and help. Liban had left Somaliland because of hunger and to escape the harassment his family suffered. Even now his British passport was held up in Hargeisa because no elder would claim a Yibir as part of his clan and the Yibir could not appoint an Aqil of their own. In Egypt, Ajis would share cups with Liban, eat with him, befriend him because there was no one to judge them but their acceptance was a vapour that would evaporate under a Somali sun. A Yibir wore the name of their clan like a yellow star, it marked them as low, dirty, despicable. A Yibir learnt from infancy that they had nothing to be proud of, no suldaans to boast about, no herds of camels, no battalions of fighters. In a land of scarcity and superstition, myths were hard currency, and rather than claiming a Sharif, a descendant of the prophet, as their first father, the Yibros had a pagan, an African magician who believed he could defeat the Muslim missionaries. For this heresy they had been cursed to be hewers of wood and drawers of water, to work leather and metal while the Ajis roamed with their noble camels. Even when Ajis wiped their hands after touching him, Liban had learnt to avert his gaze, pretend that it was natural for them to believe he could contaminate them but the further he fled from Somaliland the less his Yibirness mattered. In Egypt all the Somalis wore the same yellow star, their black skin taught the Ajis what it was to be despised.

More Somalis greeted Liban and Jama; all had cigarette packs in their hands, they spent the day in the sun, tiring their bodies so they could sleep soundly at night. Underneath their apartment, on the ground floor, was a cabaret club and music pulsed through the walls up to their cramped apartment. The men sometimes poked their heads into the cabaret where a dancer called Sabreen had befriended them, she was a beautiful Punjabi who they called 'Hindiyyadi', the Indian girl, she had large brown eyes and suggestive lips. Jama's chief pleasure in Alexandria was to creep down at night and watch through the alley window as Sabreen danced cobra-like from the depths of a large basket, cavorting and jiggling in the shisha smoke. Soon Liban began watching her, and then the other Somalis, until Sabreen had a dedicated following of Somali alley cats peering in through the window.

Jama joined in with the daily routine of Liban and the others, buying cheap cigarettes at the dock and selling them for a penny profit. He slipped out alone one day to change his inheritance into Egyptian pounds and never mentioned it to Liban or the others. He had to shred the prayers that had protected the Adeni notes for so long, collecting all the sacred wisps of paper and stuffing them into his trouser pocket. He boasted of his life in Gerset to all and sundry, his shop, his farm, his twenty employees, his beautiful wife. The Somalis humoured him but made alcohol guzzling gestures behind his back.

On the façades of the cinemas were film posters, blown up images of sleek men and their smouldering dames snarling down on the mortals beneath them. Jama stared up at the actors, wondering what they had done to achieve such glory; the film posters drew his gaze more than the statues and grand buildings. He grew a pencil moustache like the film men, so that he looked like a matinee idol playing the role of a man down on his luck. One day he borrowed a black jacket and a white shirt, combed his hair neatly to the side and had his photograph taken in a cheap studio. He stared for a long time at the man in the photograph. He had the same expression as the film men, but his black eyes betrayed him, they were looking ever so slightly up at the sky, waiting for the stars to take mercy on him. Jama took the strange image and thrust it into the clerk's face at the British consulate. 'Give me a passport,' he demanded in Arabic.

Jama was asked to give his name, his address in Alexandria, his birth date, which he made up, his clan and the name of his clan's Aqil, and was told haughtily that he would be double checked by the authorities in Hargeisa. He hesitated before handing over his photograph. He was the first in his family to have this paper twin made. He wanted people in centuries to come to point at the picture and say, 'This is Jama Guure Mohamed and he walked this earth.' He believed he would never die if his face survived him.

'It could take months, Jama, if they ever get back to you,' Liban said as they left the office, 'let's try our luck in Port Said in the mean time.' Jama nodded noncommittally and they sat by the duck pond in the municipal park.

Like Aden, cosmopolitan Alexandria was not an easy place for poor Africans. People looked through them as if through vapour or stared at their bodies dissectingly, commenting on their teeth, noses, backsides. Alexandria belonged to the pashas who walked down streets cleaned for them, past doors held open for them, into hotels and shops where people quivered and fluttered around them.

★   ★   ★

After three months of waiting in Alexandria, Jama was running out of money and patience, on a sultry morning, after a fretful sleepless night, he shook Liban awake. He had ten shillings left of the money Ambaro had given him. His mother's sweat had gone into this money and he wanted something honourable to grow out of it, not this sleazy vagrant life. 'Come on then, let's get out of this stinking place and try our luck in Port Said,' he told Liban.

Jama had no desire to join another army but needed to escape from the poverty of

Alexandria. He spent every day dwelling on the bitterness Bethlehem would feel if he returned to Gerset empty-handed. The apartment was a depressing place now, many of the other Somalis had left for Port Said or Haifa, and those left behind were doomed to return to their villages. Liban and Jama set off on foot for Port Said, eager to spare the remains of their money. They followed the Mediterranean coastline east for more than a hundred miles, passing through the outskirts of many small towns but when they reached Damietta, two Egyptians in tarbooshes approached them, blocking their path. The plain-clothed police officers demanded the Somalis' papers. Liban proffered his fakes while Jama left his hand-me-down papers in his shoe. The Egyptian took Liban's certificates and gave them a cursory appraisal.

'This is shit,' sneered one of them. 'You're not Egyptian, I can tell by your faces that you're damned Somalis.'

'Chief, we were just going to Port Said, to look for work, chief, that's all,' Liban pleaded.

At the mention of Port Said the police officers pulled themselves up, stuck their chests out pugnaciously.

'Working for the British, eh? I see, Gamel, I think we have found two British spies in our country, think of that.'

'Let's take them to the station, Naseer, they will turn their arses inside out.' On the spot, Jama and Liban were handcuffed together and marched into the industrial town. The locals jeered and spat at the detainees and now and again one of the policemen would shove them from behind, they were made to walk in the road amongst the donkeycarts and horsecarriages. A crowd of streetboys followed their progress after the excitement of Jama catching his shirt in the harness of a horsecarriage and being dragged along beside it; the policemen had hollered and blown their whistles in a panic thinking they were running away.

The police station was a grim place, alternately full of shouts and moans and tense silences, they were kept in a room next to the main entrance, an armed policeman keeping guard. The handcuffs were taken off them and Jama's suitcase was taken away for inspection. He let it go sullenly and they sat down to await their fate. Jama was called out first for questioning and they sat him on a broken wooden chair and stared him out. The chief policeman was fat and cleanshaven, his thinning hair stood up in a black fuzz over his head and the dark bags under his eyes gave him a threatening look but when he spoke his voice was even and dispassionate.

'How did you get here?', 'What do you want in Egypt?', 'Where did your friend get the fake document?'

At the end of the interrogation the policeman told Jama that he would be deported back to Sudan and banned from entering Egypt again. Liban and Jama were put on the next train minus Jama's rababa which had been stolen from his suitcase. The whole carriage was full of Somalis who had also entered Egypt illegally, all roamers who had only known porous insubstantial borders and were now confronted with countries caged behind barriers. Some of the detainees had been shuttled back and forth on this train in the past, and were amused when they reached the border to be told that the Sudanese would not accept the Egyptians' 'trash'. Liban breathed a sigh of relief but Jama was furious, he hadn't left Gerset just to be treated like dirt again.

Back in the Damietta police station, Jama and Liban were placed in one of the large cells while the police decided what to do with them. They were locked up with suspected murderers and rapists, thieves and madmen, drunks and drug addicts. Jama and Liban huddled together in terror as the worst men prowled around, casting wild looks at anyone who met their gaze. They had to pay for their own bread each day and water was given to them in small cups that they had to share with men bleeding from the nostrils and ears. At night, hands would go exploring and knives were pressed into backs to extort money or caresses. Jama and Liban stayed awake in shifts so that they could protect each other, Liban had a small pocket knife but the other men had daggers and screwdrivers secreted in different places. The prisoners spoke in a rough dialect that Jama could barely understand but this was a blessing as they were a verbal bunch who grew tired of the two Somalis when they couldn't understand or respond to the insults thrown at them. The balance of the cell was thrown off its kilter when a man unlike any other man was brought in. He was a giant, an African goliath, a megastructure, his head touched the ceiling and each of his thighs were wider than Jama's waist; he blocked out the light as he came in and fury was etched across his face.

'Thieves! Thieves!' he roared at the police, who scampered out afraid that one of those granite fists would come down on them. Veins stuck out all over the new prisoner's hands and over his forearms and neck, his anger sucked out noise and movement from the room. 'Give me my hundred pounds back, you Arab dogs!' he bellowed.

Jama stared up at the goliath, felt his hot breath gust over him and gathered his legs away from the crushing feet. The emasculated Egyptians had gathered in one corner for protection. The prisoner seethed in strange tongues, clenching and unclenching his fists, boxing with his shadow, a wad of tobacco forced into the side of his cheek, a bruise just perceptible along his blue-black jaw.

'Just look down,' whispered Liban fearfully. Jama tried to but his gaze was constantly drawn back to the man, the new prisoner met Jama's eyes.

'What you want, kid?' he demanded.

'Nothing,' muttered Jama, hiding his head between his knees.

'You Sudanese?' he asked. Jama shook his head and hoped the man would reveal where he came from. 'Bastards taking me to Sudan, I don't want Sudan, I live in Lebanon.'

'They took us to Sudan but we were deported from there too, they will probably send us to Palestine now,' said Jama growing in confidence.

'I want to go to Palestine too, will you speak for me? I speak Arabic badly, they don't listen,' said the man tentatively in Arabic. 'Good boy, good boy,' he exhorted as Jama nervously got to his feet.

Jama went to the bars of the cell and called for a policeman. When two policemen arrived, truncheons in hands, Jama explained that the new prisoner had come from Palestine and not Sudan and if they took him to Sudan the border police would not let him in. But they were uninterested and shrugged their assent to deporting him to Palestine as well. Jama gave the good news to the prisoner who picked him and threw him in the air, kissing him profusely on the cheeks. 'I go home to my woman! My baby! My taxi!' he yelled. Back on the ground Jama took the man's hand and introduced himself and Liban.

'My name is Joe Louis, you know Joe Louis, famous boxer? That me!' said the man crushing their hands.

'Joy Low Is,' repeated Jama and Liban trying to master the strange name.

'You speak French, garçons?' Joe Louis asked. 'I speak perfect French,' but Jama and Liban shook their heads.

From that evening Joe Louis treated Jama and Liban like his sons, paying for their food, giving them cigarettes, and protected them. In broken Arabic he told them about his life in Lebanon, he had a French wife, a young daughter and made a nice living as a driver and occasional boxer. He had gone to

Palestine to fight in a match against British soldiers but had got into trouble.

'Palestines bad bad people, everywhere they call me Abid, you know Abid? Slave! Me slave! So I fight, I fight too much, so they call police, take my taxi, and bring me here, dirty Palestines, spit on them.' Every night Joe complained about the Palestinians until Liban and Jama were convinced that they were the most dangerous, bigoted, savage people on earth and were afraid of their upcoming deportation. When the day came, Joe Louis took their arms and they were all put on the train to the border. The armed police played cards and smoked in the carriage, leaving the mostly black deportees to sleep out the long journey through the Sinai desert. Deep in the night, Joe Louis became agitated, fidgeting and looking furtively around him. Jama in the throes of sleeplessness watched him. 'What's the matter, Jow?'

'I gonna jump off train,' whispered Joe.

'Why?' Jama whispered back, aghast.

'They will send us prison in Palestine, I want wife and baby, no wait.'

Jama glanced through the window at the black and silver desert and knew his friend was making a mistake. 'You will die, Jow, you'll never see your wife and baby again,

314

hallas, I also have a wife and she would be very angry if I did that,' warned Jama. Joe looked out at the desert and his face was twisted in doubt. 'Don't do it Jow.'

Joe flung his hands up in frustration. Jama watched Joe out of the corner of his eye but he didn't move, he fell into a heavy sleep, filling the air with his loud snores. Jama wished that his own father had fought to get back to his family the way Joe did. In the morning, a senior policeman entered the carriage, a fat blond child in a strained white shirt and navy shorts holding his hand. The senior policeman stopped in front of Jama and called for his deputy and a man in a crumpled uniform hurried towards him.

'Have these boys been given breakfast?' the boss asked, looking at Jama and Liban's dry white lips.

'No sir,' said the deputy.

'Get them food and water. What have they done?' said the boss.

'They came into Egypt without papers, sir, we are taking them to the Palestinian jail.'

The boss looked at Jama and Liban, like dishevelled crows they sat there, with messy black hair, their thin limbs visible through their dirty clothes, and back to his plump cheeked son.

'Let them go at Al'Arish, they won't

survive prison,' he said before dragging his son into the next carriage.

The deputy kept his word, bringing them bread and water and when they reached Al'Arish, Jama persuaded the deputy with a little of Joe's money to let Joe alight with them. An old policeman was sent with them. Al'Arish was a beautiful seaside town with a yellow beach caressed by white surf. Palms on the shore shook their fronds in delight. They were herded onto a jeep at the police station and swept over the border into Palestine. They reached Rafah in a few hours and the sergeant turned to face them, with a dirty finger poking into their faces he shouted, 'You blacks come into Egypt again and I'll personally make sure that you all spend a year in jail, understand me? Yallah, get out!'

Joe opened the door of the jeep and pulled Jama and Liban out with him, screaming back at the deputy in his own language. Joe took charge now that they were in Palestine, walking them towards a British army canteen he knew from his taxi-driving days. Jama was fearful of the reception they would get from the Palestinians but all they saw were a few old men with heavily-laden donkeys. To the side of the road, Joe saw the walls of an orchard and peered over, he threw Jama and Liban over the top and then jumped over the high wall as if it was a chicken coop. Inside, the orchard was a sight worthy of paradise with bright globes of nectar hanging heavily from green trees. Jama felt as if he had not tasted an orange in centuries. They crept into a corner and ravished the trees, eating orange after orange, they sat in the cool fragrant shade and gorged themselves. The sticky juice ran all over their arms and chests and attracted bees but it was worth it. Before they could doze, they heard the orchard gate scrape open and an old man's lamentful mutterings, and they fled back over the wall. On reaching the canteen, a Palestinian chef raced over to them and embraced Joe wholeheartedly, without any of the bigotry Jama had expected. Joe threw his heavy arm over the Arab's shoulder and led him away to talk quietly. When they returned the chef asked Jama and Liban if they had really worked as galley boys on British ships and they convinced him with enthusiastic tall tales. The chef offered them work in the kitchen.

Joe held Jama's head. 'Petit garçon, you have no problem now, good pay, good food, Allah rewards the kind,' he said, kissing Jama on the cheeks before pulling out money from his pocket and shoving it into their hands. 'Take, take, merci merci.'

Jama and Liban weakly resisted before accepting. Joe stayed for a last meal with them before wandering away with old acquaintances and disappearing into a truck. He gave them a thumbs-up before zooming off into the distance and returning to his wife and daughter. Jama felt as if a mantle had been pulled off his back. As darkness fell, Jama and Liban grew afraid, they were the only Africans in a congregation of Arab men and they had lied to them.

'What will happen tomorrow when they realise we don't know what we're doing?' asked Liban fearfully.

'I don't know, but we've eaten their food now, they're going to be angry.'

The chef cheerfully brought them dinner and laid down canvas sheets in the storeroom for the night. 'See you bright and early, boys, I need the best of you two.' Jama and Liban smiled and nodded at the chef, pretended to bed down but instead they sat up, waiting for the dawn. When the first slivers of light were visible through the barred windows, Jama and Liban grabbed their meagre belongings and ran away. They were afraid of the Arab soldiers but more importantly they had not left home to work in a canteen in a Palestinian border town and their destiny demanded another throw of the dice. They avoided the road, walking along the sand dunes, just keeping the stretch of road in sight. They had made a mistake in not bringing food and water and by midday they needed to rest under a tree.

'You only see a dead man resting under a tree,' panted Liban. The gravity of their situation was beginning to dawn on Jama when a group of dark men appeared in the distance.

'Police, police!' hissed Liban. 'Quick, behind the tree!'

Both Jama and Liban nudged the other, believing their harsh breathing would give them away, but it was the banging of their heartbeats that seemed so loud. They could hear footfalls and voices a few metres away; the language sounded strange to Jama, guttural and accusational, and it took him a few moments to recognise it as Somali. He poked his head out and saw Bootaan, Rooble, Samatar, Keynaan and Gaani from the flat in Alexandria walking past, arguing amongst themselves.

Jama ran out after them. 'Waryaa! Waryaa! Wait for us!' he yelled.

The men looked back in shock before falling about in laughter. 'Would you look at them, you look like jinns,' laughed Rooble, picking leaves out of Jama's hair. 'What happened to you?' he asked.

'We got jailed in Port Said and they brought us here,' said Jama, delighted. It had been a deep worry to him that no-one knew where they were, Bethlehem would never know what had become of him.

'Where are you going now?' asked Gaani of them, as if they were crazy children.

Jama and Liban looked towards each other, 'We don't know,' they said in unison. The older men, older only by a few months or years, tutted and shook their heads. 'First get to Gaza, there is a Somali man always at the bus stop, Musa the Drunk, he will find you. Tell him to put you on the bus for Sarafindi and in Sarafindi there are four Somali men working for the British, one of them is your people, Liban, and one yours Jama, but they will all give you money and then you can go where you like,' counselled Samatar.

'Yes, that's right, that's what you should do,' agreed the others.

They pointed out the way to Gaza and then turned back towards the Sinai. Jama and Liban followed the route the men had cursorily pointed out. Most Somalis avoided sharing the precise routes and tricks that they hoped to benefit from themselves, they did not want to be beaten to a ship, and careless words might put border guards on their trail.

They turned away from the road when they heard an army truck approaching, but it was travelling so fast it was upon them in seconds.

It slowed down beside them and Joe Louis stuck his head out of the passenger window, squinting in disbelief. 'Jama? Liban? Garçons? Where you walking to?'

Jama and Liban raced each other to the window to explain their predicament, Jama forced his voice over Liban's, 'He was a very bad man, Jow, we woke up in the morning, worked for him and then he sent us away, he wanted to give the work to his Arab friends.'

Joe kissed his teeth. 'So where you want to go?' he asked.

'Gaza,' replied Liban, annoyed that Jama was doing all the talking. Joe pulled them into the truck and took the wheel from the driver. He rushed them to Gaza bus station, tearing past the checkpoints in the powerful and unquestionable army vehicle. Liban slept next to Jama, his head thrown back in exhaustion, while Jama massaged his painful feet and revelled in the power and luxury of driving in a motor car. The Bedu walking along the road, dragging their donkeys behind them, looked infinitely hopelessly poor in comparison. Joe drove at dangerous speed but was a born driver, an equal match for any hazard the road jinns threw up; he drove with one hand, his face relaxed and content, staring at the open road. Joe let them out at Gaza bus station and with a paternal slap on their cheeks he disappeared for the last time.

As Samatar had said, Musa the Drunk quickly found them. They shared the same mishmash of features as him, an awkward alchemy of eyes, noses, mouths, hair textures and skintones that belonged to different continents but somehow came together in their faces. He was completely incongruous in the quiet bus station, a shabby middle-aged Somali man, barefoot and balding, with the sharp smell of alcohol emanating from somewhere about his person.

'My sons, my sons,' Musa slurred, staggering with alarming speed towards them; he shamelessly scratched his balls before grabbing them in a fevered embrace. Jama and Liban were embarrassed by him, they looked terrible already but his company gave their appearance another level of seediness and destitution. Musa was lonely and talkative, the poster-boy of failed migration, his thick ribs stuck out from a soiled, buttonless shirt, he spoke little Arabic and had zero interest in what the locals thought of him. After listening to their story, Musa ushered them to the stop for the Sarafindi bus, they sat on a bench, stinking in the sun,

Musa talking loudly and obscenely, 'I've had her', 'I've done her', 'He wants me'.

Jama and Liban cringed beside him and feared he would attract the police to them but the Palestinians completely ignored him. Jama gave Musa money to buy food and he scuttled off to their relief, they took all the deep breaths they could before he returned and brought his miasma back. Sitting with him depressed Jama. As Musa continued to talk he could see the remnants of what had been a sharp witty mind, but it had been pickled in gin and blunted by isolation.

Musa told them how he had ended up in Gaza. 'I have worked for the British all my life, I was their donkey, but most of the time a happy donkey, I learnt how to read and write English. I got a good wage, lived in nice quarters, had a household back in Somaliland, but they sacked me, my wife divorced me, and I have stayed in this bus stop for some years now. Whenever I want to leave, I will just take one of these buses.' As Jama listened he could see his own life taking Musa's terrible trajectory, see himself forever poised to try the next place, only to belatedly grasp that the good life was not there. Jama looked at Musa and realised that not even a mad man would have left everything he had on the advice of a ghost.

'You can't force your fate,' mused Musa.

'Come with us to Sarafindi,' suggested Liban, but Musa shook his head silently, adamant that he had business in Gaza.

Jama started to question his own journey. He had spent all the savings his mother had left him, was living on what charity others gave him in a strange hostile land and had no realistic hope that he would ever become a sailor. The bus came while Jama was in this funk, and he boarded it simply because he had nothing else to do. Musa ran alongside the bus waving and panting, but Jama didn't wave back.

'What a fool,' Jama seethed.

'Oh leave him be, poor man doesn't know today from tomorrow.'

'That's his own fault,' Jama argued.

'No, that was his fate. Who knows, it could be ours.'

'I would rather die,' thought Jama, he was in a belligerent mood, a Shidane mood, his patience and optimism exhausted.

'You Ajis always think everything is owed to you.'

'What?'

'Deep down, you're surprised when things don't fall into your lap,' Liban persisted.

'You don't know what I've been through, Liban, nothing has ever fallen into my lap!'

'It has, think about it, you have a strong clan behind you, someone, wherever you go, will give you food and water, will think you're important enough to milk their camels for.'

'Liban, shut up, what camels are you talking about? From the age of six I slept on the streets in Aden with any passing maniac liable to drop a rock on my head. You had a father watching over you, a mother, sisters, cousins,'

Liban stared at Jama, lightning in his eyes. 'Yes, I had a father, a father who could only watch as my mother was beaten up by an Aji, for a goatskin of water she walked miles for!'

'Ooleh! shut up you two!' yelled the bus driver. Liban moved clumsily to a seat at the back of the bus.

'Suit yourself,' yelled Jama.

★ ★ ★

Sarafindi was a town holding its breath, within a few months it would be a ghost town with stray dogs sleeping on mattresses and storing bones in the deserted kitchens. If only a place could speak, or howl or bark a warning. In April 1947 the women of Sarafindi collected olives, gave birth, drew water from the well, and arranged marriages as they had done for hundreds of years on their native soil. The soil in which their mothers, fathers and stillborn infants were held. But Sarafindi held a secret; during the hot, quiet summer, a rolling black barrel filled with explosives and fuel would trundle along the main dirt path and stop outside the beyt al-deef. After the blast would come men carrying machine guns, ordering everyone to leave. Destroying the old mudbrick homes with grenades.

The sprawling British garrison was the only clue to the coming tragedy. Jama and Liban waited sullenly outside this garrison for the Somali askaris. 'I'm sorry that happened to your mother,' Jama said.

'I shouldn't have shouted at you, brother.' Liban held out his hand, Jama took it and shook it hard.

They spotted the askaris late in the afternoon, three Somali men in their thirties and forties in tidy uniforms. The askaris knew the procedure; they each gave a pound to the boys and Jama's clansman walked them to where the other Somali worked. The clansman's name was Jeylani and like the others he repaired shoes, holsters and other leather goods for the British soldiers; he was a former nomad who had been taught how to work leather by Mahmoud, the Yibir man they were about to meet.

Jeylani was not impressed by Jama and Liban's escapades. 'Go home, boys, you look intelligent, I know you speak good Arabic but don't waste your lives being pushed around in Arab lands. Go home, there is nothing for you here, there is going to be nothing but violence. My advice is that you head into Jordan, then Saudi, do your pilgrimages and then get a boat home. Every day I see boys like you fleeing from God knows what.'

Jama listened carefully to what their elder was saying and nodded in agreement, but Liban walked on ahead with his wide, optimistic strides, certain that he would never return to Somaliland a poor man. Mahmoud was a kind, relaxed man, with deep wrinkles across his forehead, he poured tea for them and asked how they had found him. He smiled knowingly at mention of Musa the Drunk, and was quick to give his share of the langaad, tipping Liban with an extra pound as Jeylani had done with Jama.

Mahmoud took a deep breath and said bismillah before biting into a slab of bread and meat. 'I was just telling these boys to go home, to stop wasting their time here,' Jeylani said.

Mahmoud waggled his head. 'Oh, they won't stop until they have tried and exhausted their luck. I didn't either, only after the seventh failed attempt to cross to Port Said did I give up,' Mahmoud laughed.

'Each time I walk, they pick me, I walk, they pick me up, my feet were cut to shreds!' he said lifting up his black army boots. 'If you two are desperate to get to Egypt and have better luck than me, I will tell you everything I know, no-one knows that route better than me.'

Then Mahmoud began a finely nuanced recital of roads that led to Egypt, referring to an internal map that included humps in the sand, electricity pylons, noteworthy birdnests, forks in sandy paths, shallow marshes in the Red Sea. So detailed, in fact, that Jama and Liban had to ask him to repeat everything from the beginning, they could not read or write but they memorised everything with a skill only found in the illiterate. He ordered Jama and Liban to follow the coastline of Palestine during the day and sleep in villages at night, and to avoid any wealthy areas.

With the few pounds they had collected in their pockets, they left Sarafindi and began to walk. Jama was still tempted to turn in the opposite direction and go to Jordan and then Mecca but Liban would not hear of it and deep down Jama was frightened of going alone. Only later in life do we see the tugs of fate with clear eyes, the minute delays that lead to terrible loss, the unconscious choices that make our lives worth living; fate told Jama to head west rather than east, and with that all those old prophecies that had followed Jama, of wealth and incredible voyages, became flesh.

The Palestinians they came across were not recognisable from the portrait of irascible bigots that Joe Louis had painted. Each night Jama and Liban turned inland and went to the nearest village and each night they were accepted and led to the beyt al-deef, the guesthouse for strangers that every village, however poor or remote, maintained. The hospitality was usually brisk and business-like but very generous; every household brought something, bread, water, meat, eggs, milk, fruit, dates, rugs and blankets. No questions were asked of the strange boys and no one reported their presence to the police, they treated Jama and Liban as otherworldly spirits who would report their compassion or meanness to a higher authority. The growing tension between Jama and Liban dissipated in the comfort they found in the beyt al-deef. They talked late into the night about the lives they had left behind. Liban had been born into a family of musicians and had served in Eritrea, somehow managing to avoid the battles; if he weren't Yibir his life would have

been enviable. Liban was cheerful, thoughtful, selfless, he revived Jama's spirit and
brought back his belief in a different kind of
life to the one he had struggled with. The
journey to the Egyption border was almost
fun. The long day's walk gave them a purpose
and they competed to see who could go
faster; at night they relaxed and enjoyed the
good food. Near Khan Yunis, they stopped to
rest at a village and found a wedding in full
flow, the guesthouse occupied by a band
armed with ney, darbucka, oud and kanun.
They hovered at the entrance listening to the
songs until the singer beckoned to them to sit
down and they crept in. The music thumped
at the walls and glided over them and out
through the window. After a large meal of
mansaf, the men went out to perform the
dabke, twirling handkerchiefs over their
heads. The musicians whipped the guests into
a frenzy, the beats on the darbucka working
faster and faster, until Jama and Liban lost all
shyness and added their feet to the dancing
centipede. Unlike in Somaliland and Eritrea,
the men and women celebrated separately,
but the chants and piercing ululations of the
women could clearly be heard even when
the men began to tire and drift away.
When the bride arrived, she was a sight to
behold, seated sideways on an elegant horse,

her head covered by a shawl twinkling with coins, her proud mother, aunts and sisters flanking her in gorgeous dresses. Bethlehem would have looked so beautiful in those clothes, thought Jama, regretting his own rushed wedding. The bride took all attention away from the musicians and only then did they quieten down, playing delicate wedding songs as Jama and Liban laid out their rugs under the stars.

They walked beyond Khan Yunis and a few days later crossed the border into Egypt. They kept clear of Al'Arish, and almost ran to Romani, delighted to find there the pylons that Mahmoud had described. It was the last outpost of civilisation before they crossed the Sinai Desert, there were no more villages to sleep or be fed in. By the sea at Romani they nervously approached a group of fishermen resting around a fire, pushing each other to speak to them. Jama asked them for any leftovers they might have but they gesticulated to the empty bowls and fish bones. One man passed over his bowl and Jama handed the tiny handful of rice to Liban, expecting another bowl to be forthcoming, but there wasn't, and within a few seconds Liban had wolfed it all down. Jama would have kicked Liban if the fishermen weren't watching, but they watched and laughed at the choked-down annoyance in his face. They passed fresh water to Jama and he drank enough to fill out his stomach before handing it to Liban.

'Where you boys from?' they asked.

'We're Egyptian, we wanted to find work in Palestine but the police told us to go back, so we're walking to Port Said,' Liban lied, afraid they would alert the Camel Corps.

From Romani to Port Said was the deadliest, most treacherous part of the journey. There was just sea on one side and murderous desert on the other, they would not be able to find food or water, and if they were caught by the midday sun or the police they were finished. Mahmoud had warned that Somali skeletons lay on that stretch of sand, and it was the most perilous journey of all the journeys in Jama's life. Liban and Jama decided to rest hidden in the sandbank until sunset, so that they could travel in the cool night and evade the Camel Corps. Sunset came and they scuttled out of the sandbank like crabs, the moon lighting the way forward and the crash of waves applauding their progress. The realisation that they had forgotten to buy food and water was a dreadful one when it finally came to their awareness, but they felt superhuman, unable to turn back.

Jama turned to Liban and said, 'If I can't

walk with you, don't wait. GO! And if you can't walk, I won't wait for you, I'll go on so at least one of us can survive.' They shook hands and carried on side by side.

Neither fell back, their desire and hunger were too strong, their paces identical, unstoppable. In sixteen hours they walked more than forty miles, they resembled two slivers of soul light more than men made of flesh and blood. They broke the tenets of human survival; dehydrated, starved, exhausted, they did not stop, they would not stop until they got to Port Said. The land began to fragment into reedy marshes as they reached the end of the Sinai. Jama and Liban held on to each other when they saw how close they were to their promised land, the white light of the Port Said lighthouse was calling them in.

A salt lake yawned between Port Fuad on the east and Port Said on the west, Mahmoud had told them it was too deep to cross except at one point, where the pylons were planted on each bank. Mahmoud's memory was photographic and as he had said, the water between the pylons was shallow and thick with salt, they waded slowly across, both frightened of the water that reached above their waists. Jama crossed the waters of the Red Sea with his father's battered suitcase held up over his head and his heart in his mouth. They reached the other bank panting with relief and excitement, they had performed a feat of human endurance, but the Nubian man shouting 'Hey, Hey!' and running at them with a stick had no concern for that. The Nubian chased Jama and Liban, caught the weak men in his strong hands, put them in a car and drove them to a nearby villa.

He went and told the manager that he had found two layabouts crossing his water, but he was in no mood for action, his hair was stood up, sleep in his eyes. 'I don't give a damn about them, look at the time! Don't wake me up again, you fool.'

The Nubian sheepishly led them out of the villa. 'You want to buy me a tea?' he asked audaciously, but they were so happy to be let loose that they agreed.

The last task was to cross the Suez canal and with the pounds given by the Sarafindi men, they bought two boat tickets.

'Mahmoud said it was gate 10 for the garden, didn't he?' checked Jama.

'Yes,' guessed Liban. All they knew was to head for a garden where there was a teashop frequented by Somalis.

'We'll sit apart in case one of us gets caught,' ordered Jama as the boat arrived. He sat next to a Bedouin and made small talk to calm his nerves.

'This is gate 10,' said the Bedouin man at last and Jama signalled to Liban, bade the Bedouin a safe journey and disembarked. Liban wanted to rest on a park bench but Jama was unable to stop, he was a bloodhound with a scent, and he led Liban out of the garden and finally to the teahouse.

'Oh God, it cannot be, you little hoodlums!' the crowd shouted as they caught sight of Jama and Liban. Jama looked around as if in a daze and saw all the boys he had met outside Rafah, the ones who had told him to go to Sarafindi in the first place. They had made the same journey across Palestine a week earlier and were still recuperating. 'Tell them the news then,' said Gaani, his face full of mischief.

'The teashop owner has some bad news for you,' said Keynaan gravely.

Jama's knees buckled. 'What?'

'I'm sorry to say both your passports have arrived and are waiting for you in Alexandria,' the chai wallah boomed.

The men picked Jama and Liban up and threw them into the air, cheering and singing.

Jama and Liban held hands over the men's heads and shook with hunger and happiness. They knew they might now make something of their lives.

Name: Jama Guure Mohamed
Date of Birth: 1/1/1925
Eyes: Brown
Hair: Black
Complexion: Man of Colour
Nationality: British
Place of Birth: Hargeisa, British Somaliland

This thin description of Jama in the dark green passport was all that the western world needed to know about him; he was a subject of the British Empire. The passport determined where he could go and where he couldn't, the ports where his cheap labour would be welcome and the ports where it would not. In Alexandria, Liban and Jama were constantly asked by the other Somali boys to show their precious passports. The documents were passed around in awed silence. Jealous boys leafed through the pretty watermarked pages and fingered the embossed lion and unicorn on the cover, stared at the black and white snapshot, scrutinised the cross that Jama had made as his signature, wondered if they could do it better.

'You're going to become Fortune Men', 'No more jail for you', 'Sell it to me' they said before handing the passports back.

Liban and Jama were now gentlemen; all they needed was a job to enter the richest caste of Somali society. Stoking the boilers of steamships could earn them in a week more than they had lived on in a year. To find work they rode the train back to Port Said, leaving Keynaan and the others still waiting for their passports in Alexandria. Liban sat back in his seat, smiling at the countryside running past the train confident that the British Consulate would now save them from harassment. Neither Jama nor Liban knew anyone in Port Said but they expected to turn up and find a ship ready to take them aboard. The reality would turn out that way for one of them but not the other.

Liban and Jama found lodgings with other prospective sailors, and the word was sent out that they were looking for work. A Somali elder who had remained in Port Said after losing an arm aboard a British ship was the local headhunter, spending his days arranging work for clansmen. As Ambaro's clansman rather than Guure's, the Somali elder was not compelled to help Jama but he called him in for an audience. Liban was less fortunate, he was the only Yibir in all of Port Said and with scarce work for Aji Somalis, he was locked out of the old nomad's network. As Jama was shuttled from one meeting to another, Liban was left to wander around the docks, looking for work as a stevedore or panhandling for food. With a useless passport in his pocket he thought of the walk from Romani with growing bitterness as a failed escape from a family curse. The Somali elder had found an Eidegalle sailor on a British ship sailing to Haifa and the sailor was sure that with a certain kind of sweetening, the captain would take Jama as part of the crew. The Somali elder arranged a collection and raised five pounds from Jama's clan, this was smuggled to the ship's captain, who then signed Jama on as a fireman. Within sixteen days of collecting their passports from Alexandria, Jama had his first navy job and Liban was wondering where else in the world he could go.

Jama gave Liban all the money he had before departing for the ship. 'When I come back, brother, I'll help you find a job,' said Jama.

Liban nodded as if he believed him and embraced Jama in his new shirt and trousers. 'Take care of yourself,' said Liban, hiding his envy and sadness.

Their goodbye was protracted and uncomfortable, Jama kept trying to reassure Liban. 'Who knows! Maybe when I get back you'll be away working.'

'Go man, don't keep him waiting,' said Liban finally.

* * *

Jama's clansman walked him to the ship that had taken nearly a year of his life to get to. She was a leviathan, the tallest, longest, greatest thing he had ever seen, stretching like a steel town along the canal, her black hull bobbing gently in the water. Near the prow of the ship, stencilled in white metre-high writing was 'RUNNYMEDE PARK LONDON'.

Jama stopped at the gangplank and took a last look at Africa. Beyond the faux European skyline of Port Said lay his heart and home, the mountains and deserts of Somaliland and the valleys of Bethlehem. He knew that if he died this would be the last thing he saw in his black eyes. The hot red dirt of Africa, scintillating with mica as if God had made the earth with broken diamonds, would not be found anywhere else. But like the Somali women in Aden, Africa struggled to look after her children and let them run with the wind, giving them freedom to find their own way in the world. Jama placed both feet firmly onto the *Runnymede Park* and waited to be borne away.

Exodus, May 1947

'I think this is going to be a strange voyage,'
said Abdullahi, Jama's clansman. Abdullahi
had been told at first to expect a short trip
to Haifa then Cyprus, but on the journey to
Port Said he had seen the captain in huddled
conferences with military men. He took Jama
to the cabin that they would share: a small
porthole funnelled in light and two bunk beds
with thin mattresses stood with a night table
and lamp between them, five-star accommo-
dation by Jama's standards. There were
twelve Somali firemen to stoke the engine
and the rest of the crew were white British
men, all senior to the Somalis. Jama was the
youngest on board apart from a slip of an
English galley boy with fine blond hair.
Abdullahi took Jama from fore to aft, into the
holds, around the engine room, through
the coal bunker, past the steering room to
where the lifeboats hung lifeless. Jama was
happy, happy, happy, and when Abdullahi
presented him to Captain Barclay, he
genuflected, curtsied and held onto his hand
as if it was the hand of the emperor of the
world. Jama's pay was set at £19 a month, a

quarter less than the British sailors, but still a fortune to a boy who had once fought cats and dogs over bones. Jama asked what they would be transporting. 'Jews,' said Abdullahi.

Jama's work could not have been simpler. He had to shovel piles of coal into the giant furnace in the boiler room while a trimmer wheelbarrowed the coal in from the bunker and deposited it at Jama's feet. Four hours of work, eight hours of rest; by the time they had reached Haifa in Palestine, Jama had fallen easily into the rhythm his life would run by for the next fifty years. In his hours of rest, Jama observed the construction of a cage on deck. A small lavatory block had been built inside the cage but that was the only sign that it was being made for human habitation. Haifa port was a battleground when they docked, five hundred gunners of the British marines stood alongside tanks, trucks, military jeeps, their guns aimed at a broken-down steamship renamed *Exodus* 1947 and the unruly Jews onboard it. Four thousand refugees were trying to force open the British quota into Palestine and were in sight of the Promised Land. The *Exodus* had been rammed by three British ships, including a navy destroyer, and it now lay motionless like a gutted whale, with Jewish refugees peering out of its bowels. The refugees from Auschwitz, Bergen-Belsen, Treblinka were once again separated from their belongings and marched into shacks where they were sprayed with DDT and pushed onto the waiting prison ships. The hard young men and women on board the *Exodus* had to be forced from the wreckage with baton and gunfire and three corpses were bundled by the British into waiting ambulances. Jama watched in amazement as thousands of bedraggled people trudged towards the *Runnymede Park*, towards his pristine ship, old men hobbled along as best they could, while children with lost eyes stifled their tears. They looked nothing like the turbaned Jews of Yemen, these pale, haggard people. They looked over their shoulders, at the black jute sacks of clothing, food, jewellery and mementoes that the British had prised off them and dumped haphazardly on the dockside, a desperate cry rang out when part of the pile collapsed into the water and sank to the bottom of the sea. Eighty Royal Marines boarded the *Runnymede Park* along with the refugees, the glossy young men with tanned skin and sun-kissed hair squashed under red berets seemed like a different species of human to the thin, angry former Europeans they were pushing into the hold. After the Haganah zealots had been identified and placed under guard, women, children and the elderly were allowed on deck. Some refugees had salvaged all the clothes they owned from the jute sacks and now they peeled them off, clothes from their past lives, from the death camps, from the DP camps, their history folded into a few items beside them. Unlike the marines who only had eyes for the bewitching Hungarian girls with the sorceress green eyes and wide feline faces, Jama's attention was caught by a woman sat boulderlike by the railings away from the other refugees. She was heavy-set but made larger by the woollen coat she continued to wear in the heat, an infant slept at her breast, and something about her gave Jama a powerful sensation of Ambaro. It was as if his mother had been transplanted onto the ship. For a long time Jama watched her stare into the sea, unconcerned with the hustle and bustle around her. She adjusted her headscarf and cast a weary look over the potato sacks that contained her worldly goods. Jama could feel she had been through something terrible but would stubbornly survive it, just like his own mother would.

'Oi sambo! Stop mooning at the white women and get back to your cabin,' yelled the donkeyman at Jama, beckoning with his thumb to the hot cabins below. Jama, only understanding the tone and hand gesture, turned to obey his superior.

'Leave him, Bren, he ain't hurting anyone,' called down an engineer who had observed the exchange. Jama loitered by the metal steps to see if he could decipher what the Ferengis were saying about him.

'Poor fella, yer true to yer title, Bren, you ride those Mohammeds as if they were donkeys. My 'eart goes out to 'em, poor, puzzled, uncomplaining, ostracised buggers never complain,' said Sidney the Engineer.

'I've got to, matey, they might be quiet but they're conniving bastards, they'll have our jobs and our birds as soon as we turn our backs,' replied Brendan the Donkeyman.

'Good luck to 'em, if I owned these ships I'd employ 'em too, they're like fucking barnacles, however bad it gets they hang on. Don't see 'em bellyaching like you paddies, live off a stick of incense a week or a whiff of an oily rag, ain't surprised the bosses wanna keep 'em on. As for our women, you know you ain't that scrupulous in your dealings with coloured girls when we dock in Bongo-Bongo land either,' teased Sidney.

The cabin rocked Jama gently to sleep, the distant roar of the engines and sea becoming part of his dreamlife. He had the top bunk and his dreams often made him leap from it;

he would wake up suddenly on the floor with a sore hip or elbow. It was usually hyenas that pursued him, frothing at the mouth as they pounced, or Italian gunmen kicking in the door and opening fire at him with machine-guns.

Small muscles had formed on the top of Jama's arms and his cheeks had filled out with the regular meals. Good dreams consisted of feedings that never ended, dish after dish served on the plastic trays he had grown to love. The white steward would smile and proffer the strange canned beef, the sweetcorn, sardines, freshly baked bread. The hot noisy inferno of the engine room never appeared in his dreams but dominated his waking life, every eight hours he went down and fed the glowing fire, communicating over the scrape of shovel and coal with hand signals and lip reading. The ship was a world propelled forward by Jama and the other Somali firemen, an ark with more than two of each, English, Irish, Scottish, Somali, Polish, Hungarian, German, Palestinian; the *Runnymede Park* carried them all on her back away from the Promised Land to an unknown shore. The Jewish refugees had been told that they were being taken to a camp in Cyprus, but that was a lie, Cyprus lay far behind them and they were heading for Europe, to be made an example of. The eighty marines kept a close watch on the young men and women, fearing the Haganah militants amongst them. At night a huge lamp was shone into the cage and over the Mediterranean, casting a ghostly eye over the bundled families and mysterious sea. The refugees were separated, with the most virile and threatening held under guard in the hold. Women, children, the elderly and sick were allowed on the deck to visit the hospital, to prepare their meals of rotting army rations, and for the elderly to teach Hebrew to the children. There was little interaction between the crew and the refugees, but one day a determined-looking man made a beeline for Jama and presented a navy sports jacket with gold buttons. 'You buy!' he declared.

Jama tried the jacket on, '£1,' Jama held up one finger and through hand gestures the Jew and the Somali haggled hard, to the death, until they agreed an acceptable price and shook hands.

That was the only time the refugees acknowledged Jama, usually they looked through him with a baleful expression of suspended animation, of people caught between life and death. Even the children had suspicious adult gazes, demanding chocolate without childish gaiety but with a bullying tone learned in the camps. The woman who had reminded Jama of Ambaro was forever on deck, her overcoat folded underneath her large bottom. She had two daughters around six and eight years old as well as an infant son and her girls were the happiest on the ship. Jama gave them the Bourneville chocolates he bought in the ship's store. The mother never noticed when they ran up to Jama and pleaded for the red and gold wrapped chocolates he kept in his pocket, neither did she help the women prepare the rations during the day. Instead she sat with her face upturned to the sunlight and ignored everything.

Haganah activists circulated secretly amongst the passengers. When a careless marine told one of them 'We're sending you bastards back to where you came from', the news spread within minutes and created a kind of millennial hysteria. 'Palestine! Palestine!' was the chant. The refugees had borne the filth, heat, worm-infested soups, fungusy crackers, and varied deprivations quietly for three weeks but now they exploded with angry yelling faces, painted gentian violet to heal the blisters and rashes that had erupted onboard. By the time the ship docked at Port-de-Bouc in France, a swastika had been painted over the flying union jack and the marines had to force the seething purple masses back into the cage. Each day there were bomb scares and the marines treated all of the refugees as potential terrorists. The British refused to give the refugees water and rations in the hope of forcing them to disembark and in response a hunger strike was defiantly declared. The British pleaded and threatened, the French tried to mediate, but the refugees were adamant they would only disembark in Palestine. One woman had given birth in the cage and Jama could still see her lying in her blood and gore, her baby wrapped in a dirty rag from her skirt. He did not understand why they would not get off the dirty, hostile ship. If he had not bent with circumstances he would have been broken by them, but these people seemed to want to be broken or at least did not care. The hunger strike fizzled out with the arrival of manna on launches operated by Haganah agents and paid for by American Jews, each day crates of Irish stewed steak, French sardines, American evaporated milk, Assis jam, French baguettes were brought aboard. The marines bayoneted the cans, to prevent smuggling they said, but mainly out of jealousy as they were still eating the army rations. Even the crew looked on in envy at the refugees' food aid. Books were also delivered by the launches, torahs, novels, dictionaries, the British confiscated these fearing the propaganda secreted within them. Food was the only succour the refugees had. Even the weather had turned against them, it was the hottest summer on record in the south of France and the holds became ovens, the steel walls scalding bare flesh, the air fetid and unbreathable. The British were called Nazis, Hitler Commandos, the *Runnymede Park* a floating Auschwitz. On this floating Auschwitz, the sailors and soldiers fished, sunbathed, and swam in the Med in their free time, just as SS men had frolicked in the death camps.

After the heat came the deluge, a four day storm that forced all fifteen hundred refugees into the holds. The sky was black, strong winds tossed the ship from east to west, rain poured through the grills and the holds filled with inches of bilge water mixed with vomit. The British Nazis waited for the storm to break the refugees' spirit but still they refused to leave. While the refugees relived the Old Testament on the *Runnymede Park*, Jama and a few Somalis went on shore leave. A bus took them to Marseilles and Abdullahi showed them around. They went down touristy Rue de Joliette, along Vieux port, ate in La Canabiere and ended up in the seedy Ditch, in an African bar run by a Senegalese man. An American named Banjo sat by them and played wild songs, the Jelly Roll, Shake that Thing, Let My People Go. Jama danced Kunama-style to the strange music and the bar filled with black sailors from the West Indies, United States, South America, West Africa and East Africa. Banjo introduced them to his friends Ray, Dengel, Goosey, Bugsy and a pretty Habashi girl called Latnah. There was no need for translation between them, they were spiritual siblings, that they had washed up in this bar to spend the night together was all they needed to know, the money that passed from the sailors to Banjo and his friends was irrelevant.

The twenty-eight days docked in Port-de-Bouc passed quickly, spent either in Marseilles with Banjo and the other panhandlers, or on the ship sleeping and resting. The British crew drank the days and nights away, arguments breaking out like summer storms and when they were particularly violent, Jama would lock his cabin door and cower in bed. The Somali firemen would force him to open the door and tell stories to calm his terror, of lands where the men dressed like women and women married trees, of sailors thrown overboard after petty arguments, of stowaways found too late. One of the sailors had earned the epithet 'Grave reject' as he had survived three torpedoed ships during the war, appearing on the surface of the water as if by magic even though he was unable to swim. Another sailor had been to Australia and met an old Somali man living alone in a desert outpost; he had arrived in the last century as a camel trainer and now couldn't remember a word of Somali. Australia, Panama, Brazil, Singapore, these were names Jama had never heard before, they might as well have been describing moons or planets, but these countries were now part of his world. Then they started to talk about women.

'The thing is, you can't trust women, look at the kind of job we do! We're gone too long, they end up thinking that we've forgotten them, so they forget us,' Abdullahi said.

'That's not true,' cut in Jama.

'What do you know about it? The only thing you do in bed is piss yourself!' jeered Abdullahi.

'I'm a married man, with a wife ten times more beautiful than yours!' shouted Jama.

'Oh yeah, well if she's that beautiful and delicious, you have left your dinner out for another man to eat,' snorted Abdullahi. Jama turned his back to all of them and sulked.

For all their stories, the sailors had to admit that Jama had chanced upon a very remarkable ship for his maiden voyage. On the twenty-eighth day, very distinguished men with medals covering their chests came onboard and read out a declaration to the assembled refugees. Through the many interpretations of the Somalis who had a little English, Jama learned that the British were threatening the Jews, giving them a day to surrender or be taken to Germany. One Somali said that the Germans were the arch enemies of Jews, and this was a very grave threat that the Jews could not ignore. To show their serious intent, the British handed out leaflets to the refugees and wrote the threat in many languages on a blackboard, when the British finished talking, the Jews defiantly applauded and went back to the cage. That night launches filled with Haganah agents sidled up to the boat and with megaphones encouraged the refugees to stay onboard. The British silenced them with a siren but it was too late. The next day as the six o'clock deadline approached, only a solitary self-composed little girl, around twelve years old, left the ship. The rest stood to attention like legionnaires under their general, Mordechai Rosman, a partisan leader who had led a band of fighters out of the Warsaw ghetto. With his long hair and bare bony chest, Rosman looked like an ancient prophet lost amidst the modern world, where the Pharaoh had gas chambers, the Promised Land was subject to United Nations resolutions and only desperate Somalis tried to wade across the Red Sea.

With only one less passenger, the *Runnymede Park* set off for Hamburg. Despite their defiance, something had been lost amongst the refugees, they finally realised that they were prisoners, in no position to negotiate or barter, and worst of all they felt alone, as if the world had forgotten them. More children were born on the way to Gibraltar, where the ship refuelled. These babies were prisoners of the British, but also of their parents' dreams. Jama was back to work but even he was infected with the melancholy of the refugees, a ship full of heartbroken people has a particular flavour, a certain energy that is hard on the soul. Jama only had to look into the faces of the refugees to be sent back to his own nightmares, to feel again deep fear, despair and self-hate. The refugees had been treated like animals, had been mocked, beaten, degraded by men revelling in their power, as had Jama, and that humiliation never left anyone. It sat on their backs like a demon, and these demons would intermittently dig their talons into their flesh and remind them of where they had been. Jama approached the large lady one day, her daughters didn't run around anymore, just sat quietly next to her. He pressed a couple of chocolates into the mother's hand, she hid them in her bra and took Jama's hand, her large brown eyes read his palm while he tried to remember his words of Hebrew.

'Shalom!' Jama said.

'Shalom,' the woman replied, stroking the lines on his hand, she nodded her approval; she saw a good life in his hands.

Jama pointed to his chest and said, 'Jama.'

The woman held out her hand, 'Chaja.'

★ ★ ★

At seven in the evening the refugees gathered on the deck, all but a few women on laundry duty found whatever space they could to sit or stand around the cage. These meetings were called regularly to solve disputes between the refugees, or between the refugees and the British but sometimes the people gathered just to talk and sing. Jama, Abdullahi and Sidney were the only crewmen who seemed interested in these powwows, and they joined the refugees whenever they were called. Under the glare of the searchlight, ghostly figures complained about the mothers who did not clean up after their children in the latrines, the noisiness of the

British marines walking along the duckwalks at night, sometimes even disputes from the war or before the war were brought up. An old man in nothing but his undergarments was squaring off with a much stronger bare-chested man.

Jama asked Abdullahi what the old man wanted. 'He says this young man stole his property before the war.'

Sidney was laughing at the amateur boxers, as were some of the refugees, but Jama worried for the old bearded man. His bony legs could barely hold him up but he persisted in shoving and enraging the younger man.

The old man cried out in English, 'I used to be somebody! I had a name that was respected, I owned a farm, a flour mill, a forest!'

The men were separated and a young woman stood up to speak. 'I knew this man in Poland, he was a friend of my father's, he taught Hebrew to my sisters and me. When the German and Polish soldiers came, he saved my life. He hid me in a barrel in his flour mill while the rest of my family were walked to the river and shot. I saw their naked bodies floating down the river. If it wasn't for this man I would be in that river with them, if he says this man stole his property then it is the truth.'

German burghers spoke after Hungarian farmers and Red Army soldiers, some described pre-war lives of furs, chauffeurs, governesses while others had only known the misery of pogroms, bitter winters and poor harvests. Even now, good fortune was sprinkled haphazardly and confusingly, many refugees had lost forty or fifty members of their family while others were still huddled with their children and parents. Abdullahi translated as much as he could for Jama while Sidney scribbled things down in a little notebook. The children were given time to speak, a little girl with a crooked back told the people that her family had fled to Uzbekistan during the war and when they had tried to return to their village in Poland her parents had been attacked and killed. She was now one of the many frail orphans onboard the *Runnymede Park* who believed that Palestine would be a land of peace and milk. All the refugees spoke of Palestine as a kind of paradise where orange trees grew and birds sang, it had no relation to the poor Arab country that Jama had passed through.

Chaja stood up, waiting for her chance to speak; she was impatiently tapping her feet, grasping her son to her hip. A young Polish partisan was speaking about the need to fight for a Jewish homeland. Many of the young people had been part of Zionist groups in their villages and their hunger for a homeland now coalesced with a desire to avenge their families. The partisan seemed unable to see a future without more violence, more battles, more ghettoes, more blood on the streets. 'If they do not let us live on our land, we will crush them like ants, we will smash their heads against boulders and walls,' he said in heavily accented English.

Chaja pushed him aside and stepped under the huge lamp. 'I have lived through Polish hell, Russian hell, German hell and now British hell but I swear by God that I will not condemn my children to Palestinian hell. I have lost my husband and son already, watched their ashes blow out of Nazi chimneys, I want peace, just peace, give me a little scrap of wasteland as long as my children can eat and sleep in peace. My father was a philosophy teacher but my daughters cannot even read, you think they can learn while you are fighting and smashing heads? Take your violence and murder to people who have had enough of comfort and peace. I want nothing from guns and bombs. You think you are David from the bible but we are not your worshippers or subjects. In Palestine there must be no war, if there is war we may as well stay in Poland, or go to Eritrea, Cyprus or wherever the British want to send us.'

Chaja spoke until her throat was raw and thick veins stuck out along her neck, she brandished her baby like a weapon, thrusting him at the partisan. Jama barely understood what she said but he was moved by her, the partisan looked so weak beside her, if Jama had to follow either one of them he would follow Chaja. He had seen how strong women were better leaders than strong men. With the Italians he had learnt how to destroy but the women of Gerset had taught him how to create and sustain life.

The refugees remained quiet after Chaja's speech, they nursed their dreams of peace and dreams of war in silence. They were in an airtight bubble on the ship, cut off from the rest of the world, unable to comprehend real life any more; farms, school-houses, synagogues were all things of their imagination now. Eventually a teenage boy pulled out a harmonica and played to them, children clapped and sung 'Hatikvah', serenading their fearful parents with sweet wavering voices.

Jama, Abdullahi and Sidney clapped along. Jama remembered sitting as a child beside his father under the gigantic moon of the Somali desert. Old men dominated the evenings talking about trade and clan disputes until they grew tired, then the young men would take their place to sing love songs and recite poetry that gloried in the richness of their language. Jama wished that his mother had had her chance to speak out like Chaja, to show those men all the workings of her wonderful mind and all the courage in her heart.

★ ★ ★

The journey to Hamburg brought back all the memories the refugees had been suppressing for months, choked down by fanciful ideas of a Palestinian Jewish heaven. On German soil there could be no denial of what had happened, the smell of burnt corpses returned to nostrils, and the pain of unending hunger tormented stomachs whatever food they were given. Brendan the Donkeyman had no time for the refugees, he called them 'smelly ungrateful yids' and encouraged the soldiers to take a hard line with them. The soldiers were angry and resentful; they had been duped along with the refugees, having been told that they were only to escort the ship to Cyprus. Now, they vented their frustration whenever they could, shoving the children, refusing small requests and talking loudly as the prisoners tried to sleep. It was a quiet ship that approached Hamburg, the long, slow funeral march had come to an end. 'We have returned. We have returned to Auschwitz and Bergen-Belsen,' cried one man.

'I lost twenty-eight of my family here,' said an old woman. The refugees broke out in wailing and rent their clothes, even Mordechai Rosman watched the dark land appearing through the fog with his head bowed, his arms outstretched as if on a crucifix. The *Runnymede Park* waited while the two other prison ships, the *Ocean Vigour* and *Empire Rival*, were cleared out, British troops and German guards dragged out frenzied men and women, American jazz blaring out to muffle the screams. A homemade bomb was found on the *Empire Rival* to the pleasure of the British; at last their suspicions had been confirmed, the purported refugees were actually dangerous terrorists desperate to injure their British guardians. The bomb was safely detonated on the dockside, but the refugees on the *Runnymede Park* would suffer for it. Batons went flying, hair was pulled out, soldiers kicked Mordechai Rosman down the gang-plank, possessions were thrown into the sea. Jama came on deck during this festival of violence, he had never believed white people could treat each other with such cruelty, but in front of his eyes was proof.

'Wahollah! My God, this is terrible!' said Jama as he saw Chaja trying to escape down the gangplank, her head bent down to avoid the blows as her children skidded and tripped beside her.

'And good riddance!' bellowed Brendan at their backs, sticking his middle finger in the air.

The Jews were handed over to the smirking Germans and the *Runnymede Park* became a ghost ship. After the AB's returned it to a semblance of order, Captain Barclay told the crew that they were going to Port Talbot for dry-docking before returning to Port Said. Jama would earn eighty pounds for this journey. His aim was to return to Gerset with two hundred pounds, and buy a prize camel and a large store and house for Bethlehem but the other sailors laughed at his plan.

'Forget it, boy, we're leaving this ship at Port Talbot. All the work is here, why do you want to return to stinking Egypt? If you stay on, it will be without any of us,' said Abdullahi.

'So what are you going to do?' asked Jama.

'Get another ship from Port Talbot or Hull, we get English wages on ships from England, a quarter more.'

The prospect of even greater pay was seductive but Jama worried that Bethlehem would give up on him, a year had already passed without any contact between them. She wouldn't wait any more, he thought. What if she had found someone else he wondered, a Kunama, or some rich Sudanese merchant? As a child Jama had wanted desperately to have wings, to go home now was like asking Icarus to set fire to his wings midflight, but he could not fly forever and keep Bethlehem.

Without the distraction of the refugees and soldiers, the *Runnymede Park* was now an ordinary freighter and the typical tensions in a mixed crew became clear. The British cooks would prepare pork products alongside the Muslim men's food, the British would mock their accents and skinny bodies, the drunken behaviour of the AB's was abhorrent to the Somalis. The AB's liked Jama though, his youth brought out a paternalistic kindness, and his inability to understand their insults meant his happy, ingenuous demeanour was not diminished.

They mispronounced his name Jammy, 'Hey, Jammy', 'You finished, Jammy?', 'Want a jammy biscuit, Jammy?', they enjoyed using his name and as the chill of the North Sea deepened it was 'Want a jumper, Jammy?' and

362

'Bet you're not used to this,' with exaggerated shivers.

The older Somalis told Jama that he was being mocked but he found it hard to care. His earlier fear of the white men had subsided, the British had given him work, high-paid work and for that they could say what they liked. The AB's were positively loving in comparison to the Italians he had worked for, they never hit or humiliated him, they were nothing to be scared of despite Brendan the Donkeyman's efforts. Brendan stalked around after the Somalis, his large baby-blue eyes threaded with red veins, he had buck teeth that stuck out from his puckered mouth, and his hair was balding in patches across his skull. The Somalis called him Sir Ilkadameer, 'Sir Donkeyteeth' to his face, and he would glow at the 'Sir', believing Ilkadameer to be a native term of respect. Sidney would call the Somalis to join the rest of the crew for fag breaks and Jama would converse slowly in sign language and broken English. Sidney was especially friendly to Jama. When he invited him to his cabin Abdullahi forbade him to go, but Jama went anyway. Sidney had a large cabin to himself in a quiet part of the ship and on the white wall he had stuck up pictures of white women in underwear that made their breasts point like goat horns. The only other picture on the wall was a yellow hammer and sickle on a red background. 'You know what that means, Jama?'

Jama thought it must be something to do with his work, maybe he was a farmer as well as sailor and he shook his head not wanting to embarrass himself.

'It means I believe that workers like you,' he poked his finger in Jama's chest for emphasis and then pointed at himself, 'and me should unite, together, understand?' His fingers were now knotted together, caressing one another.

The smile fell from Jama's face, the intertwined fingers meant only one thing and he didn't want that, but what about the naked women, perhaps they were just to disguise Sidney's real intentions?

He turned to the door but Sidney grabbed his shoulder. 'Hold on a second, take this,' he shoved a fat dictionary into Jama's hand, 'I'm sure you've been about a bit, I would like to hear about it someday.'

Jama took the dictionary and ran out, giving a cursory 'tanks much' to Sidney.

★ ★ ★

For Jama, the rest of the journey to Port Talbot couldn't have been more peaceful. He met Sidney occasionally in the fag room, and when he didn't repeat his hand caressing, Jama brought the dictionary with him and asked for help in learning to read. Sidney read out articles from TIME, following the words with his finger while Jama looked over his shoulder, the smell of cigarettes and the pleasure of reading would forever become entwined for Jama. He now understood that the war that had ravaged Eritrea had blazed across the world. Jama stared at the photographs of Hiroshima, Auschwitz, Dresden. Naked children screaming with hollow mouths appeared in all the photographs calling to each other like Siamese twins who had been torn apart. African, European and Asian corpses were piled up in the pages of the magazine beside adverts for lipstick and toothpaste. Already the world was moving on, from sombre black and white to lurid colour.

Sometimes Sidney stopped reading and reached for a map. 'Over here in Burma was the worst hell, North Africa was a picnic in comparison, I can handle desert heat but a man isn't made to fight in a jungle, gave me the fucking willies. Me and the Somalis in the battalion were going barmy, when you can't see the sky or feel a breeze it does something funny to a fella, the Japs would just appear out of nowhere, slit your throat and jump back into the bushes. Look, a Somali mate put this on my arm.'

Sidney rolled up his sleeve and revealed a dark blue snake cut into his flesh. Jama touched the livid serpent resting on Sidney's bicep like a python bathing on a hot boulder. It reminded him of the signs nomads cut into their camels. The snake was Jama's totem, perhaps Sidney would put one on his arm.

'I thought I was gonna die in that place, honestly and truly, I'm surprised to be sitting here, between Hitler and Hirohito I thought my number was up.'

Jama rolled up his sleeve, and gestured between his small hump of a bicep and Sidney's.

'You want one?' laughed Sidney

'Si.'

'You worked for Italians, eh? Well, I'll make more a hash of a tattoo than an Italian would fighting, better you get one done in London.'

Jama took the map out of Sidney's hands, found the pink spot Idea had said was Somaliland, he moved his finger along the Red Sea coast, beyond Gerset, into Sudan and Egypt, to where a sea separated his old world from the new.

Sidney put his blackened fingernail in the blue sea of the cold north. 'That's where we are, lad. Right up in the North Sea. You're a long way from home aren't you?'

Jama nodded.

Sidney ripped a piece off the map, took a pen out his shirt pocket. 'Jama, I live in London, by the river in Putney, if you ever need anything, come by and give me a bell.' Sidney wrote down his address in awkward capitals and gave it to Jama.

Jama walked the perimeter of the deck, the searchlight was switched off and a full moon beamed down on the sea, its reflection floating on the indigo waves. Light from the ship scintillated and sent stars over the water. Jama breathed in the cold salty air, found the star of Bethlehem and blew a kiss to it. A whale cruised in the distance, cutting slowly through undulating waves, and Jama turned around to show someone the whale but the deck was deserted. He had never imagined such creatures existed, but every day brought new wonders, monsters and knowledge. Bethlehem would never believe his stories, how could he explain the size of a whale to her, how it shot a geyser from its back, how it lived in ice-cold water. Jama closed his eyes and pictured Bethlehem's night time routine; she would check her chickens were safely locked up, then the goats, she would then take the half empty pan off the fire and store the remains for breakfast. The day's labour over, she would find Jama's star, send her love and then stretch out her lovely limbs on the mat that still smelt faintly of him and sing herself to sleep.

Port Talbot, Wales, September 1947

The *Runnymede Park* hung close to the white chalk of England before reaching the Bristol Channel and Swansea Bay. Beyond the tubes, funnels and chimneys of the steelworks, thick smoke hung over Port Talbot. Jama went to Captain Barclay and received his fortune of eighty pounds in an envelope thick with notes. Another hundred pounds and he could live like a king in Eritrea. When Captain Barclay asked if he would be staying on the *Runnymede Park*, Abdullahi, the serpent in paradise, whispered in his ear, 'The next ship will earn you twice this one, if you stay on for woman you will be the biggest fool in the world.'

Jama wrung his hands, looked over his shoulder at the broad sea, squeezed the envelope in his pocket. 'I'll come with you.'

Captain Barclay shook their hands in farewell and gave Jama his leaving card, his behaviour had been marked down as 'Very Good'. Jama stepped down onto his Promised Land and put a handful of cold earth into his pocket to take back to Gerset one day. Sidney gave Jama a salute as he left for the train station, a canvas sack thrown over his strong back.

The Somali men found their way to Port Talbot high street, and people observed their progress as if they were invaders. Jama felt very conspicuous; everyone was so pale, their skin looked cold to the touch. It was September and a chilly wind swept through the cramped streets and vague specks of rain floated in the wind. Workmen spat and made obscene gestures as the Somalis walked past and wild-haired women stood in doorways, some holding their brooms out in front of them like weapons, others with come hither looks in their eyes. The Ferengis' clothes were made for fatter people, large holes gaped in their stockings and the cardigans had been patched and darned. They found the Eidegalle hostel, a damp, brown building in a particularly poor part of town. Here they would sleep, eat, socialise; it was their bank and post office, their only sanctuary while they stayed in the wild west. A Welsh woman named Glenys worked for Waranle, the hostel owner. She was a bubbly woman, her blonde-white hair curled and face painted every day. Glenys enjoyed using her smattering of Somali, 'Maxaad sheegtey, Jama?' she would say in her sing song voice, 'What you saying, Jama?'

The older men did not enjoy going into

town. 'What's the point? They look at us as if our flies were open.' Only rarely could Jama persuade Abdullahi to take him out. Abdullahi would always wear shirt, tie, waistcoat, best suit, trilby to impress on the locals that he might be coloured but he was a gentleman of means. Jama eschewed the stiff itchy jackets and knitted hats that Glenys tried to force on him. He hated the smell of damp wool and this foreign wool brought his skin out in red welts, he went out in just his thin Egyptian shirts to everyone's disapproval.

'Look at this, Jama, another sign, No blacks. There aren't any other blacks in this town but us! Let's go back to the hostel,' fumed Abdullahi, pointing out the hand-written sign on the pub door.

'This is just like Eritrea.'

'Of course, and you better get used to it, it's like this all over the world for black men.'

A girl was watching from a café doorway and beckoned them over. Abdullahi tugged at Jama's sleeve to ignore her, but Jama could not, he walked over to the entrance and sat down at the wooden table.

'There's nothing to smile about, Jama, she's just too desperate to refuse our money,' Abdullahi chastised. He ordered two teas and sat in his finery looking forlorn amidst the cheap clutter.

They finished the tea and Abdullahi left a penny tip for the waitress. 'Thank you, sirs!' she exclaimed and bowed before them. It was the first time a Ferengi had ever bowed to Jama, he gave her another penny to see what she would do. She kissed Jama on the cheek, closed the café door and ran with her money over to the grocers.

'That's probably the biggest tip of her life,' laughed Abdullahi.

'Honestly?'

Abdullahi continued, 'Oh yes, they have a saying in this country, all fur coat and no knickers, understand? On the outside everything looks grand and pompous but underneath,' Abdullahi waved his hand disgustedly.

'Underneath it's just abaar iyo udoo-lullul, hardship and banditry, yes I understand,' laughed Jama.

★   ★   ★

After their few excursions outside, Abdullahi said it was too cold for him, he would not go out again unless it was to sign on for a ship. Jama became miserable in the hostel, he brooded on his loneliness and felt as if Bethlehem was lost to him, separated by time and distance. He sank deep into melancholy. Jama spent all his time in his freezing bed, in a room that stank of damp and gas, a sooty old paraffin heater burned all day giving him headaches and nosebleeds. Out of the dirty window he could see the faded green hills, moulting in patches like a sick jackal's fur, kissing the low dark sky.

One day, Glenys knocked on his door. 'You alright, Jimmy? Haven't seen you downstairs for days.'

Jama pulled the blanket up to his neck, he didn't understand what she wanted.

'You looking right peaky, lad, get up and I'll take you out for some fresh air, you can't keep this fire on all day with the window closed.' She threw Jama's clothes at him and walked out.

The sailors were playing cards downstairs; they wolf whistled when they saw Jama and Glenys walking out together.

'Waryaa! Where do you think you're going with her?' Abdullahi yelled.

'I think she is going to take me to her doctor,' Jama stuttered.

'That better be it, Jama, you come straight home after you've seen him.'

'I don't know what you're saying Abdullahi, but you should keep your nose out of things that don't concern you,' said Glenys before bundling Jama out.

Glenys was twice Jama's age but she aimed

to show him a grand old time. 'Doctor? Doctor?' attempted Jama a couple of times, but Glenys had other ideas, they had ice creams and donkey rides on the beach, they climbed the foreboding hills, she showed him the violently green countryside and the fat Welsh sheep.

Finally she treated him to afternoon tea. 'See you didn't need any stuck up doctor, did you?' Glenys giggled, happily buttering Jama's scones for him.

Glenys' big mistake was to show Jama the funfair as they walked home; one look and he was gone. Machines dedicated to fun and excitement had never existed in his world and here was a whole field of delirious mayhem, light bulbs of red yellow blue green flashed and popped, burnt onions and sugar perfumed the air. Raucous songs and melodies played cacophonously over one another, interrupted by random bangs and pings. Most of the rides stood idle but the cheaper ones were flying, the screeches of girls and boys howling down. Rides to frighten, to elate, to compete in, every emotion was for sale, when the girls saw the dark handsome sailor there was a stampede towards him. He was prised from Glenys' grip and taken away by a troop of Welsh Sirens who wanted toffee apples, bumper car tickets, goldfish, all the things they knew Jama could afford.

Every evening Jama snuck out. 'Where are you going now?' Glenys would ask if she caught sight of Jama skulking away.

'To buy a jumper!' he would reply before running off, but he was meeting Edna, Phyllis, Rose, or any other of the fairground girls. The girls cheered when he turned up, and he never got bored of spinning and whirling with them, but his real downfall was the bumper cars. A fix of five minutes cost sixpence, and he drove the cars from afternoon to late in the night, a pretty girl's thighs squashed by his and another squealing in delight when he crashed into her. He paid for all the girls and even a few boys. 'What's he about?' the boys asked.

'He's a prince from Africa here on holiday,' the girls insisted.

Jama finally had a chance to play and live his lost childhood and his father's motoring dream; the frustrations of a caged, demeaned, stunted life exploded out of him in that fairground. Each evening his precious pile of English money diminished until only the shiny bottom of the biscuit tin stared up at him. Now when he went to the fairground or to the café with only lint in his pockets, he sat watching, hoping that one of the girls would sit by him, but Edna, Rose, Phyllis and the others coolly cast their gaze somewhere else. Jama became just a crumpled figure on the edge of their sugary world.

'Eighty pounds! Eighty pounds! You spent all your money on those hussies!' fumed Glenys when she heard he had run out of money. 'Well, back off to the dock with you then, there is a ship to Canada that's looking for firemen, you better get on it, laddio.'

Abdullahi concurred with Glenys for once. 'We're signing on for that ship, I'll take you to put your name down.'

The ship was taking coal to St John's, New Brunswick, Abdullahi took Jama to the British Shipping Federation office, he gave his name, and then put his fingerprint and shaky cross next to the man's calligraphy.

'You can take your wage now if you want but you will have to wait two months for the next payment,' Abdullahi explained.

'Tell him to give it to me, I owe money to Waranle.' They walked down the street, Jama counting the money.

'Now in Canada, you will have to wear a jumper, coat, hat, none of this nakedness you have got used to, the cold there will kill you straight, it's happened before to foolish Somalis,' Abdullahi admonished.

'Twenty-four pounds!' Jama exclaimed.

'What did I tell you! English wages.'

'How long will the voyage take?' asked Jama.

'What's it matter? The longer it takes the more you'll get paid. You still want to go back to Africa?' laughed Abdullahi.

'I have to.'

'Don't have to do anything, all these men are killing themselves to get here and you wanna go back to one meal a day, heat, thirst, you're a strange boy to even think about it,' Abdullahi tutted.

As the departure date neared, Jama tried to believe that Abdullahi was right, that to return to Africa would be the worst mistake of his life. That he would never have this chance again, that he owed it to himself to go to Canada, that Bethlehem would accept anything if he came home a rich man. All of this became a kind of philosophy passed on from Abdullahi, that grey seas would be their goldmines, seagulls their pets, hairy blue-veined Britons their companions. Women and Africa were not a part of this brave new world. Beyond the rationing, the bomb sites, the slumlike housing, the angry dungareed men, Port Talbot was still the Promised Land, with every new technology obtainable, gas cookers, vending machines, top class radios, picture houses. Even though many white people pulled faces when they saw him, there were unexpected kindnesses. Old ladies who invited him into their small cosy homes, men who offered to escort him home on foggy nights, housewives who rushed up to shake his hand and thank him for his war effort. There were enough humane Ferengis to make life interesting.

* * *

Life carried on peacefully until one day a stranger came to the hostel, a dapper Somali from London. He was looking for Jama.

'What do you want him for?' Abdullahi challenged.

'Family business,' replied the stranger shortly.

'I'll go get him for you, sir,' said Glenys, dashing up the stairs. 'Jama, Jama, open up,' Glenys said, hammering on his door, 'there's a nice looking man asking for you!'

Jama alarmed, rushed down the stairs behind Glenys. A black-suited man sat opposite Abdullahi in the sitting room.

He stood up to greet Jama saying, 'Long time no see, cousin.'

Jama grabbed hold of Jibreel's hand. 'Man! Where has this ghost appeared from?' was all that Jama could say. Jibreel's askariness had disappeared and a film star stood in his place, shiny black hair, neat thin moustache, black hat in his hand, he was more debonair than anyone Jama had seen.

'Let's go to your room, I have news.'

Sitting in the grey room, with wallpaper falling down around them, Jama's heart stopped when Jibreel delivered his news. 'Your wife has had a child.'

'Allah!' exclaimed Jama.

'Manshallah, Jama! Praise God, I leave you a little sad boy and now you're a father before me.'

'Allah!' Jama said again.

'Leave God alone!' laughed Jibreel.

'How do you know?' Jama asked when he had finally composed himself.

'Your mother-in-law wants you to come home, she has been telling every Somali in a hundred mile radius. An Eidegalle man passed through Tessenei and came by ship to East London where the news reached me. When I heard that you had arrived here, I couldn't keep the good news to myself, could I?'

'I have to go to Bethlehem, what can she be living on? I didn't leave her any money, my poor Bethlehem,' Jama embraced Jibreel. 'But I've taken the Ferengis money, they'll make me go to Canada,' he cried.

'You've signed on for another ship?'

'Yes, it's leaving this week, they know my name, where I live, everything, they finger-printed me!' Jama wailed.

'Settle down, we'll sort something out,' soothed Jibreel.

Jama hid his face in his palms, imagining Bethlehem nursing his child all alone in their tukul. On the ship his love for her had been like a dove in a cage but it now stretched out its wings and soared. 'Is it a girl or boy?'

'Jama, I have a letter here from your wife.'

'Read it to me outside, I can't breathe in this room.'

They walked to the freezing docks, the sea a thrashing grey whale beside them, the wind tearing through Jama's thin shirt. They sat on a wall, smoking Jibreel's cigarettes, while Jama's heart flipped over every second.

'Ok, I'm ready.'

Jibreel pulled out an envelope from his jacket pocket, it was covered in finger prints and worn in places, it had clearly passed through many hands to reach him. Inside was a sheet of blue paper covered in Arabic script. Jibreel read to Jama:

My Heart,
I have been trailing your vapours since you left, I don't know whether you are alive

or dead. *I even went to a fortune teller in Tessenei and he saw you in the grains of his coffee, he told me that you're safe, on a sea surrounded by Ferengis and Yahudis, but I don't believe him. My stomach has been growing ever since you left and we now have a son, I came here to the scribe because your boy is a small, sickly thing and I don't want him to pass away without ever seeing you. Life is silent without you, the birds don't sing anymore, even the baby is quiet, we sit together in the evening wondering where you are. Sometimes I am angry but other times I feel nothing because I doubt whether you were ever real, whether our marriage was just a figment of my imagination, whether my child was put in my stomach by sorcery. Nothing grows here now that you have left, our fields and stomachs are empty. I am sending this letter out into the universe in the hope that you will remember me, come home one day and tell me that you are real.*

    Bethlehem

Jama hid his tears from Jibreel. 'What is the quickest way of getting to Eritrea?'

'You can either go to Aden and get a dhow to Massawa, or go to Egypt and travel down through Sudan.'

'Which is cheaper?'

'Through Aden.'

'Let's go then, I have no time to waste.'

They finished their cigarettes and walked back to Waranle's hostel. Abdullahi looked harshly at Jibreel as they walked in. 'What's going on, Jama?'

'I have a son,' Jama replied with a weak smile.

'And what? We all have sons, daughters, doesn't change anything.'

Jama's face fell, hearing Abdullahi unable to even extend a kind word cut into his heart. Abdullahi was not someone to take counsel from; he was embittered, chasing money around the world without any meaning to his life.

Jama rushed up to his room, packing clothes into his father's suitcase. 'You know, Jibreel, that day you walked me to meet that man, the man from Gedaref, after he told me my father was dead, I sat there until nightfall unable to move, but I promised myself something. I might have been a scrawny, snot-nosed little boy but I promised myself something, that I would never abandon a child of mine, never.'

'Then you became a man that day,' said Jibreel.

'All that hardship my mother and I went

through, the hunger, the insults, the loneliness, how could I do that to Bethlehem and my son?'

'You couldn't, Jama, you don't have the stomach for it.'

'Let's go, I'm ready.'

Jibreel paid Jama's bill with Waranle, and a leaving party gathered around the door. Glenys kissed Jama goodbye. 'Good luck, son.' The sailors shook his hand, gave him a few coins for his child.

Jama found Abdullahi in the sitting room, sullenly drinking tea. 'I'm going, Abdullahi.'

'Well go then, fool!'

'What will happen about the wage I've taken?'

Abdullahi raised his eyes to Jama. 'I'll tell them you're at death's door and you will have to pay them back if you ever return.'

Jama let out a long sigh. 'Thanks, Abdullahi, for everything, see you in Africa maybe.'

'Not in a thousand years,' sneered Abdullahi.

★ ★ ★

The train pulled in at Paddington, 'London,' crooned Jibreel. As they walked through the great city, Jama looked up and saw blackened buildings that looked like the nests of huge violent birds.

'London's beauty is not in its buildings, Jama, but in its people, you go to Piccadilly Circus and it's like walking through the crowds on Judgement Day, people flee from all over the world with bits of their villages hidden in their socks and plant them anew here. Just in Leman Street we have a Somali barber, a Somali mechanic, even a Somali writer amongst the Jewish grocers, Chinese cooks and Jamaican students.'

Jama dug out his Welsh soil from his pocket and showed it to Jibreel. 'I'll plant this in Eritrea,' he laughed.

Jama stayed with Jibreel in his room in Leman Street, talking late into the night. 'I wonder what he looks like. I hope he has his mother's big eyes,' Jama mused.

'Imagine all the generations that have gone into making your son, marriage after marriage, the men, the women, some forgotten, some remembered, Kunama, Somali, Tigrey, farmers, nomads, all to make this little worm,' Jibreel said sleepfully.

'I still can't believe it, only when I see him will I really know what it means,' Jama replied, eyes wide awake in the dark, 'but I know what I will name him.'

'Oh yeah?' slurred Jibreel.

'Yes. Shidane.'

* ★ ★

While they waited for the ship's departure date, Jibreel taught Jama how to Brylcreem his hair until it was just so and then they promenaded around London. At the Serpentine Jama told Jibreel what had happened to Shidane, at a café in Trafalgar Square he described Bethlehem's beauty, along the Southbank he explained how he had walked from Palestine to Egypt.

Jibreel listened and smiled. 'I think you are lying to me, Jama. The last I remember of you, you were always sulking, pushing your bottom lip out, you tried to turn all of us into your mother, feeding you, nursing you, giving up our mats for you.'

Jama laughed, an ocean of time separated him from that little malarial boy in Omhajer.

Finally, on a bench near Putney Bridge, Jibreel was able to tell Jama where he had been.

'After you left Omhajer, there was meant to be an offensive against the Ethiopian fighters, the Italians brought out huge guns, tanks, poison gas, everything, they meant business this time. The night before we were meant to leave, I thought to myself 'Do I want to die for them, is there nothing else?' Before the sun came up I fled, I walked all the way to

Djibouti then through both Somalilands. In Kenya I stopped, I worked as a shoeshiner at Nairobi station, without shame I polished shoes next to tiny little boys. With a bit of money in my pocket I left again, in Tanganyika I worked for Omani Arabs, then I got sick of that and jumped on a lorry to Rhodesia. There I worked on an Englishman's farm, and he said to me 'Oh you're Somali, you must be trying to find work on the ships,' and I said to him 'What ships?' and he explained how so many Somalis were working for the merchant navy because they paid so well. I was off! I left that stupid farm and went to find a big port, from Rhodesia I walked to South Africa, and then I had to walk all across that damn country until I came to Durban where the British navy were. I stowed myself onto a British ship, five years to the day I had left Omhajer, I was caught and put in chains, when we got to Liverpool I ran away and joined another ship!'

Jama and Jibreel competed over who had walked the furthest, starved the longest, felt the most hopeless; they were athletes in the hard luck Olympics.

'Look here, in that prison cell in Egypt, there were men who were bleeding from every hole in their body and we had to sit in that blood day and night,' Jama boasted.

Jibreel scoffed, 'Luxury! Do you know how many times I have been attacked by leopards, I have their teeth marks all over my back, lions have stalked me, white farmers have shot at me. Man! You wouldn't believe the trouble I've seen, you have spent most of your time in an Eritrean girl's arms.'

They laughed over the things they could speak about, the rest was left to rust in the locked chambers of their hearts.

Jibreel intended to make London his home, he had grown used to the fast life that sailors lived, and could not imagine returning to Somaliland with his new bad habits.

'Everywhere I go I meet Somalis, always from the north, standing at a crossroads, looking up to the sky for direction, the poor souls never know where they're going. They all say the same thing, there is nothing in our country, I'll go back when I can afford some camels. I think that there are more Somalis at the bottom of the sea or lost in the desert than there are left in our land. They leave to become drivers, askaris, sailors, whatever, anything as long as it takes them far away.'

Jama thought about what Jibreel said. 'It's because we are nomads, land is the same to us everywhere we go, we only care if there is water and food to be found. When I was farming in Gerset I felt this patch of land is mine, this tukul is mine, I planted this tree so I want to see it grow, now I think wherever my family is that is where I belong.'

'You're Cain and I'm Abel. Give me open skies, wide horizons, and new women. Deep down I will always think that the only thing that comes to a man who stays still is death.'

Jama could not stay still; he wanted to pick Bethlehem up and swing her around, to pepper his quiet baby's face with kisses and make him laugh. With the twenty-four pounds from the Canadian ship he would take Bethlehem wherever she wanted to go, share the wings that fate had given him. Jama intended to buy her jewellery in Keren, take her on Hajj to Mecca, take her to the cinema in Alexandria, make up for every day that he had left her alone.

'Is this address nearby?' asked Jama, pulling out the scrap of paper Sidney had given him.

'Yes, I think so.'

They left the riverside bench and walked up the high street. Jibreel asked a bus conductor for directions and he pointed out a side street. Jama pressed the bell and then stood well back; Sidney appeared through the green leaded glass, a huge bearded merman.

'Aye aye, comrade,' Sidney boomed.

Jama held out his hand and Sidney

grabbed it, nearly pulling Jama's arm out of its socket.

Jama pointed to his companion. 'This Jibreel.'

'Come on in, lads, I won't bite.'

Sidney lived in a flat shared with other navvies. Newspapers, heavy boots and letters lay forgotten along the dark hallway, he ushered them into his room.

It was as sparse and tidy as a hermit's cave, books were neatly stacked along the skirting board, cold air hissed through the windows and only the sickle and hammer flag covered his thin mattress.

'What can I do for you, mate? You got into trouble already? Wanna cup o'splosh?' Sidney held up his mug demonstratively.

Jama shook his head, pointed at his bicep. 'Tattoo?'

'What a persistent little sod! I didn't realise you were so envious of mine. Alright, let's go, just don't go telling your mum that I took you.'

The sailors took the number 14 bus to Piccadilly Circus, past the boys waiting under the electric signs for their girlfriends and into the dirty red streets of Soho. Jibreel whispered warnings into Jama's ear. 'The needles are dirty, only Ferengis do it, you'll change your mind,' but Jama didn't listen, it was the only way to take home everything he had seen and done.

'I've got another lamb for the slaughter,' Sidney called to the tattooist; he was another burly merman, his arm a picture house of fancy women and animals.

'Tell him I want a black mamba,' Jama ordered Jibreel.

The pain was excruciating, fire lapped along his veins and bit at his bones, but with relief Jama watched the bad blood welling out of him, the blood that had pumped fear and grief and pain around his body for so long. From the fire emerged a beautiful black snake. Jama, the black mamba boy, had become a man of the world, his totem etched into his skin as a mark of where he had been and what he had survived.

'Sterling job,' admired Sidney.

Jama traced his fingers along the red ridge of ink, the snake pulsated under his fingertips, as if it had crawled out of the earth, through his mother's bellybutton and into his mouth, to watch the world from his arm.

'Your wife will hate it,' frowned Jibreel.

'No, I'll explain to her what it means.'

'Come let's go, we have to get up early for the ship tomorrow,' said Jibreel shaking his head.

The steerage class ticket to Aden dampened in Jama's clammy hand. 'I should buy them something from here,' he panicked as the barrowmen of East India docks pushed past him. He blew white smoke over his cold hands and nervously stamped his feet on the icy crystal ground.

'Leave it, I'm sure they'll be happy with your pocketful of dirt, but . . . here, take this.' Jibreel pushed five pounds into Jama's jacket pocket.

'Take it,' ordered Jibreel, 'I should have known that day I saw you, careering around Omhajer with your big knees, crying out for Eidegalles, that there wasn't any distance you wouldn't travel for your family, but times are changing now. You might be able to bring your family back here, I have seen quite a few of our women pushing those baby carts.'

They embraced before Jama climbed aboard the P&O ship, his father's tattered suitcase somehow still holding together, even with the many new dreams and fears squeezed in amongst his clothes. Jibreel raised his hat to him and walked along the frozen dock with long elegant strides, his black overcoat merging into the dark dawn light. The ship pulled away, sliding along the oily serpent back of the Thames, with Jama leaning over the rails, taking long full draughts of London before it disappeared. The great city was painted in grey watercolours, with cooing pigeons nestling in her blackened arches and spires. The world beckoned to Jama and he wanted Bethlehem to see it all with him, he would never have to struggle alone now and nor would she. They would pack up their bags and move like nomads over Africa, over Europe, discovering new worlds, renaming them 'Jamastan' and 'Bethlehemia' if they wanted. Rich English youths were gathered around a gramophone on deck. 'Tell ol' pharaoh to let my people go,' growled Louis Armstrong. Jama let his legs move to the swinging jazz, let his hips whine a little, his shoulders shimmy, anything to free the music trapped within his soul.

★ ★ ★

Above him, the stars were hot diamonds piercing the black flesh of the universe. Looking up, Jama knew that his loved ones were with him, his mother, father, sister, Shidane and maybe Abdi were roaming through the sky, arguing, laughing, watching. He would join them eventually but not until he had devoured all the seeds that the pomegranate world offered. He wanted to be a flesh and blood father to his son, a flesh and blood husband to Bethlehem, and to not observe the hustle and bustle of life but to be it. He felt at the centre of the world, a smiling Somali man in a white t-shirt was the sweetheart of the stars, the world was a cocoon of love enveloping him, all fear and pain suffocated in its folds. 'Hoi hoi,' he called to Bethlehem's star, he would come home to her a different man, and he knew that she would be changed too. She would be like his mother now, flinty, brave, iron-eyed, with a child growing out of her back. He was ready for that, he was ready for anything that life had to offer.

Acknowledgements

Many books and articles informed this novel but there are a few that deserve special mention: *Banjo* by Claude McKay, *Eritrea 1941* by A.J. Barker, *The Yibir of Las Burgabo* by Mahmood Gaildon, *Exodus 1947* by Ruth Gruber and *An Account of the British Settlement of Aden in Arabia* by Captain F.M. Hunter.

I would like to thank my father, Jama, for many things: laying his life before me — both to admire and to embellish, for his unwavering support in writing this book and for surviving everything with peace and love in his heart.

I am indebted to my mother, Zahra Farax Kaaxin, the next book will be for you hooyo. Wax kasta ood ii karikarto waad ii kartay libaaxaday.

Yousaf Ali Khan set this book off on its journey into the world.

Butetown History and Arts Centre, Abdi Arwo and The Arts Council enabled me to start writing.

My earliest readers Hana Mohamed, Dr. Lana Srzic, Dr. Srinika Ranasinghe, Khadar Axmed Farax, Abdulrazak Gurnah, Liz Chan, Sabreen Hussain thank you.

My family in Hargeisa, Abti Maxamed Farax Kaaxin, Edo Casha and Edo Faadumo, Liban, Hamsa, Saciid, Abbas, Naciima and all my cousins, thank you for making my journey to Hargeisa so memorable.

To the friends and family who gave me encouragement or necessary distraction: Ahmed Mohamed, Nura Mohamed, Mary Mbema, Rosalind Dampier, Sarah Khawaja, Attiyya Malik, Danielle Drainey, Mei Ying Cheung, Emily Woodhouse, Sulaiman, Lies and Saleh Addonia.

Selma El-Rayah, as-saayih extraordinaire, you championed me and spread the word far and wide.

Abdi Mohamed and Osman El-Nusairi gave me their time and knowledge.

Chenoa Marquis thank you for that day in the Rhodes House library.

Dr. Virginia Luling, your timely assistance helped me trace Ibrahim Ismaa'il's magnificent autobiography.

My gali-gali boy Ben Mason, you saw the pearl in the oyster shell, and your faith and counsel has been invaluable.

To my insightful, exacting, humane and funny editor, Clare Hey, thank you. You brought out this novel's truest and most beautiful face.

I would like to express my gratitude to everyone at Conville and Walsh and Harper Fiction for making this novel happen.

ECHOES OF A PROMISE

Ashleigh Bingham

When Victoria Shelford runs away to sea in the name of love, her parents disown her, and she feels the pain of her father's rejection keenly. Nevertheless, Victoria's wandering spirit is not dampened, and she sets off to exotic Kashmir to find a new life. Here, she encounters the unpopular and grim-faced Andrew Wyndham, whose misspent youth has left him with empty pockets as well as a closely guarded secret. Victoria is intrigued by Wyndham, but the complications that beset his life mean that it is hard to get close to him. Can Victoria succeed where all others have failed?